ALSO BY ELIZABETH GRAVER

Have You Seen Me?

Unravelling

The Honey Thief

AWAKE

AWAKE

ELIZABETH GRAVER

HENRY HOLT AND COMPANY
NEW YORK

Henry Holt and Company, LLC
Publishers since 1866
115 West 18th Street
New York, New York 10011

Distributed in Canada by H. B. Fenn and Company Ltd.

Library of Congress Cataloging-in-Publication Data
Graver, Elizabeth, 1964–
Awake / Elizabeth Graver.— 1st ed.
p. cm.
ISBN 0-8050-6539-3
1. Xeroderma pigmentosum—Patients—Fiction. 2. Identity (Psychology)—Fiction. 3. Mothers and sons—Fiction. 4. Sick children—Fiction. 5. Camps—Fiction. 6. Boys—Fiction. I. Title.
PS3557.R2864N54 2004
813'.54—dc21 2003055253

Henry Holt books are available for special promotions and premiums. For details contact: Director, Special Markets.

First Edition 2004

Designed by Kelly S. Too

Printed in the United States of America
1 3 5 7 9 10 8 6 4 2

To Lauren

We grow accustomed to the Dark—
When Light is put away—
As when the Neighbor holds the Lamp
To witness her Goodbye—

A Moment—We uncertain step
For newness of the night—
Then—fit our Vision to the Dark—
And meet the Road—erect—

And so of larger—Darknesses—
Those Evenings of the Brain—
When not a Moon disclose a sign—
Or Star—come out—within—

The Bravest—grope a little—
And sometimes hit a Tree
Directly in the Forehead—
But as they learn to see—

Either the Darkness alters—
Or something in the sight
Adjusts itself to Midnight—
And Life steps almost straight.

—EMILY DICKINSON

AWAKE

ONE

A long road leads to it. There is no sign. No Indian name on a wooden plaque, no GO SLOW CHILDREN, just a left turn off the highway, a right turn off a single-lane tar road, then a dirt road appearing before the headlights of the van, the unfurling of a path we never thought we'd find. Max in the back, that first year, his arms pale in his short-sleeved shirt, his face pressed to the window. Are we almost there, Mom? Yes, I think we're almost there. Ian at the wheel, leaning toward the dashboard. I sat next to him, my penlight tracing our path on a map. We were late. We'd gotten slightly lost, my fault. Behind Ian, his head on a rolled-up sleeping bag, Adam slept.

What I remember of that trip, our first trip there, was a sense of moving toward a place I'd been wishing for—quietly, almost unconsciously—for the past nine years, even as I'd thought it didn't exist and never would. What I remember, too, was the feeling of entering a made-up story, for I'd often told Max about a land where night was day and day night, where children ran outside when the sun went down and flowers bloomed white so you could see them in the moonlight. As we drove up the dirt road, a deer stepped out of the woods and Ian slammed on the brakes. For a long moment, then, we all stared, human and animal, the deer so close you could see the flare of its nostrils, the raised tendons in its neck. Be careful, I said to Ian after the creature had plunged back into the brush. Be careful, please. It was something I said too often in those days. I am, said Ian. I always am.

A startled deer. It stopped to look; we all looked back. Be careful. Already in my mind it was a story for Max, to help him remember as he—if he—grew up.

It was after ten when we pulled up to the camp. The lodge was dark and massive, built of wood. In the driveway we saw minivans like our own, and station wagons, and a smaller car or two. Lanterns hung on poles along the drive and swayed in the breeze, making it look festive, like a wedding. The license plates were from everywhere, Arizona and Quebec, Illinois and Alabama, all of us come like pilgrims, gripping tight our hope. Ian parked the van and turned off the motor. Are we there? asked Adam sleepily. From behind, I felt Max's hand on my neck. He'd crept close, his fingers twining through my hair. All right, said Ian. Shall we go check it out? But we just sat, my hand on top of Max's now, pressing down. From inside the lodge came the sound of voices and a child shrieking, then a piano being played by someone who didn't know how.

Who knows how long we might have sat there if a figure

hadn't appeared on the front steps and waved. Ian rolled down the window and said hello.

"You must be Ian and Anna." The man came over and stood by Ian's door, then looked into the back of the van. "And Max and Adam. Welcome. Hello. I'm Hal. Were the directions okay?"

"Perfect." Ian flicked on the overhead light.

I leaned across him. "We got a little lost, but not because of the directions. I missed a sign. Sorry we're late."

"No, no." Hal shook his head and handed Ian a heap of cloth—four blue T-shirts, it turned out, printed with a glow-in-the-dark CAMP LUNA above a winking crescent moon. I'd seen his picture on the Web site, but of course he looked different in person, his face more animated. "You're not late," he said. "You're just in time for dinner." Then, as suddenly as he'd come, he turned and disappeared inside.

Ian followed. First Ian, then Adam, then Max. Max wore a fanny pack around his waist with Who, his stuffed owl, zipped inside. We left our bags in the car. None of us wore the shirt. I went last, making my way up the stone steps into the entry hall, wishing Max had stayed behind to hold my hand. Over the years, I had become more rather than less timid. Now I felt like a new girl at a school dance, filled with both curiosity and queasiness: the camp would live up to our expectations; we'd be disappointed; Max would make friends, or else turn away and sulk. The other children would be—

Here I had to stop a moment. The other children would be what? Hurt. Scarred. Dying. Some of them would be dying—if not now, then over the next few years. I'd known this before, but never so strongly as when I stood on that threshold. It was as if we'd been separated years ago from a tribe we'd never asked to join, and now here it was, a reunion, a gathering—*Come in, come in, you're family*—but what was this family? A fluke in wiring. A random, costly mix-up in some DNA.

It was Hal who came to get me. I must have seemed dazed. He looked at me; I looked away. He touched, I think, my arm, and the moment, well, the moment passed like any other, as most beginnings do.

"Are you all right?" he asked.

"I'm fine." Suddenly, oddly, I was. I smelled food cooking and heard laughter coming from inside. "I can't believe we're finally here," I said. "Max has been waiting for so long."

Hal nodded. "Alida too. My daughter. Do you want to meet her?"

I followed him into a central room with high ceilings and a huge stone fireplace. People turned briefly to look at us, then returned to their conversations. A woman walked by with a pot of steaming soup, her round face flushed. I scanned the room. In the corner, squatting over a stuffed animal, was a small girl with dark hair that fell nearly to her waist. As we approached, I saw that her skin, at least in the dim light, looked normal. She wore the blue camp shirt and a red polka-dotted skirt.

"Hi, monkey." Hal touched the top of her head. "I've brought you Anna Simon, Max's mom."

She looked up.

"Hi there," I said.

She put her hand on her father's foot. "Where's Max?"

"Max is—" I saw him standing across the room, next to Ian and Adam, and another man and boy. "That's him, right over there."

"The Max *I* know"—she pushed her bangs off her face and

turned to look—"takes his boat to an island where there's monsters in the trees."

I nodded. "He likes that story too."

"But he's got straight hair and no XP. And a mother."

"This Max has a mother too." Who, I wondered, did she think I was? "And a father and brother. Adam. He's also here. He's thirteen. How old are you?"

She scanned me up and down, her eyes, like her father's, so dark brown they seemed black. Then she pulled on his arm. "Tell her, Daddy."

"You don't know how old you are?" Hal asked.

"No, but in days, tell her. In minutes."

"You're . . . over two thousand days old. More minutes than I can count. In years, you're six."

"Am I older than Max?"

"Max is nine," I said, "in boy years. In girl years, you might well be older."

Hal laughed. "She's on to us. Come, let's go meet him."

"He's a little shy—" I started to say, though I'd vowed not to step in for Max. But already they were walking across the room.

Picture your child as one in half a million, with a condition so rare that it takes months, after he's born, for it to be correctly diagnosed. Picture the white cotton weave on his blanket when you put him in his car seat under a tree, how within minutes, the open weave of that cloth has imprinted itself on his skin like a tattoo, a rising, welting rash. Allergies, says the doctor, prescribing cortisone, but meanwhile the infant is still swelling, blistering, his eyes squeezed shut, his mouth an open ring of pain.

Picture the hike you take with your baby strapped to your chest, a rocky climb to the top of a mountain in New Hampshire, the fresh young family, the older boy who clambers, sturdy, up the rocks. How the new one cries and cries, howling so hard that as you rush back down the trail, you can think only of wanting to tuck him back inside you, return him, unbirth him.

Tests and speculations, then, charts and results, until—finally—a name: xeroderma pigmentosum. You've never heard of it. The words are twisty, warty, on your tongue. Xeroderma pigmentosum. XP. Flawed DNA repair system. Hypersensitivity to ultraviolet light. Skin cancer, eye cancer, at a thousand times the normal rate. Only a thousand known cases worldwide. The X moves into your house. The P moves in. You gather up the facts, gather up the children. A new planet, this, and you, it seems, the only people on it. Once you were a lover of light, a traveler of lands. Now you darken the windows, batten the hatches, close the doors. Slowly, as time passes, this begins to feel like all you've ever known. You grow accustomed to the dark. You live—you often even love—your life.

Then picture this:

A room, a house full of children like Max. They looked fine. Yes, some of the kids had faces dusted with dark freckles, or pockmarks on their chins, or crutches. And yes, one boy wore thick, owlish glasses and squinted when he spoke, and another child had blisters on her lips, but really, unless you knew, this could have been any group of kids, girls with butterfly clips in their hair and cut-off shorts, boys in backward baseball caps, kids bare-legged, dark-skinned, light-skinned, curly- or straight-haired, chattering with one another like old friends. I sat on a high wooden chair in the corner and watched. It might have been a church social, or a birthday party, or a camp that specialized in archery or arts and crafts. Only the parents looked a little different—hovering, maybe, or extra animated, buoyed up by the newness of this place, this group. As I looked around, a woman caught my eye. She waved as if we'd already met, and I hesitated, not sure the gesture was meant for me, and then waved back.

I should introduce myself, I thought, together with Ian and the boys, but they were nowhere to be seen. My old worry, then, so quick to return. I spotted Ian talking to someone and went to him.

"Hey." I tried to keep my voice casual, but he knew me better. "Sorry to interrupt, but have you seen the kids? I thought they were with you, did they—"

"Outside." He pointed toward the porch. "Anna, this is Carole."

Carole. Yes. I took a breath, shook her hand. Pleased to meet you, Carole, mother of Nicole. From Alabama. Pleased.

Outside. Of course. It was dark out, and we were deep inside the woods. The doors could be opened, the breeze let in, the kids let out. Except what about those woods? Bears, holes, poison ivy—and, somewhere nearby, a lake.

Absently, Ian took my hand and patted it. Already, he and Carole were talking light meters and lotions, homeschooling and field trips, doctors and gene therapy research. Inclusion, I heard him say. Lead a normal life, hope for a cure. Carole nodded and leaned toward him, and I felt a twinge of jealousy, or was it excitement? It was so unusual for us to be out together among strangers. For a moment, I tried to see Ian from outside, as if we'd just met. He is quite handsome, Ian, in a blue-eyed, clean-boned, Irish way, and his voice is reassuring and sincere. Back and forth they went, and I knew he was impressing, and I knew I was not. Silently, I waited for the moment when I could take my leave.

"I think I'll go explore," I said when there was a gap in the conversation, but just then a gong sounded, a hollow, echoing noise.

"Dinner!" called a voice I recognized already as Hal's.

People started toward a doorway. In the crowd I spotted Max's dark-blond hair, Adam's brown. They had changed into the camp shirts and were moving among a group of children all wearing the same bright blue. I reminded myself to retrieve their own shirts, which they'd probably dropped in a corner somewhere. The dining room was huge, the table long enough to seat us all. On the wall was a stretched zebra skin and two crossed spears next to a faded, tattered poster: SAVE THE SPOTTED OWL. A copper chandelier hung over the table, looped with yellow streamers and cutout tinfoil moons. There was, I noticed suddenly, copper everywhere. The windowsills were covered with it. Hammered copper pots hung from the walls. A side table covered with dimpled copper sheeting threw back the light. Beside it stood the gong we'd heard, a copper disk on a wooden stand.

Ian held out his arm. "May I escort you, madam?" he whispered, and I had a moment of gratefulness that he was nervous too, or that he knew I was.

The soup had alphabet noodles floating in it, and other pasta shaped like stars and moons. I stared into my bowl at the letters—E, A, J, X—and tried to make a word, but nothing formed. I looked over at my children. Max was sitting quietly now, holding a spoon but not eating. Adam was next to him, spooning steadily, his head bent toward his soup. For an instant I saw them from outside too: a pair of fine-boned boys with the same elfin nose and high forehead, Adam so much bigger, always hungry, Max a picky eater who examined each bite as if it might be laced with arsenic. They'd just gotten summer haircuts and had that shorn, bare look, as if their ears and necks were pinker, younger, than before. Max glanced over at me. So here we are, his eyes seemed to say. So here we are—and now? I raised my eyebrows at him and smiled, but his own face stayed sober, almost accusing, as if to remind me that, having brought him here, I was now accountable for anything that might come to pass.

Eat, I mouthed, tasting a spoonful of soup. Until I swallowed it, I didn't realize how hungry I was. Someone passed a basket of bread. Mothers reached into their purses and pulled out pills and vitamins, which they handed across the table to their children. The soup was vegetable broth with a slightly spicy aftertaste. The next time I looked over, Max was eating, too, and listening to the boy on his left. I ate, and ate some more.

Toward the end of dinner, Hal rose from his seat. "Welcome to Camp Luna." He lifted his glass and looked up, his eyes circling the room. For a moment, he met my gaze, and it seemed he was about to say something (to me? I didn't know, yet, that he had a gift for making everyone feel the brush of his attention). Then he moved on. As arms raised and glasses clinked, I brought my own glass to Ian's.

"To Max," I said softly

"To Max," I heard Hal echo, and though his tone was warm, I heard my words turn selfish, too specific, in his mouth.

"And to Étienne," he added, "and Alida, Sara, Tommy, Anil, Nicole . . . "

As he spoke, the names became a sort of litany, almost a prayer, and I remembered, in the vivid yet unreliable way of something long forgotten, hearing the mourners' kaddish chanted at my grandmother's funeral as a girl. No, not the mourners' kaddish. What was wrong with me? I felt under the table for Ian's hand. This was a list of the living, of the loved.

"More wine?" a man near me asked.

"Oh, please." I held out my glass, which I hadn't realized was empty.

"More cheese?" Ian asked, though already he was dropping it on my plate.

"*More More More*," I said. It was the title of a storybook our boys had loved when they were small. I could feel time compressing, all of us growing younger, older. In houses throughout the Adirondacks, families were brushing their teeth, saying good night and climbing into bed, but here, among this odd and rogue-gened tribe, the day was just beginning. I leaned back in my chair and looked around. Max, I knew, would love it here. He had—we had—been alone together for so long.

You may have heard about places like Camp Luna, specialized ones for kids who wouldn't make it at Girl Scout Camp or 4-H Camp. There's one in the Berkshires, not far from where we live, for children who've had heart surgery, Camp Open Heart. There are camps for Down's syndrome kids, camps for children who have cancer or are HIV positive or asthmatic. Diabetics have their own camp on the Jersey shore, with a refrigerator full of insulin. Ian has always found it troubling, this siphoning off, the separating the good eggs from the bad, the regular children from the ones with something wrong. Too much like a leper colony, he said once. Hey, folks, it's easy, just stick these kids in the woods where nobody can see their sores! He wanted Max mainstreamed; he always has, even though Max himself has forever been a wayward, watchful fellow (XP or not, somehow I think he'd be this way), all darts and glances, shy smiles, sudden moves. A lot, I guess, like me.

For me there was, from the start, something moving, even magical about these camps for the crooked children of the earth. Fifty blind kids, fifty scarred kids—it might have been fifty girls like the one I'd been—uncomfortable in their skins, fast in their movements, unable to find the right words or meet the shifting demands of the social world. Suddenly, where once these children had stood out, now they were among familiars, lost in the crowd. I'd seen the way Max hovered at the edge of the gym class he took at home and preferred to hang out with a troupe of imaginary friends or with me. I'd seen how he and Adam had been growing more and more apart, as one boy stayed up in his room while the other flung himself into the lit, green world.

For a year or so, I'd been logging on to the computer to check out the XP Society Web site or read the e-mail messages on the listserv I'd joined, though I never spoke up on it myself. The messages could be banal or long-winded, but I didn't mind, so relieved to find that there were others like us, people with the disease in Tunisia and Paris and Nepal, in Puerto Rico and Japan, Nebraska and Arizona—not many, but there they were, and the parents told stories, asked questions, and now and then an adult with XP even wrote in, and each time I thought *Yes, she has a job; he has a girlfriend; they have whole lives,* the messages like a balm delivered through the liquid plasma of the screen.

It was mid-February of Max's ninth year that I first showed him the camp on the computer. It was close to midnight; we were taking a break from his lessons, Ian and Adam asleep. The link to Camp Luna sat on the Society's home page below a photo of a canoe on a lake. There were two kids in the canoe, wearing tank tops and orange life preservers and holding their paddles aloft. You could tell from their red pupils that a flash had gone off, but still the photo had an air of light about it, the glint of water, the reach of arms. Perhaps it was this image, newly posted, that made me bring the camp up to Max, when other nights I'd passed it by. Or maybe something else: a readiness. I went to the link; I clicked.

"Come see," I told Max. "It's about a camp for kids with XP."

He slid into his desk chair, and then we were there, on the black page with its winking yellow moon, while outside the real moon shone and, next to me, my boy's eyes looked at a screen that might, for once, lead into a world of actual flesh and blood. I started skimming the text on the home page: Secluded lake . . . for children with XP and other light-sensitivity disorders . . . limited spots . . . free. (Could it be true? How had I not noticed it the year before?)

Before I could read further, Max took the mouse from me and clicked on an icon that led us to pictures of the previous year's camp. There were children mugging for the camera and gathered around a campfire, girls with their arms draped around one another's shoulders, kids angling toward a volleyball. Max studied the photographs. I watched him watching, tried to let him be. He'd only ever met two other children with XP, both at dermatology conferences where we'd gone to meet the scientists and look for help. Those kids had been much worse off than Max. One had been diagnosed late and had needed over forty surgeries to remove cancers; the other had the strain of the disease that leads to neurological damage—at twelve, she was deaf and could neither walk nor talk. Max clicked again and we saw a lake, a string of lights, three adults on a bench, holding up some sort of papier-mâché beast. Again he clicked. A child looked out at us, his skin pocked, his grin lopsided as if part of his jaw had been sliced off.

"All right," I told him, my voice thin, but still he wouldn't stop. He went through all the pictures, once and then again, leaning ever closer.

Finally, he sat back. "Say we're coming. So they save us a spot. Okay?"

"Hold on, sweetie," I said. "We need to talk to Dad first and figure out our schedules. He has summer school, and Adam's signed up for soccer camp, remember? There are a lot of things we'd need to find out."

"Dad—" he started to call, heading for the door.

"No." I got up and stopped him with my arm, then leaned back and clicked us to the home page, away from the wounded boy. "Tomorrow's a school day. We'll ask him later."

I didn't tell him that I had, in fact, read about the camp on the listserv the year before and suggested it to Ian then. He had dismissed it for a hundred practical reasons and (though he didn't admit it) a deeper one—he didn't want Max dumped into the collective stew of the disease. I hadn't pushed. I hadn't even investigated further. We'd grown comfortable in our lives, all of us wary of change. Instead of camp, we'd gone on a short vacation to southern Maine, staying in Ian's cousin's empty summerhouse. We took the kids to an amusement park one night and to an outdoor movie on another. On our last night, we raced down a long beach, singing and throwing pebbles into the phosphorescent tide.

All that was nice, but the house had picture windows we had to cover with flattened cardboard boxes and black garbage bags, and the town was so small that no stores stayed open late. When we walked down Main Street in the late afternoon, people stared at Max, who was covered head to toe—ski mask, sunglasses, high-tops, gloves. Yes, we know it's hot out, I'd wanted to shout. Keep your eyes to yourselves! But oh the sea was vast, and the paths outside the house were lined with crushed white shells, and everything tasted of salt. I came home with both a renewed hunger for the outside world and a newly kindled anger at its obtuse and sunny ways. Was this the beginning, a gradual tilting of the scales? Next year, I remember telling Ian, next year it's my turn to pick.

Now Max stood by the door and hopped from foot to foot. I squeezed myself between him and the door. "Let's do some spelling."

"No, Mom, please." His voice rose. "Really, he won't mind if I wake him, he never—"

"He needs to sleep so he can work tomorrow. You know that. Okay, *camp*. Four letters, starts with . . ."

He sighed, then rattled it off.

"Yes. *Luna*."

"Um. L-U-N-A."

"Great. *Marshmallow*."

"M-A— I don't know. What if tomorrow there's no room left?"

"That won't happen overnight. Sound it out, possum, you were doing great."

"Do they eat them there?" He twined his arms around me, smelling of soap and the faintest glaze of sweat.

"Possums? I hope not."

He swatted at my behind. "Marshmallows."

"Oh. Probably. It's a camp."

"Can I go, Mama. Please?" Butterfly kisses up and down my arm.

I kissed him back, once, on the nose. "I think there's a good chance. We can try to work it out for a week or two—that's all I can say right now. I'm sorry. I need to talk to Dad."

He detached himself from me and began tearing around his small room, loping past the closet, climbing the bunk bed, jumping down to trace his hand along the windowsill, where he stopped to play with a corner of the window film.

"Don't peel it," I warned. "Try to settle down. After spelling, we can go outside."

"Adam goes to camp." Now his voice was bitter, almost defeated. "Everybody goes except for me." He threw himself onto his bed and spoke into his pillow. "Why won't you just say yes?"

I should, of course, have made sure the camp was certified, real. I should have asked Ian first, consulted Adam. We were a tight, well-oiled machine, my little family. When one part moved, the rest followed; things rarely happened without consultation, by themselves. I looked up. Max's eyes watching me over the pillow were too wise for a child his age. It was partly the faint web of wrinkles around them. It was partly the longing there, the way it was all bound up with too much knowledge—of the danger of just one minute under the sun for this boy born into the wrong elements, a fish spawned out of water, a land bird hatched under the sea. He asked for so little, really, when it came down to it. He lived with such grace inside his box.

"All right," I told him. "You can go, if they have room."

He smiled broadly, a child again, and sprang up, high-fiving the air. Then he stopped, suddenly serious. "Will you come with me?"

I nodded. "It says the families go, too." Already I was panicking at having made a unilateral decision, but I also knew I couldn't undo it, not once I'd said the words.

"And Dad and Adam?" Max was almost shouting.

"Shhh. You'll wake them."

"We'll all go," he said happily, as if everyone had just agreed.

The spelling words I chose that night all had to do with summer camps, though I'd never attended one myself—*swimming, lifeguard, firefly, cabin, badge, craft, mess kit, outhouse, matches.* Max tossed them back at me, always a good speller, and then we stopped so he could go downstairs for recess, a half-hour romp around the yard.

As I stood on our back stoop, I knew he wasn't alone there, not like he usually was, a boy running solo through the cold night air while up and down the block, the neighbors' children slept. He wasn't there at all that night, though his body circled and his lungs drank air. Already, I knew, Max was chasing after the children he'd seen on the computer screen. They would gather; he would gather with them—rare moths, regular old kids. He was throwing twigs onto a bonfire and watching them burn, kneeling by the lake, draping his arms around his friends to pose for the camera, their eyes briefly blinded by the flash.

TWO

My first labor was short and hard, a slippery passage. By the time the pain became impossible, it was too late for drugs; Adam was coming, he was coming, he was there. But Max was breech in my belly, his head tucked underneath my heart, his feet dangling down. He'll probably turn, the doctor kept saying, and as my due date approached, I did what I could to coax my fish to flip. I played the radio between my legs, dove to the bottom of the swimming pool at the Y, balanced on all fours like an inverted red-faced camel, turn, baby, turn.

He wouldn't. Of course not. Already stubborn, already shrewd, my younger boy, my last. All along, as I bent my body into unkind shapes, I knew he wouldn't turn. Inside you, they're hairy for a time—lanugo, it's called, a soft down, a primate-harkening fur. Max should have kept his coat; it might have shielded him. Or stayed inside me, where the atmosphere was sunproofed and he was double-skinned. Pure chance, I can hear

Ian saying. Pure chance that one was breech, the other not. Pure chance that one was sick, the other not. Three weeks before my due date, they decided to try to turn him. A *version*, it was called. A gentle manipulation, said my doctor, while we monitor him on ultrasound. Their version. Come on, little fellow, good boy, come along now. Flip. To say it hurt doesn't begin to describe what it felt like, the sickening, pure white pain of something completely at odds with itself, so unlike the pain of Adam's birth, where everything conspired to push him down and out.

They gave me intravenous drugs to relax my uterus. Dizzy, I kept saying, I'm really dizzy, and they flipped some levers on the table and tilted me head down, like a baby entering the birth canal. Then they were pumping something else inside me, I was impossibly cold, my arms shaking, my legs, a fish out of water, the thump of fin, dry gasp. What happened next I only know as it's been told to me: how my blood pressure dropped, the baby's too, how our heartbeats, tandem hoofbeats on the Doppler, slowed. Some kind of reaction to the medication, they said later. They put me under, cut Max out. After he was born, he wasn't breathing, and they intubated him and took him to another floor, but I knew none of this as it was happening, suspended in a watery, sleep-swept region like the one he'd come from. When I woke, I said, Where's my baby, meaning Adam, and the nurse said they're helping him, they're making him better. Adam, I said, trying to sit up, hands suddenly appearing to restrain me. Then Ian's face above me. He was, I remember, a peculiar shade of gray. Adam's with my mother, he said, touching my face. The new baby is fine, they're just checking him out in the pediatric ward. So he's not fine. No, I really think he is. Then why—

On my belly, I wanted him, or no, something more extreme, in my womb, back inside me, for I had loved being pregnant those last few months, once the nausea was over, had never minded how big I got; it made me feel so whole, so doubled, harboring a complex, private world that ran itself. I could have stayed that way, pregnant, for sixteen months, like a rhino, or twenty-two months, like an elephant. I knew, of course, that I couldn't keep the baby inside me forever, but a little late, a little later, that would have been nice. They made a gash in me, then closed it like a zipper. More than once in the months that were to follow, I would picture opening myself with one sure tug and popping him in again. Just for a time, so I could fix him, or, if that proved impossible, so we could all get ready. Then to the sun, the light.

"Oh come on, Anna, he's perfect," I remember Ian saying a few weeks after Max's birth, for he was a newborn of uncommon good looks—a beautifully shaped head from the C-section, lots of curls, his eyes a complex blue that already hinted at the delicate gray-brown they would become.

"He has a constant rash," I said. "He *hurts*. I'm telling you, something's not right. Adam didn't have this."

"It's hot out, that's all. Look at me." He showed me his arm, the beads of sweat, the bug bites. "He just has to adjust. Remember, your body had climate control."

Over and over, in those early days, Ian told me I was a worry-wart. He wasn't the only one. Dr. Orleans, Max's pediatrician, said the same thing. Put a hat on him, she suggested. With flaps. Mild sun allergy; keep him in the shade. From the beginning, I knew it was more than that. I remembered how, from birth, Adam had turned toward the light as if it were a food source or human voice, tracking it with his eyes. Max winced away from the light, hunching inside his blanket like a stunned turtle. One day Ian brought home an article on postpartum depression. A few days later, he told me we could try again in a few years, go for a third child, since he knew I was disappointed not to get a girl. I might have gotten angrier if I hadn't been so tired, so filled with rising dread. I couldn't seem to concentrate on anything but this tiny aching baby and my own body, which was cut and leaking blood, still, and milk, and demanding prodigious quantities of food. Even Adam seemed suddenly more self-sufficient, stacking blocks and eating rice crackers on the floor as I tended to Max, in a way that left me both stricken and relieved.

One afternoon, while Ian was with the children, I went to the town library and looked up sun allergies, with the help of a friendly librarian and a database I had no idea how to use, until I came across the précis of a scientific article: "Gene Therapy and DNA Reconstructive Possibilities for Patients with Xeroderma Pigmentosum." How new the words were to me then, how strange and hard to say. The article itself was in a medical journal the library didn't carry. I ordered it on interlibrary loan, photocopied the précis, and called Dr. Orleans, who said she would look into it and call me back. I called my old college roommate Sophie, now a doctor in Chicago, and she promised to hunt down more articles for me. It was two days before Dr. Orleans called.

"I really doubt it," she said as I plugged one ear to block out Max's crying. "It's very, very rare, and there are many more common things that could be causing a reaction."

An hour later, she called again while both boys were napping. "Let's go ahead and keep him out of the light," she said, as if she were his mother too. "Just while we investigate, to be safe. I still think it's probably a minor thing."

"What do you mean, out of the light?"

"Out of the sun."

"What if it's cloudy? I mean, if I want to take him on a walk in the stroller, or out in the yard? I also have Adam, I can't just—"

"Of course not. Put up the stroller hood and give the baby a sun hat, and maybe carry an umbrella over him."

Then she paused. In my stomach, something flopped, a quickening, almost.

"Actually," she said, "I take it back. Let's play it safe and keep him inside, with the shades down. I know it's a nuisance, but hopefully it won't be for long. I need to look into this and get you hooked up with someone at Children's. I'll start on it right now."

"But you still think it's probably not . . . xero—" I stumbled.

"It's so rare," she said. "Practically unheard of. I've never seen a case, and neither has anyone else in the practice. How's he doing otherwise?"

"He's, you know, nursing and pooping and sleeping. He's adorable—we think so, anyway—in that old man baby way."

"Enjoy him," she said. "It goes so fast."

A few days later, after I'd read the whole article but before we had an official diagnosis, I came home from a postpartum checkup to find Ian outside with both children. It was late afternoon, a cloudy day. Adam and Ian were leaning over something—a caterpillar or an anthill—in the yard. Max was on the porch in his car seat, with the hood up and a crocheted blanket slung between the hood and base of the seat, creating a sort of tent. Through the layers, I could hear his thin, catlike cries. I lifted a corner of the blanket and looked inside. He was tightly swaddled with a hat on, but his face was exposed, and his eyes were full of what I can only call despair.

I whisked everyone inside, sent Adam into his room with a box of crayons and a pad, unswaddled Max, and held him under the light above the kitchen table, where I could see—on his face, his neck, even one ear—a spreading rash.

"If you ever do this again," I said to Ian above the baby's howls, "I'll take them and never come back. This could kill him, don't you understand?"

Ian squinted at me. "Listen to yourself. It's five o'clock, it's not even sunny out, and he was wrapped from head to—"

"It doesn't matter, it's *light.* You didn't protect his face. I told you—any light." I started dabbing at Max's face with a wet paper towel, which only made him scream harder. "Oh, my baby," I kept saying. "Okay, all right, all right now, shhh." Baking soda, I remembered about burns, but mixed with what? Cortisone cream, Benadryl, somewhere we had some. Noxzema? Toothpaste? Not on the skin of a newborn.

"Stop it, Anna, he hates that. You're torturing him."

"*I'm* torturing him? Look at him. Look!"

We both leaned over Max. His cheeks were pocked with small red welts and rising blisters, which seemed to multiply as we watched.

"Jesus," said Ian. "It was only for five minutes, while Adam ran around the yard, he was so cooped up, I thought . . . I read that with sun allergies a little exposure can help, if you're careful. Dr. Orleans said she wasn't sure what was wrong, remember, there were several possibilities—"

Ian reached out, but I drew Max back, against my chest.

"This isn't an allergy, it's irreparable damage. Read the stuff I left you. And Sophie sent more articles today. You just ignore—"

"I didn't ignore it. I put sunscreen on him and covered him up, and with the porch roof and . . . and the hood and blanket and, I mean, it's such a cloudy day, I thought—"

"Sunscreen won't do a thing but irritate him. Shhh, baby. Shush . . . okay, we're sorry, Daddy's sorry, it's okay."

"So he can never go outside? You mean, at all?" Ian said it as if it were dawning on him for the first time. Max was beginning to quiet down by then, though his skin would take weeks to heal.

"Not during the day. It'll—" I couldn't say the word. "Not when there's any light. Only at night."

"That's insane." His face twisted, and for a moment he didn't look like himself, and I felt afraid in a whole new way. "People can't live that way, it's not possible," he said. "They have to be able to find a cure for this thing, if he really does have it, or a . . . I don't know, a cream or something, to block the light."

"Well." I shrugged. "They haven't. Not that we know about."

"I'll start looking into it," Ian said. "There must be a solution to this or we would have heard about it more. I mean, who can live like this?"

"People do," I said, thinking, *until they don't;* fewer than 40 percent survived past the age of twenty. "It's extremely rare," I said, "and there's very little research. It's an *orphan disease.*"

I'd been reading everything I could find, and already the words felt oddly familiar on my tongue, as if I'd mastered the lingo, explained our situation to doubting family and friends. Really? But the baby seemed fine when we saw him, so cute. . . . Did you have an amnio? . . . Have you taken him to Beth Israel, my cousin's a chief resident there—in cardiology but maybe he could help, he's really smart. And invitations: Can you come to our picnic, do you guys want to go swimming? Oh, sorry, sorry, Anna, I forgot. An *orphan disease*, as if it had no parents—except it did, Max did, and we were them.

"What?" Standing beside me that day, Ian crossed his hands over his chest. "Orphan disease? What's that supposed to mean?"

"That nobody wants to fund the research—it's too rare."

"Lovely term. Very nice." He took Max from me. "You're going to be okay," he murmured, sliding his finger into Max's tight grip. "I'm sorry," he said—to me or to Max—and I put my arms around his waist, and we stood there rocking, my head bent over the baby's.

"Mommy." We turned. Adam was standing in the doorway.

"Oh, Addie." I reached out my arms. "Hi, honey. Come here."

He held out a piece of paper.

"You finished your drawing?" I asked. "Can I see?"

He charged toward us, tumbling forward. He always looked as if he were about to fall but rarely did. When he reached me, I started to hug him, but he pulled back to show me his drawing, purple scribbles with fanged orange teeth.

"Ooh." I said. "Scary. Is it a monster?"

"It's Max," he said. "When do we bring him back?"

Without thinking, I took Max from Ian. "Back?"

"To the hospital."

"Oh, no." I shook my head. "We don't bring him back, he lives with us. That's what having a brother means, you get to teach him how to be a big—"

"He means because Max isn't feeling so great," Ian said. "We might want to take him to the hospital so the doctors can make him better, right, Adam?"

"Is that what you mean?" I knew it wasn't, and for a moment I pictured it too—returning this infant. Not quite what we had in mind, cash or store credit, please come again. "This is a huge change for you," I said. "Come here, baby."

Adam let go of his drawing, and it floated for a second before sliding under the table. "Daddy," he said, and climbed into Ian's arms.

Max had stopped crying, though his eyes were still swollen, his mouth pursed shut. My back, my head, everything hurt. My shirt clung to me where my milk was leaking through. One of my nipples was bloody, cracked. Across the kitchen, Ian's face seemed mottled, bruised, as if he were the one who couldn't tolerate the light.

"We'll need blackout shades for every room," Ian said. He put Adam down and went to pull the curtains even tighter. "I'll go tonight, after they're asleep. And I'll see what else I can find out. I know you already did, but maybe there's more."

I nodded, suddenly too hungry to speak. I put Max in his car seat, knelt down and started rummaging through the fridge, stuffing a carrot stick in my mouth, swiping my finger through a tub of hummus, looking for cheese, but we'd run out. We needed to go shopping. You walked down the aisles and picked out groceries. You paid. It was simple. We could do it.

And then Max was crying, a squall of hunger now—a normal cry, not pain, not sun. For me.

"I'm hungry," Adam announced over the noise.

I bit a grape in two and popped half in his mouth, half in mine. Then I laughed, and when I met Ian's eye across the room, I saw that he was laughing too.

"Everyone is hungry," I said. "And everyone shall eat."

And so we moved back inside our lives, together again, sealed in our house now, our living bodies asking us for food. We had so much to learn, so much to forget—the trips we'd planned, the camping equipment stowed in the attic, our early hikes together, the skylights and windows we'd been drawn to when we first saw the house, the art studio Ian was going to build for me, our taken-for-granted pleasure at watching our children move slowly, steadily, into the world.

Adam leaned against me. Ian picked up Max. These are my people, I remember thinking. The ones I've made my life with, the ones I've made. I handed Adam a carrot stick dipped in peanut butter and reached for Max. Still chewing, then, I put my baby to my breast.

Later that first night at camp, Hal gave us a tour: of the lodge and outbuildings, the lawn, boathouse and shoreline, all the places that would later become part of my inner landscape, my private property. The lodge was built to last, with great beams bisecting the ceilings, a kitchen sink the size of a bathtub, a linen closet that could have housed a queen-sized bed. The house Ian and I owned was dollhouse small, its ceilings so low I could touch them with my raised palm. Our cabinets were laminate, not oiled wood, our sink a postage stamp of fiberglass. In our kitchen, you could reach from the stove to the sink to the fridge without taking more than two steps. In the lodge, I felt small, dwarfed, yet somehow also larger, too, as if a space had been opened up inside me and I might step through it to become another person.

"Here," Hal said that night, stopping by the door that led to the front hall. He showed us the double doors, a sensor and a bell; it would ring during the day each time somebody came within thirty feet from inside or out. "That way, the kids, if someone's around, will have time to run upstairs before any light gets in."

Ian grimaced. He disliked such tricks of technology, the shrill solace of a warning bell—anything that made an XP house, an XP kid stand out from all the rest. At home we simply had a handwritten sign asking visitors to ring the doorbell and wait two minutes before opening the door.

Behind the lodge, a long slope—the lawn. At the bottom, lights, then darkness beyond. We followed Hal to the water's edge. "If you're quiet, you might hear something," he said, and after a few minutes it came, a cry from across the water, mournful and hollow—*Oo-ah-ho*—almost like a human in distress. "The common loon," Hal said, raising his hands to his mouth. "*Oo-ah-ho!*" He did the call so expertly that to my untrained ear he might as well have been a waterbird. I was standing behind him with my flashlight on, and for a moment I saw his arms as wings, his hair as a bright plume.

"And sometimes," he said, "they laugh, or wail. *Kee-a-ree, kee-a-ree!*"

It was then, beneath those odd bird calls, that I got my first glimpse of Hal's sadness. I'd already been told by another parent that his wife had died five years earlier, and somehow I knew, I think I knew, that he had practiced these calls with her before she died. As we turned away, I pictured my own hands cupping my mouth, the uttering of an old—or was it an anticipated?—grief. I'd lost nobody so far. Not really. Still, I could feel the ache, of a man for his wife, of a girl for her mother. Of a mother—*let* me think it—for her son. Ian didn't like to talk about the possibility of losing Max so I tried not to bring it up, but the less I spoke of it, the more it pressed against the edges of my thoughts. The sounds rose up inside my throat; I cut them off.

In the dark, as we followed Hal about, Max stayed close to me at first, toying with my elbow, which he'd always found comforting, that jut of bone and skin. When we came to an outbuilding, Hal turned on the light and the group crowded in behind him. The room was lined with old wooden desks and chairs. Three computers sat on the desks, each with a different screensaver—a city skyline full of blinking lights, a night jungle, a black sky stocked with shooting stars.

"We're still building shelves and desks in here," Hal said, "but I got the computers hooked up so you could stay in touch with your friends."

"Can I check my e-mail, Mom?" Adam asked.

On one screen, cartoon monkeys swung, chattering, from branch to branch. On another, a star fell with a whistling sound and disappeared. I shook my head. "We just got here. Not right now."

"I know I'll have messages."

"After the tour, Adam, okay?"

As we left the computer room, Ian and I dropped a few steps behind.

"Wired." He let out a low whistle. "They call this a summer camp? Where are the outhouses? Somebody's got major bucks here."

"Shhh," I said, and then, in a whisper, "Lucky for us."

As a boy, Ian had gone to a camp where you had to build your own shelter, catch fish, pick dandelion greens and blackberries for meals. He was suspicious of money, the product of his practical

Irish-American mother, and he had a complicated ethos that valued both self-reliance and teamwork in ways I still found confusing. As for me, I'd never been to summer camp; my mother must have been afraid that something would happen to me, or maybe my father was too cheap. Instead, I'd taken classes at the Jewish Community Center, and baby-sat, and gone with my mother and brother to the municipal pool, where the mothers did an awkward breaststroke with their necks thrust up so their hair wouldn't get wet and the chlorinated water burned your eyes. You could only get chips there, in tiny bags half full of air, and melting Popsicles that attracted wasps and bees. Did I mind the creamy imported cheeses here, the antique mission furniture, the bells and whistles? At home, I lived entirely within our means, a genuine fan of castoffs, yard sales and bargain bins, but didn't our boys—didn't we—deserve a holiday?

We saw, that night, the boathouse and the dock, the tennis courts, the hangar where the summer people used to keep their planes. We saw the wooden rotunda, its latticework twined with moonflower vines, the flowers white flares. Slowly, we made our way down branching paths, losing kids to Ping-Pong in the boathouse, to horseshoes and Frisbee on the sloped lawn, which smelled of cut grass and crushed thyme.

"Can I?" Adam asked at the trampoline, and before I could answer, he was up there, springing high to land on his knees, twisting in the air, his body wiry and confident. A wall of netting circled the trampoline but it still looked dangerous, and I moved closer.

"You want a turn?" Ian asked Max after a few minutes, but Max shook his head. "Are you sure?" Ian nudged him gently. "You can control how high you bounce. Adam, why don't you let your brother have a turn?"

"I said *no*." Max turned away. There was a trampoline at the gymnastics class he'd started taking after we got a donation from 3M to tint the gym windows at the elementary school, but he'd refused to try it, just as he'd refused to vault over the horse or climb the rope.

"You can try later if you change your mind," I told him. "Or not."

I looked up the hill. The group had moved on.

"Come." I took his hand. "If we hurry, we can still catch up."

Hal conducted the tour of the grounds as if he were the owner, or not quite—as if he were the caretaker, or the gardener who had coaxed each carrot from the soil. Though he wasn't a large man, his voice was deep, and it was clear he really loved this place. As we continued, more kids began to lag behind, and some of the adults started flagging too. But I liked being on a tour; it made me feel like a child being taught about the world. *This is the garden, this is the boathouse, this is where we wash our clothes*. I liked not being the one in charge. Gone was my date book filled with doctors' appointments, practice schedules, home-schooling units; gone, my shopping lists and coupons—BUY TWO GET A DOLLAR OFF, BUY FOUR GET ONE FREE. When, finally, we returned to the porch, Hal put down Alida, who had been riding on his shoulders, and she leaned against him, swaying.

"I think this monkey needs a nap." He ran his fingers through her hair.

"No nap." Alida rubbed her eyes.

"All right, but rest. I'll carry you."

People started off in various directions. I looked around. Ian was a few feet away, but Adam and Max were nowhere to be seen.

"Where are the kids?" I asked Ian for the second time that night.

"Adam went to check his e-mail. Max is"—he pointed—"there." He had, I realized with a start, been keeping track while I had not.

I heard Max before I saw him—a cry of pleasure, a bursting laugh. He was down below, where the lawn leveled out. As we moved closer, I could see that he was climbing through the opening in the netting onto the trampoline. Ian and I went down the porch steps. Almost in unison, we turned off our flashlights and crept over to watch from beneath the shadow of a tree. By the time we got there, another boy had joined him; through the netting, I could make out the child's thick glasses, his round, pleased face. Max bent his legs and stumbled, let out a low cry, righted himself, bounced a few inches off the surface, bent his knees and bounced again. Across from him, the other boy bounced too.

This, before us, was our small, our caged and cagey boy, our second son, my shadow, the one who never left my side except to circle our yard or hole away in his room. This was the Max of public scowls and private deep affections, of bursts of temper and hours of solitary observation, looking at the computer screen, at the kids outside his tinted windows, at his books and collections: Pokémon cards, nocturnal stuffed animals, hospital bracelets, stamps. This was the boy who knew the names of all the planets and a slew of constellations but had never ridden a school bus, or played at a friend's house in the afternoon, or run with a pack of boys into the woods.

From perhaps thirty feet away, Ian and I stood, and when he tucked his arm around me, I moved in front of him, leaned back into him, felt his mouth against my head. I traced his forearm with my fingers—the soft hairs, the familiar skin that was slightly darker than mine and tanned more easily but held the same recessive gene. His hands moved down. He cupped my hips, and I arched to bring us closer.

The world dropped away, then. The many details of my life became tiny, nearly invisible, hard to track. The laughing boy on the trampoline might have been our child or somebody else's, a gymnast we were watching, a perfect form seeking flight. I might have been fifteen or fifty, a mother or not, married or not. A body, I was, for a moment, as Max leaped high and staggered low and leaped again, Ian's hands on my hips, my eyes filling—but why?—with stinging tears.

I turned to Ian and brought my mouth to his. We kissed there, then, standing in the shadows while Max lost and found and lost his balance on the trampoline. We kissed with the kind of hunger nearly always reserved for strangers, or for lovers who've been apart for much too long—wandering the world, perhaps, or locked inside their heads. We met each other's mouths with as much ease and abandon as this new place seemed to have, this land where clearings held tables full of paint and paper, where lanterns seemed to burn of their own accord and wary children leaped to life.

Later, of course, I learned that people had worked for months to ready the camp, not just Hal but also the volunteers: Charlie, from town; Andrew and Kaylie, who hung the lights from the trees, refilling them each time the kerosene ran out; Jess and Amy, born-again Christians whose sister had died from a hole in the heart and who tended tirelessly to our kids. Later, too, I learned the history of the lodge, its copper imported from the

African mines where Hal's wife's family had made its enormous fortune, its chairs and couches worn smooth by privileged people long since dead. How, when his wife died of breast cancer, the whole thing went to Hal, who'd been, in his youth, a poor Jewish boy from Brooklyn. Later still, I learned the back ways: the servants' staircase, the meat locker off the kitchen, the dank basement smelling of mold, the far garret bedrooms that trapped the heat at night, making it hard to breathe.

That first night, though, everything was simple. I kissed my husband. I watched my child jump. It was dawn by the time we went inside and slept, mid-afternoon when we woke for breakfast. In the tinted daylight, I could see sores on the campers' skin, dry scaly patches, and scars where cancers had been removed. Adam was tired. Max was quiet again, drawn inside himself. Across from me, Ian talked to a man named Josh about the research of a scientist in Seattle who was studying XP. That morning, for the first time in months, we'd had sex when finally we went to bed, and though I'd showered, I still felt raw and salty at breakfast, even sore.

I sat between my two boys and ate quietly, methodically, lifting my eggs to my mouth with a tarnished fork etched with a monogram, EKP. After dark, Hal announced at breakfast, he'd take a group out fishing in canoes.

Fishing, I thought, and I pictured not the hook and rod, not the shout of a child reeling in a fish, but the deep, still waters, how free the fish were and how silent, turning first here, then there, with a flick of tail, a flair of gill, while overhead, canoes passed by filled with this group of people (how small we were, how thin-skinned, lovely and determined), laboring our way across the lake.

THREE

Once, long ago, when I was perhaps four or five, friends of my parents invited us to a summer party at their country house. We drove for miles, and by the time we got there, it was dusk. There was a house—there must have been a house—but I don't remember it. I remember a field, a wide cast-open swath, and the way the parents sat talking on the patio while the kids ran out into the grass. I was a child of the suburbs, the daughter of a nervous mother, but that night my mother sank deep into her lawn chair, sipped her wine and let her children go.

Grass on my legs, scratching me, I remember, and the sound of my own heart, and the way I was hurtling along—heedless, reckless—somewhere new in the world. There were other children there but I couldn't see their faces, so I didn't need to ask their names or tell them mine. Flung laughter, we were, forward motion. When the fireflies started to blink, jars appeared, and we ran after the insects, closing our hands around their lights and dropping them into the jars. I wasn't much good at catching; I was better at watching, at running, and after a while a tall girl handed me a canning jar and told me to stand with it so the bigger children could fill it up.

My breath steadying, then, evening out. The jar in my hands, a round of cool, hard glass. I stood very still, unscrewing the lid when a child appeared with a firefly and using my palm as a shield to keep the other bugs inside. How capable I was—suddenly I knew it of myself—and how astonishing the stuttering, live lights I held, like nothing I'd ever seen.

Standing there, I felt, for the first time in my memory, suspended inside a moment that I knew was about to pass. I could see it all before it happened: how the bugs would be set free or die; how the parents would call us and, named, accounted for, we'd leave the field, we'd come. Too-bright light inside a house, then. This is Annie. Say hello, Annie. This is Susan, Jamie, Paul. You must be dehydrated, have something to drink. My mother scrubbing my face and hands, taking off my sandals so she could check my feet for ticks.

Already almost over, I thought as I stood in the field. A boy came up to me. I unscrewed the lid and the firefly joined the others and the boy wheeled off into the night.

Already almost gone.

A place like that, Hal made of his camp. A place—it was the first time I'd come across one in my adult life—that felt like a more sustained version of my moment in the field. What do we each leave on earth after we're gone? What will I leave? Hal's camp was his gift. In honor of his wife, it was, and for his child, and yet he loved other people's children too—loved ours—and not in an abstracted or blanket way, but as he got to know them, watched them, learned their ways. Those were the easy parts, the rest perhaps more complicated. How much he needed everyone to like him. How full of want his eyes were when he looked around at us, his left hand trembling sometimes, wishing, though I didn't yet know it, to grasp a cigarette. How angry he was, and how well he hid it—like the rest of us, I suppose. At least like me. Everyone was drawn to Hal, almost everyone, women, men, children, just as we were all slightly afraid of him—for how he kept the place running at such a steady shipshape clip, for how his voice could have a pierce to it and was, for all its charms, not easy to dispute or to ignore.

Each evening we had activities: face painting and volleyball, story circle and midnight water polo. A fencing team came out one night to give a demonstration and lesson, the masked fencers dodging and sparring like giant leggy insects on the lawn. Another night, a battered silver truck carrying two ponies pulled up and several clowns emerged from the cab with painted-on smiles, their noses glowing red balls. As the children played, the parents did too. We played card games and board games and sang songs while a volunteer strummed on her guitar. We cleared and set the table, cleaned string beans and peeled potatoes, but these things did not feel like chores, somehow, not like they would have at home. I loved the kitchen with its sweet smell of gas and rows of drying herbs. I loved the enormous washing machines and dryers, the laundry bags marked with other people's initials, the horsehair pillows on the couches, the cookie jar shaped like a ship. I loved how you could chat easily with someone by the sink, on the porch, then climb the stairs to your quiet, gabled room.

For the first time in years, I spent chunks of time with adults other than Ian. I drank wine on the porch with Marnie, mother of Tommy, the boy on the trampoline. Carole and I went on walks. More and more, as the nights went on, our children disappeared, clustering in small packs, taking off down paths into the woods, where counselors waited by campfires or crafts projects. For the first time since Max was born, I didn't always know where he was. Often, when the kids were off together, a group of parents would go down to the lake to float on inner tubes or sit on the raft, where we'd talk and laugh. We laughed about funny things—a child's comment, a joke—but we also laughed in the way of people sharing something tight, private and indescribably painful for the first time. I know, we kept saying. I know. And somehow, as we sat there, the world turned comic, bright and giddy. That happened to us too, we kept saying, and it wasn't so much that misery loves company as that this particular company let us wrap our misery in the skewed, cartoonish colors of a joke.

We laughed longer, louder than the stories were funny, until our stomachs ached and our eyes watered. I was not quiet in this group. I was not unfunny. "Remember?" I'd say to Ian when he was on the raft too. "Remember when?" And if he smiled a bit stiffly, laughed a bit briefly, I'm not sure I noticed, too high on the moment, too full of my newfound friends. "Once we were waiting in line—" said Carole, said Françoise, said Hal. "Once her doctor told us—" Then to the water, a jump, a dive. Marnie's crawl was steady. Hal did a jackknife. He might have been a boy, all of us children, the darkness that forgiving, the only light coming from some flashlights strung around the raft. The arc of her arm as it sliced the water; his body springing, folding and unfolding, going down. For a long moment, nothing. Then he surfaced, breathless, grinning. I stood, curling my toes around the edge of the raft. The wood was wet and rotting, as soft and slippery as kelp. I shut my eyes and jumped.

By the seventh night, everyone was ready to take a break from activities and catch up on sleep. Most people weren't accustomed to the hours we were keeping. The non-XP siblings and the parents with day jobs were used to getting up for school or work, and even those of us who stayed up late at home, like Max and I, didn't stay up *this* late, collapsing into bed here just as the sun began to rise. That second Saturday at dinner, I watched as, all around me, eyelids drooped and mouths stifled yawns. Adam had already gone to bed, complaining of a headache. Max sat next to Ian, his head on his father's arm. Even Ian, who has always needed less sleep than the rest of us, had a glazed, vacant look in his eye. He and a few other fathers had started making a ropes course the night before, and his hand was bandaged from where he'd gotten a splinter and tried to extract it himself.

"I'm exhausted," Marnie said as we got up from the table. "Being on vacation is a lot of work."

I finished off my glass of wine. "You don't want to swim tonight?"

She shook her head. "I can barely move. I think I'll just mellow out and rest."

The thing about me, though, was I wasn't mellow, I didn't want to rest. I was buoyed up, flying. How can I explain? It was, perhaps, most like my first year at college, away from my parents and our manicured New Jersey suburb. Suddenly there I was, at this experimental school in the Berkshires where we had no grades, no curfews, just a hilly green campus filled with buildings where we were meant to read books, sculpt and draw, make friends. I hardly slept for weeks. I talked, read, wandered.

In my first art history class, I met Sophie, who became my closest friend. I met a brown boy with a glossy black ponytail and made out with him on the roof of the planetarium, where the asphalt shingles still held the day's last heat. Or it was like the first time I went to Europe and traveled alone through France and Italy, getting off at whatever village struck my fancy and soaking in the foreign language, the foreign food, the slant of perfectly foreign light.

Every once in a while, things hit you so hard you can't close your eyes for a long time. I was forty-one my first year at Camp Luna. I had one son who was thirteen, another who was nine. I'd been married for over fourteen years. Our life as a family wasn't easy, with Max's illness, but neither was it extremely difficult, as lives go. We loved one another. We were kind most of the time, and tolerant; we gave hugs, told jokes, forgave one another's moods. We lived as well as we could in a small space. What I hadn't quite allowed myself to consider until then was how cramped I was, how much I wanted to stretch my limbs, my mind. I took a walk that night, alone. I left Ian playing a half-hearted game of Scrabble with a few other parents, left Adam sleeping upstairs and Max eating cookies in the kitchen. Before I went, I put on jeans, hiking socks and a long-sleeved flannel shirt. I tucked my hair into one of Adam's baseball caps, sprayed myself with Off!, slung a water bottle around my neck and grabbed a flashlight from a basket near the stairs.

"I'm going for a little walk—be back soon," I said, first to Ian, then to Max, and each of them barely looked up.

Hal passed me in the front hall as I was leaving. "Anna." He looked me over, from my sneakers to my cap. "Are you off on a safari?"

I flushed. "I wish. Just a little walk."

"It's beautiful out, nearly a full moon." He cocked his head toward my flashlight. "You almost won't need that. Where are you going?"

"No place, really. Along the shore, maybe, for ten minutes. Just to get some air."

I could tell he didn't believe me, and as soon as the words left my mouth, I knew not to believe myself.

"You could take a trail," he said. "They're marked with glow-in-the-dark markers."

"I don't want to leave the kids for too long."

"There's a battalion of grown-ups here," he said, "including Ian, right?"

I nodded. "I'm just not used to leaving them, especially Max."

"Most parents feel that way at first. Often, though, it's the siblings who end up being a little lost."

"Really? Does Adam seem lost to you?"

He considered. "Maybe, or maybe he's just keeping his own counsel. I hardly know him. I'm sure you're the better judge."

I pictured Adam over the past week, how he had hung back much of the time, carrying around a book or his Game Boy, or going off to check his e-mail. He went to bed earlier than most of us, spent more of the daylight hours awake, but wasn't that to be expected since it was what he did at home? He was in a new place, where his brother was in the limelight. And he was thirteen. At home, where he rode his bike to soccer practice, fielded phone calls from both boys and girls, did his homework swiftly and well, he struck me as anything but lost.

"This is a funny setup for him," I said. "He's really attached to his friends, and he wanted to be at soccer camp. He'll go when we get back. He's the most popular kid in his class at home, but here—" I shrugged.

"Everything is different," said Hal. "Turned on its head. No former rules apply. Is that it?"

"I guess so. Something like that."

"It's like one of Alida's favorite songs." With his eyes trained on the wall above my head, he began to sing:

"If buttercups buzzed after the bee,
if boats were on land, churches on sea,
if ponies rode men and if grass ate the cows,
and cats should be chased into holes by the mouse.
If summer were spring and the other way 'round,
then all the world would be upside down."

When he finished, he dropped his gaze, suddenly bashful, I thought, though it seemed unlike him and I couldn't be sure.

"That's great," I said. "Where did you learn it?"

"Robin knew it, from her childhood. I might be missing a few lines, or even verses. Probably I am."

"Will you sing it again?" I asked. "Or write it down?"

A spiral of my hair had come untucked from Adam's cap, and as Hal leaned forward across the hall, I realized he was about to tuck it in. I pushed the hair back myself and glanced at him. Between us, the air was almost visibly taut. He straightened up, laced his hands together and let out a little sigh. Suddenly I saw myself as he must have seen me: uptight, flinching, too ready to interpret. He was an affectionate, physical man, after all. His hands were always gesticulating, smoothing the hair of a child. Clearly I'd spent too much time away and had forgotten how to read the casual, friendly gestures of the world.

But then he smiled, ever so slightly. "Some former rules apply," he said.

I felt a spasm in my belly, deep and almost painful. So we were flirting—obviously we were, just as obviously as Ian was sitting in the next room, I was married, this was a harmless little game. Hadn't I seen Ian, after all, flirting with some of the mothers? I had. I could feel, as I'd watched him talk to them, the pleasure passing back and forth—from the conversation, yes, the common ground, but also from the lilt of Françoise's accent and the way you could tell that Carole had once been a teenage beauty like her daughter. These women were drawn to Ian—for his skill at playing with their children, for his thoughtfulness, but also (why not?) for his blue-gray eyes and capable hands, and the way he lived inside his body with such ease. It didn't bother me to see this, not in any serious way. If anything, it made me appreciate Ian more. And I trusted him, just as I trusted myself. Anyway, all around us—like insulation, like electric fences—were our children.

"If you take a left down the road," Hal said, "you'll come to a trail after the field where the cars are parked. There's a lantern where it starts. It goes up Fir Mountain. It's not far."

He met my gaze. His eyes were slightly almond-shaped, with lashes so thick they must have drawn comments when he was a boy. At their corners, a spray of fine creases—worry or laugh lines or both. *If buttercups buzzed.* For a moment, I allowed myself to look. Then I turned away.

"Have fun," he said sweetly, though underneath, I could swear it had another, angrier sound: Fuck you.

Go, I told my feet, and, obligingly, they trotted me out the door.

I took a left down the road, turned where a lantern hung on a post. After a few minutes, I shut off the flashlight and walked by moonlight, but once I entered the woods it grew darker again, so I switched the light back on. Before we'd come to the camp, I'd thought I had good night vision, but away from the lights of our town I found myself in a different kind of darkness, one where I might easily lose my way. One of the campers, Helen, was here not because she had XP but because she had a rare light-sensitivity eye condition that left her nearly blind by day but able to see unusually well in the dark. Each night, we watched her change from a groping, clingy girl into a leader, pointing to objects in the distance—across a field, far off in the sky. She was two people, almost, each half of her hiding, patient, while the other half emerged.

Sounds I could hear in the woods, though I couldn't see their sources: twigs cracking, the crossings of small animals, a high-pitched chirping—crickets? tree frogs?—in the trees. I walked steadily at first, quickly. Behind me I could feel the presence of the lodge, bulky and stolid, and of the people breathing inside it, my three and all the others, some of whom I was beginning, now, to know.

In front of me, a path. It turned and wandered, rose. I aimed the light downward, careful not to trip on roots or stones. Before I had children I'd been a hiker, and now we occasionally took the boys to the countryside at night, but it had been years since I'd gone up a mountain path, and as the climb grew steep my muscles ached. As a girl, I'd lived near a swatch of suburban forest, forbidden to my brother and me, who were instructed to play on our square green lawn with its strangely opulent flower beds separated by brick borders from the grass. Though my mother loved her garden and filled it with the lushest, most fragrant blooms, she was afraid of wild animals, ticks and poison ivy, murderers and stalkers, holes you might fall into, trees you might fall out of. Afraid.

But sometimes, when my brother and I were with a sitter or our mother's back was turned, we'd go anyway, scaling the fence at the end of our yard, crossing two other backyards, a street, a polluted, foamy brook, until we entered those woods. Strangers had sex with each other there, rumor had it. Teenage girls went in for a smoke and never came out. I'd heard the stories, but I couldn't seem to care. There was so much to see in the woods—ferns that grew as high as your waist, mushrooms that bruised purple when you touched them, a pair of panties left in the crotch of a tree, a muddy American flag. When I kicked over a log with my sneaker, hordes of potato bugs scurried out before returning to the soil. I always knew I couldn't come back smudged with dirt or covered with leaves, so I played carefully. Later, with Ian, I drew closer. He loved camping, and in our first summers together we'd take a tent to southern New Hampshire or Vermont, hike all day, then duck inside our tent and peel off each other's sweaty hiking clothes. After Adam was born, we took him with us in his baby backpack, with a net hung over him to keep the mosquitoes away. I'd nurse him on a log, wade with him in a muddy brook, dry him in the dappled shade.

I don't know how long I climbed that night. I kept thinking I should go back, check on the kids, get some sleep, but meanwhile my legs were taking me higher on the path. I could feel my own pulse, and the spit in my mouth, and a tight, pressured feeling behind my eyes. The blackflies seemed to stay away from me; perhaps I moved too fast for them, or maybe it was the Off!. I walked and walked, gripping the flashlight, brushing twigs out of my way. At one point I heard a loud noise to my left, something large—a deer? a bear?—moving through the bushes. I turned off the light and stopped. The noise stopped too. I started up again. So did the noise. "Hey-ho, nobody's home!" I sang out and charged forward, leaving the sound behind.

It was only as I neared the top of the trail, the trees thinning, sloped rocks covering the ground, that I realized how long I'd been away. The sun was starting to come up. I could see it behind the mountain across from me, rising from behind a hump of land. I took off Adam's cap, shook out my hair, and sat on a rock. It was going to be a clear, breezy day, and as it grew lighter I realized, as if for the first time, that in daylight you could see across lakes, over treetops and hills, the whole world in front of you. I looked down at the lake, across to the mountains, then turned around to look behind me—more mountains, dense with pine trees, and, behind them, more mountains still. Far below, I could see the thin ribbon of a highway, a logging truck hauling its load. If I looked west, I thought, I'd almost be able to see my parents in their California bungalow and my brother and his wife and kids, who lived near them in the next town over, in a big, brand-new house I'd not yet seen. If I looked east, I could nearly see our own house, the drawers full of clothes, the fish in their tank, the burrowing gerbil—fed, while we were gone, by the neighbors' daughter.

I could see, too—or feel, as if they'd followed me up the mountain path—my two children in the lodge, Adam sprawled on top of his sleeping bag, Max in the other twin bed by now, curled into a ball, his owl in his arms. And Ian in the room next door—our room, while we were there. Had he remembered to take his bandage off while he slept, to let his wound breathe air? Had he made sure the boys took showers before bed? Would he worry about me, gone so long? Would he come looking? *No former rules apply.* We had loosened our grips on each other, freer, now, to come and go. Ian was always saying I should get out more. He would, I told myself, be asleep when I got back.

The sunrise was everything the clichés promise, streaks of bleeding color—salmon, yellow, toffee-pulled gray, diluted pink. Watching it, I thought of the Hudson River School painters, with their dramatic vistas, cliff faces and streaks of light. Often, in the foreground, the artist included a broken tree stump, a memento mori to remind the viewer of life's fragility, but in college, when I first saw the paintings, this never carried much weight for me, not next to the power of those rising cliffs, that brimming sky. Now, though, the sky seemed fragile as an ancient piece of fabric—touch it and it tears. As I watched, the colors lightened to butter yellow, palest gray-white, then to a beige, thinning translucence so temporary it would be impossible to paint, at least for me. I want Max to see this, I found myself thinking. I want him to live in the world, no matter what the price. And then (for such thoughts were always followed swiftly by their opposites), but no, just let him live, that's all—in a room, underground, it doesn't matter. Just let him live.

I climbed down the mountain in the early light of day. As I walked, I plucked off bits of things, remembering them from years before—the chewing-gum burst of a sarsaparilla stalk, the powdery pink underskin of birch bark. The trip down went much faster than the trip up, and my legs felt long and limber, my blood fast inside my veins. The lodge, when I reached it, looked grim and heavy, and for the first time it seemed to me a shame that Hal had needed to coat the windows, for it made the place seem shrouded, blind.

Inside, I headed for the kitchen by way of the living room,

my eyes straining to adjust. All the way down, I'd been picturing the snack I would have when I arrived: homemade bread with Brie, and lemonade with mint. At first I thought the living room was empty, the Scrabble game abandoned, a newspaper lying open on the floor. But then I saw Ian, asleep on a long, narrow chaise longue, his bandaged hand tucked beneath his chin. I went over, sat by his side and touched his arm.

"Oh," he said sleepily. "It's you." He let out a sound, part sigh, part moan.

"Hey," I whispered. "What are you doing here? Why aren't you in bed?"

"I—I was waiting." He yawned and opened his eyes. "You went on a walk? You said—"

I nodded and kneaded his shoulder. "I found a trail up a mountain, and it took a little longer than I thought. It was great, though. I should show you."

He sat up, suddenly awake. "Don't go disappearing that way, all right? You were gone for hours, we had no idea—"

I winced, his voice too loud in the empty room. "I'm sorry," I said. "I didn't realize—were the boys worried?"

"We read together, and they went to sleep. I said you'd be back soon. But for all I knew, you'd drowned or . . . or fallen off a cliff. You should tell me when you're taking off for the night." He shook his head. "Where the hell were you, anyway?"

"I told you. I went on a walk." I stood. I knew he had a point, yet still I felt like he was intentionally puncturing all the private pleasures of my hike. And something else: I heard my mother's voice—stay close, stay safe. And my own voice, too. Ian wasn't the worrier. I was.

"A mountain?" he said.

"A big hill." I rolled my eyes. "A *slope*."

"By yourself? In the dark? What were you thinking? You have no idea where you are."

"I had," I said curtly, "a flashlight. There's a trail. I'm used to the dark, remember? Jesus, Ian, what's your problem? Can't you maybe say, 'I'm glad you got out, I'm glad you went for one little pathetic walk by yourself'?"

He didn't answer. I looked down at his rumpled flannel shirt, his bandaged hand. You, I wanted to say, live out in the world, with a job, a mailbox, meetings, memos. You eat lunch with the other teachers and take a run after you're done coaching—I have no idea where—and come home ruddy and cheerful, smelling of chalk and fresh air. Yes, I sometimes took a walk when he got home. Up the block, down the next block, fifteen minutes, twenty at the most. Sometimes a neighbor had gotten a new mailbox. A fence went up, a tree came down, a house was bought or sold. I never went far. There was dinner to make, my family to see, all of us together for only a brief time in the day. There was laundry to do, lessons to prepare for Max. Don't you dare tell me, I wanted to say now, where to go and not to go. But I wasn't the only one to have given things up, and my voice would have come out high-pitched and curdled, sour milk.

"You know," I said instead, "you shouldn't sleep with that bandage on. The cut needs to breathe. You're asking for an infection."

The look he gave me held too many different things inside it. Sadness and distance, exhaustion and confusion. Bottled rage. Love. He shook his head.

"I'm sorry," I said again, and this time I meant it. "I should have told you. I got—I guess I just lost track of time. I'm sorry. Okay?"

His face softened slightly. "Aren't you tired?"

"No," I said, though suddenly I could barely move. "I mean, I guess. Sort of."

"This couch is a goddamn torture rack."

"Come." I touched his bandaged hand. "Let's go to bed."

And though breakfast was only a few hours away, we tiptoed up the stairs, washed up, checked on the boys, and dropped—curled carefully, almost politely, together—into our separate, sudden sleeps.

FOUR

That year, Camp Luna ran the first three weeks of August, and while it wasn't a long period, somehow time seemed to slow down. There were eleven XP kids our first year, plus siblings and parents, close to forty people in all. There was Étienne from France, his sister, Natalie, and their parents, Françoise and Henri. They wore ironed T-shirts, that scrubbed, polite French family, and folded their cloth napkins in small triangles, like flags. There was Anil, come alone all the way from Nepal, his airfare paid for by the camp. He was eighteen, the oldest of the XP kids. He'd had two siblings with XP—both of them dead now—and a pocked face and body, a wistful smile.

There was Nicole from Alabama, daughter of Carole and John, the type who might, in another life, have been a cheerleader, a sunbather. There was Helen, the girl who could see by night but not by day, and her parents, two sweet economists who squinted at the world through thick-lensed glasses. There was Carl, son of Josh and Angela, who'd had a malignant melanoma excised six months before and had just finished his course of chemotherapy, and Sara, whose left ear had been removed to take the cancer with it. There was seven-year-old Andy, who had XP and stayed close by the side of his fraternal twin brother Russ, who did not. There were children with skin smooth or scarred, freckled or clear. The lucky ones, like Max, had been diagnosed early. The others were like a fast-forward movie, the aging process quickened. You might, had you stumbled into one of the bathrooms in the lodge, think you'd come across the accessories of a theater troupe, the sills and sinks strewn with bottles of lotion, cakes and tubes of makeup, sunglasses and hats.

There was Alida, of course—Hal's only child, born when he was forty-two to a mother who died when her child was not quite one. There was Tommy, Marnie's son, the flukiest fluke of all in that he'd come—half of him had—from a sperm bank, a catalog of anonymous donors. Marnie and her girlfriend at the time had gone over and over the list, finally settling on a cluster of features that appealed to them: dark brown eyes, a love of animals, a highish IQ score, no known family history of mental illness. Good genes. I once read somewhere that 99.9 percent of human genes are identical. It's the 0.1 percent that spins us off, makes us who we are—takes, sometimes, our very lives. Marnie got pregnant on the first try; by Tommy's second birthday, the girlfriend left.

"You mean they don't screen for it?" I asked when she first told me the story. "At the sperm bank, I mean?"

We were sitting on an overturned rowboat in one room of the boathouse, while next door Tommy and Max played Ping-Pong. It was four in the morning. We'd been talking for hours but had only now come around to this.

Marnie looked at me quizzically. "Screen? No one had even heard of it when he was born. We lived way out in rural Pennsylvania with just this little county hospital. It took over a year to figure out what he had."

"What a random thing," I said. "I mean, at least with me and Ian, we were already together, we—"

She waved away my words. "What? True love, destiny?"

"No, I didn't mean—" I said. Marnie was not usually impatient or dismissive. *You don't know me at all*, I had an urge to tell her. Instead, I looked away.

"I'm sorry," she said. "It's just I've gotten a lot of this from people over the years. Tommy wasn't a bad shopping decision."

"That's not what I meant, I only meant—"

"That I might have chosen differently? But you could have too, Anna, right?" She lowered her voice again, glancing at the open door that separated us from the boys. From the other room came the distinct sound of the ball hitting the table. "I wanted a kid so badly, ever since I was a kid myself. And Tommy's just . . . he's an amazing, good person—I mean, most kids are, of course, but he's—he's *Tommy*. My life without him would be—" She shrugged. "Nothing. A big fat blank. I wouldn't pick differently, even if I knew ahead of time." She swiped at her eyes. "Sorry. I get a little crazy about this. I was meant to be his mother. But you know what I'm saying, since you have Max."

"Yes," I said.

Really, though, I wasn't sure whether to totally believe her, or was it that I didn't know if I could speak like that myself? Was I meant to be Max's mother, in some kind of divinely fated way? Would my life without him have been nothing, a big fat blank? Mightn't someone else, perhaps someone more like Marnie, have done a better job? Max was my closest friend, my nightly companion, the very center of my life. I loved him with a fierceness that surprised me again and again and kept bringing me up against the pulse of things, the beating core. But if I'd known? Might I not have stopped at Adam, who had never gotten enough from me since Max was born? Might I not have wished for a different kind of joining—not this egg, not this sperm, but the one beside it—yes, that one, with its different, all right, its *better*—0.1 percent of genes? All of us knew the stats by now, how two parents with the XP recessive gene had a one-in-four chance of having a child with the disease. But I couldn't help wondering, what of those other three chances? What of those never-born children who might, as we sat there in the boathouse, have been asleep in their beds somewhere, storing up energy for the next sunny day of their long and healthy lives? What of all the places my boy couldn't go, the scalpel on his skin, his sense (and yet, from the other room, his shout, his laugh) of the world as a place that burned?

I hadn't been sure I wanted a second child at first. One had seemed fine; with Adam, we could wander about, take trips, go out to dinner. He was a solid, good-natured baby who slept in the movies or on a park bench and woke from his naps crowing with delight. "With one child," I remember reading in a feminist magazine, "you're a moving target. With two, you're a sitting duck." I had hoped to go back to teaching art by the time Adam turned five. I had hoped to set up a studio and paint, to have more time with Ian, to see friends. And I couldn't fully imagine dividing my heart between two kids. If we have another baby, I told Ian, let's do it later, after I'm more settled into a career. I was twenty-seven when I got pregnant with Adam, and I'd ended up where I was less through careful planning than through sudden swerves. But Ian had persisted, quietly, sweetly:

a friend for Adam, someone close to his age, a less lonely kind of life. Just think about it, he'd said. We can switch off on child care. I'll stay home for a year while you teach.

One day he drew me two diagrams—of a family of four and a family of three. It was some exercise on kinship he was preparing for his eighth-grade social studies class. *See all the nice solid corners on the square, and how much you can fit inside? The triangle's all sharp and jagged. You've got to admit, it isn't nearly as appealing as the square*. Looking at his drawings, I'd thought back to my first college art class. "Always choose an odd number of objects for your still lifes," the professor had told us. "Three or five brings much more tension to the composition than four or six." Ian's square had looked stolid, almost crude, a child's unconvincing blocky drawing of a house, and I'd wondered if partly he wanted another baby because he didn't think we quite qualified as a family the way we were, too small, unfinished, outside the norm. But I had liked the triangle for the taut lines between its points and the way its peak reached sharply for the sky.

Once Adam started preschool, though, I'd catch myself staring at the pregnant mothers of his classmates, their awkward, swollen beauty, the slow animal grace they had, bending sideways over their bellies to scoop their children up. I couldn't stop watching, but did I want to *be* them or paint them? They seemed so tired, when you looked closely. They looked so full and flushed, so taken up. Though I stretched and primed a lot of canvases, I never got much painting done while Adam was at school. How the mornings sped by—a cup of tea, a section of the newspaper, a phone call, a load of laundry, a sweep of the kitchen, maybe a sketch or two, and it was time to get him. Sometimes, in the afternoon, I'd do quick gesture drawings of Adam as he dove onto couch pillows or pushed a toy through the grass, but I never painted around him, the oil paints too toxic to use around a child, though of course I might have switched to acrylics or watercolor. It took me a while to realize that I was trying to catch him, hold him, in my drawings; he always looked more like a baby than the fast-growing boy he really was.

In the end, Max was conceived in a moment of carelessness, which was as close as I could come to moving forward with open eyes. After I found out I was pregnant, things shifted a little. Ian was so pleased, and his joy was catching, and though I'd never been close to my brother, I found myself picturing my two children together—tumbling like puppies, or bent over a book, or calling each other on the phone as adults. We would have a girl, I decided, and I saw her compact, rosy body, her long curly hair, how she would sit with me and draw, chatter and pretend, or roam with me through the woods.

When the ultrasound showed us Max—the curved ladder of spine, the gray nub that the radiologist pronounced a penis—I almost didn't believe it, so convinced I was that I was carrying a girl. By then, I could feel the baby move. By then, I was talking to it. To her. To him. To Max. Who did, as he got older, often sit and draw with me, who had, as an infant, a small pink body, curly hair. Who liked to dress up, prance and pretend in a way his older brother never did, a child of surprising outbursts and long silences, as moody as the night, for him, was long. Little did I know how much things would change after this second child was born, walls springing up everywhere as if in a fairy tale, days dwindling, our starter house remaining the only place we could afford. It was I who stayed home with Max—my own choice, I suppose, if you could call it that, for from the beginning I saw myself as his protector. Never could I have imagined how far the world would contract—a tight fist, shuttered eye, set of closing doors. Nor could I have imagined the bright spirit of my dark-bound second child, or the impossible, daily fact of knowing I might have to watch him die.

By the time Marnie and I finally left the boathouse that night, it was close to five o'clock. Day was, as they say, breaking—like an eggshell or a vase. We were quiet walking back up the lawn to the lodge, Marnie's arm around Tommy's shoulder, mine around Max's, and though it wasn't yet light, I could see the sunrise before it happened, my mind lit, still, by the walk I'd taken up the mountain. Other people were heading to bed, too, moving faster than we were. Hal passed us and whispered hello, Alida asleep in his arms. Nicole, Jess, Amy, the twins, and Étienne passed us, still talking; I could hear him teaching them French words.

I climbed the stairs with Max to the room he shared with his brother and found Adam asleep on one bed, still in his tank top, cutoffs and sneakers, and Ian asleep on the other, the night-light glowing in its outlet. I started to wake them, then thought better of it. How peaceful they looked, each curled around a pillow, facing each other. In sleep, Adam seemed younger and less guarded, and I remembered how I used to watch him doze when he was just a few months old—the twitching, veined eyelids, the mouth that moved from a pucker to a half smile to repose, his thoughts opaque. I used to think that once my children learned to talk, I would gain access to their inner lives, but their words were just as often screens as entry points. Fine, Adam would say lately when I asked him a question. Good. No problem. Sure. Whatever. My affable baby had turned, on the surface, into an affable thirteen-year-old, but meanwhile his fingers were worrying at the pimples on his chin; his eyes were glazed, or glaring, or far away.

I bent to take his sneakers off. I pulled a blanket over him and kissed his forehead. Still, he slept. He and Ian had spent the evening together. Ian had suggested it after I'd told him I thought Adam seemed a little lost. I'll take him on a canoe ride or walk, he had said. Something where we can talk. That's a good idea, I'd answered, but now I wanted to know what they had said to each other. More and more, Adam seemed to be entering a realm where I wasn't welcome. Did they talk about girls as they paddled across the lake? Did they discuss wet dreams or soccer strategies or mortality, or just sit in easy silence, something Ian has always done well?

I took Max's pajamas from where they hung on a hook. "Come," I whispered. "Let's not disturb them. You can sleep with me."

Like shifting constellations, our small family—these two stars aligned, these two separate, and then a change in the weather, the slightest seismic shift, and a different pattern forms. Mother and father, brother and brother. Mother and son, son and father. Husband and wife, boy apart from boy. Mother (or should we call her *woman*, or *organism*, breathe in, breathe out), the other three away from her, a tight, close band. Ian had drawn a square in all its symmetry. Instead we just changed and changed.

That dawn, it was me and Max. "I've missed you," I told him, as we lay in the double bed, "with all your running around. Did you have fun with Tommy?"

"He said I could," he mumbled, nestling close.

"Tommy?"

"Hal said . . . do the—" He half sat up, his words already blurred with sleep. "Take that bike. I—" Now his eyes were open, staring.

"You're dreaming." I coaxed him back down. "It's just us here. Tomorrow you can ask Hal about a bike."

"Which bike?"

"I don't know, Maxie. It was in your dream. Go back to sleep."

"Do you think Arno is okay?" he asked, of our gerbil back home.

"Yes, of course. But we can check with Rachel tomorrow."

"If Arno gets out again, he'll dig a maze of tunnels in the yard, not just for him but for the moles and chipmunks, and they can call it the Arno-reum." He snorted with laughter. "And they'll have races and I can watch through one of those scope things, like on a submarine, you know, except we have to light it somehow, and then maybe—"

"Then the animals will say, *Sleep, Max*," I interrupted. "*Sleep, Mister Max, so you can be bright and bushy-tailed when you get up*."

He squirmed beside me. "I'm *awake*. Where's Dad?"

"With Adam, remember? Sleeping next door."

"Where's Tommy?"

"Everyone is sleeping. It's that time."

Which was, of course, the farthest thing from the truth, since all across the state, all across the eastern seaboard, alarms were going off, people were rising, days starting. A woman stumbled into the shower, tipped her head back, lathered her hair. Another woman stepped outside into her garden for a few moments of quiet before the kids got up. Sixteen-wheelers turned onto highways, cars pulled out of driveways. In coffee shops, waitresses measured coffee into filters and pressed START. Hal, too, was probably awake, though I didn't know that, then. He was sitting by the window, reading, thinking, smoking a cigarette.

And so the world rose. And so we moved toward rest, Max's thoughts traveling underground, mine into the waking world. Arno and the chipmunks, he saw. Arno and the mice. Arno nose to nose with a mole, an animal capable of only the simplest kind of seeing, the distinguishing of light from dark. How nice my boy smelled; I had nearly forgotten. How particular to him were the bends and turns of his mind. This child and no other. No mistake.

The next night, as I sat with a book on the window seat in the piano room, Alida appeared and climbed into my lap.

"Hello," I said.

She twisted around to face me. "Hi."

"What's going on in there?" I tipped my chin toward the living room. Finally, the schedule had begun to take its toll on me; I kept having to stifle yawns.

"They're making a play with my dad."

I put my book down. Horse thieves, Wyoming—I'd only been half reading it, but still it felt like an effort to return to the real world. "What's it about?"

She shrugged. "I don't know."

We sat then, for a few minutes, my chin resting on her head, neither of us speaking. Alida, I had noticed, attached herself easily to people at the camp, especially to mothers, climbing onto laps, offering flowers or rocks she'd made into paperweights. At the same time, there was something slightly remote about her, almost coy—a sense that she was watching herself: girl in the lap of a woman, girl with a daisy chain. Except when she was with Hal; only then did she relax and seem to live fully inside her skin. She was so clearly his, they were so clearly each other's, their link carrying an intensity that I half envied for its purity, its lack of impediments, even as I knew the truth behind it—she'd lost her mother, he'd lost his wife.

Now she shook her head and reached to touch one of my glass earrings. "That's pretty. Can I hold it?"

I took the earring off and gave it to her, and she pressed it to her own ear.

"Anna?" she asked.

"What, Lida?"

"Will you do my hair?"

"Oh," I said. "Sure. Of course."

"In a lot of braids?"

"If I remember how. I have boys. It's been a long time since I've braided hair."

A memory came to me, then: sitting with a friend whose name I've long since forgotten in the back of her mother's car in a parking lot. It was dark out. We were alone there, I think. We couldn't have been more than seven or eight. The friend's hair was straight, blond and glossy. My own was brown and curly, a thick, unruly mass that my mother kept threatening to cut. I braided my friend's hair; she braided mine, braided and then unbraided, and it was raining out, and sometimes headlights would go by, lighting my friend's head and my own hands moving through her hair. The friend's mother, if I'm remembering right, was young and playful, not at all like my own, and when she returned she said we were both beauties—*beauties*, the word startled and impressed me—and from somewhere mysterious, she produced gold-threaded ponytail holders still in their package, as if she'd seen us even when she wasn't there.

Alida dragged a low chair in front of me, sat in it to test the height, and ran her fingers through her hair. Then she squared her shoulders. I pulled her hair back and began dividing it into two clumps.

"No." She shook her head. "Not just two braids. Lots of them."

I dropped her hair and started again. "I can try, but it might not be as many as you'd like. This will be our practice run. Once I get good, we'll do the real thing."

We sat together next to the hulking grand piano with its chipped, yellowed keys, and I made one small braid and then another, leaving them dangling down her back. The first one came out sloppy and loose, but by the second, my fingers had started remembering, and the third one was even better. We didn't talk. Alida's shoulders rose and fell with her breath, and the voices from the living room reached us in pieces: *dragon, hold your fire. . . . knock knock. . . . you are who?* I picked out Max's voice and Nicole's, Sara's and Étienne's. I picked out Adam's voice, pleased that he was participating, and Hal directing them—*that was great but a little louder next time, and sep-a-rate the sounds. Okay, now, let's start from when the rest of you swim up out of the moat, so that's you, Étienne—in French if you want, so they know they're in a strange land,* d'accord?—as if they were a real theater troupe rehearsing for opening night. Theater, I realized guiltily, theater, not gymnastics, was the thing for Max—a dark auditorium, the trying on of different voices, costumes made of velvet, brandished swords. How, as I'd watched him balk at parallel bars and rings, had I not seen it before?

Alida sat quietly. I braided and braided, falling into a trance that reminded me of when I used to paint for hours at a time.

Maybe it was her hair that brought me back, each braid end like a brush's tip, or perhaps it was the motion, repetitive and rhythmic—swab of red, swab of blue, brush to palette, brush to canvas, wash of green, of red.

Finally I finished and patted the top of Alida's head. "I'm done, but I've got nothing to tie them with."

"We need ponytail holders." Slowly, she stood and turned toward me, keeping her head erect.

"We do." I stood, too.

"I've got some in my room. Come with me?" She turned toward the stairs, holding the clusters of braids in her two fists.

Most of us were staying on the third floor of the lodge, in small wood-paneled garret rooms with slanted walls and low doorways. The staff had probably slept there in the old days, but Hal had reversed things now. The staff and volunteers stayed on the second floor, in bigger, ampler rooms, as did the families from foreign countries, as if he thought that having crossed more space to reach us, they needed more space now. He and Alida were also on the second floor, in two linked rooms at the far end of the hall. The bedrooms, he had told us on the first day of camp, were private, to be entered by invitation only. We were to make our own beds and wash our own sheets. We'll be living in close quarters here, he'd said. Our rooms will be our own.

Alida and I crossed through the living room, where the kids were still rehearsing, and up the stairs to the second floor. I waved at Adam and Max as I walked by, but they didn't notice me and I didn't call out. Alida led the way, her hands still clamped around her braids. I'd never been on the second floor except to go by on the way to our room. Old photographs hung on the walls: two men posing by a lean-to, women in ruffled dresses sitting with sketch pads on a rocky shore, a boy standing rigid on the end of a diving board, as if waiting to be told when to jump. The hallway was wider, the ceiling higher than on my floor.

Alida's room, when she pushed open the door and turned on the light, was a surprise. Unlike the other bedrooms, it wasn't pared down and camplike. This was the lush, crowded room of a pack-rat child, the bed covered with a heap of quilts and stuffed animals, the floor with crayons and paper, Tinkertoys, a naked Barbie doll, socks. I felt a moment of homesickness for our crowded house full of my boys' possessions and my own boxes of earrings, safety pins and shells. Alida rummaged in a dresser drawer and pulled out a length of blue ribbon and a key chain, which she let drop to the floor.

"My hair stuff must be in my dad's room," she said.

I bent to retrieve the ribbon. "If you have some scissors, we could use this."

It was only as she grabbed the ribbon from me and stuffed it back in the drawer that I realized it must have belonged to Robin. The room, I saw suddenly, must have been her mother's when she was little. The chipped dresser was painted with butterflies, flowers and robins, and the bed was a youth bed with a cast-iron headboard painted robin's-egg blue.

Alida stood and offered me her hand. I knew I shouldn't be going into Hal's room when he wasn't there, but her hand was waiting and my own was empty, and so—and so and so and so—I let her lead.

A futon on the floor, strewn with so many books that it took me a moment, as I stood in the doorway, to see that it was, in fact, a bed. No bulky mission furniture here. No hanging antlers, or portraits of ancestors, or copper trophies from the family mine. One wall had a large bulletin board on it. The others were bare except for a few children's drawings, each stuck with a single tack. There were books and papers everywhere, teetering in piles on the dresser, lying open on the bed, stacked under the windows. *A Sand County Almanac*, I saw as I bent over a heap. *Climate in Crisis, Stuart Little, Field Guide to Mushrooms, The Tao te Ching, Asphodel and Other Love Poems, Folk Songs from Around the World, One Hundred Rainy Day Activities, The Hole in the Sky, Standing on Earth, The Borrowers, Call It Sleep, Emily Dickinson, Jude the Obscure*. . . . Just as I was wondering when Hal found so much time to read, I noticed a pale blue book called *Say Good Night to Insomnia*. T-shirts and jeans were lying about, too, and kids' clothes, and the air smelled slightly stale but also smoky-sweet, like the sandalwood incense we used to burn in college.

On the windowsill, between a bleached animal skull and a box of crayons, I saw a tin can filled with cigarette stubs. Cigarettes? Hal, whose wife had died of cancer, smoked cigarettes? Suddenly, it made a certain amount of sense—his fidgety hands, the way his mind seemed constantly in motion, but I was also struck by how he never smoked where we could see.

As Alida searched for hair ties, I inspected the bulletin board. Alida was up there, as a laughing baby. Hal was there—it must have been Hal—a boy more pretty than handsome, fine-featured with a mass of heavy dark hair and cheekbones that left shadows on his cheeks. In his eyes, the same searching look he had now. He was standing with a man and a woman on a city stoop. I'd known he was Jewish, but it wasn't until this moment that I saw my own extended family in his: the alert, almost skittish gazes, the neat clothes and dark hair, the way the parents touched the children as if they might evaporate before their eyes. There was a Night Sky chart tacked there too, and an ad for light meters, and some photos of the camp, including one of Marnie, Max and me waving from the raft. In it, Max was clowning, one leg held out above the water. I was red-eyed from the flash and looked a little scrawny next to Marnie, but my wet hair fell in ringlets and I was smiling a genuinely happy smile.

"Do you think I was cute?" Alida came up behind me and pointed to a picture of a toddler on an elaborate rocking horse, her hair in two fat braids.

"Very," I said, just as I noticed that the window behind the girl was open, her face awash with sun.

"It's my mother," she said. "When she was little. Did you think it was me?"

I nodded. "You look a lot alike. Is that also your mother?" I pointed to another picture, of an unusually pretty, long-necked woman sitting in the crook of a tree, her arms around a branch, her legs dangling down. So this, I thought, is Robin. She looked like the sort of person who could run fast, climb limbs, give her love easily. It was hard, from the picture, to imagine her felled by a disease. For an uncomfortable instant, I pictured her behind us, watching us, willing me to leave.

"Yeah. Oh—" Alida touched her hair. "I wrecked it."

"Come downstairs. I'll fix it." I looked over my shoulder, though of course no one was there. "They're probably done rehearsing the play by now."

"Just a sec." She ran to a corner, reached into a backpack, and came out with a fistful of hair ties, leaving me to wonder if she'd known where they were all along. She sat down on the futon. "I knew I'd find them."

I turned toward the door. "Bring them downstairs. I'll tie them there."

"No. Here." She pushed her mouth into an exaggerated pout, then reconsidered. "Please?"

"I'd rather go downstairs, so I can say hi to Max and Adam."

But she didn't move, and when, despite myself, I went and sat behind her, she turned and lurched toward me in a sudden, silent hug. She smelled of apple juice, and of sandalwood, like the room, and her scalp had that powdery, slightly sour odor that stays with children long after they've left babyhood and then one day just disappears. She squeezed her eyes shut and gripped the fabric of my shirt. For a minute, I held her, rocked her. Then I smelled Hal's sleep smell—sweat, cigarettes and rising dreams—and felt a tightening in my gut, a lit, red sign: NO TRESPASSING, COME IN.

"Okay, kiddo," I said brightly, falsely. "Let's go downstairs so I can fix your hair and see my guys."

It wasn't until later, when I reached to take my earrings off, that I remembered that Alida still had one of them. I couldn't ask for it back. Not that night, and not the next, and though I doubt she lost it, she never returned it to me. The earring was Venetian glass shot through with blue and gold, a birthday present from Ian when I turned thirty-five—the age, I'd later learn, that Robin was when she died. It felt like a funny sort of secret—that Alida had it and I knew she had it, that I never spoke of it and neither did she. Around the same time, I started tucking small objects from the lodge inside my pockets, then transferring them to the inside zipper pouch of my suitcase when no one was around. A smooth wooden checker piece I found behind my bureau. An old stencil card of a rooster and the numbers one through ten. A rusty key. A photo of solemn children playing at a Scottish wedding, the girls in plaid shawls, the boys holding pine boughs and wearing kilts. Nothing of value really (or so I told myself), just small worthless objects, the detritus of someone else's family life. Not stealing, not really. I would return the things next year when we came back.

So we hide things, squirrel them away. I couldn't have said why I was doing it—some kind of impulse, a primitive itch. We had four nights left at the camp, then three, then two. We took group photographs and gave hugs as we passed one another in the hallways, already nostalgic. Write, we said. E-mail, call, write. I will, of course I will. The kids put on the play in the living room, where Hal had strung a curtain as a backdrop. Max was a dragon, Adam a soldier. Nicole sang a song about moats, her voice surprisingly throaty and adult. Ian and I sat together, loosely holding hands at the beginning, then settling into ourselves. Hal was backstage, whispering cues and handing the children props. The play was imaginative and funny, the kids charming, and I wished I'd gotten more involved. At the curtain call, I think most of the parents teared up.

"Max is really good up there," Ian said, as the actors bowed for a second time. "We should see if we can get him into the play at school next year."

"Mmmm," I answered, knowing that while it was a good idea, it wouldn't be the same, not wanting to think of anywhere but here.

Marnie promised that she and Tommy would visit from Philadelphia. We exchanged the names of doctors and researchers, of articles and funding sources, of homeschooling software and companies that made UV-blocking fabric, light meters, sunscreens, window film. A reporter and photographer came from *Parade* magazine, and Alida offered practiced answers to the questions while the other children pretended not to pose. Later, Ian found Max with a bloody scratch on his palm. When we asked him about it, he told us he and Tommy had become blood brothers. That same night, I came across Adam and Nicole holding hands in the boathouse. When they saw me, they pulled apart as if they had been stung.

At ten or so on the last night, I was packing in the boys' room when someone knocked on the door.

"Come in." I looked up from a pile of clean laundry. The door opened. It was Hal.

"Are you busy?" he asked. "Ian said you were up here . . ."

"That's okay, I was just—" I shoved some of Max's clothes into a duffel bag. In my mind, I saw Hal's room: the piles of books, the cigarettes, the bed I'd sat on with Alida. I had thought of that room often since I'd seen it, pictured myself napping there. I'd pictured Hal, too, asleep between piles of books, or tacking photos to the bulletin board, or making love with his wife, who looked small-boned, as I am, but younger, more sparkling, her features more symmetrical, her hair cut short to hug her head. Here and there, such thoughts, then on to something else. It didn't mean that much to me. My mind has always been full of such wanderings, a hundred veerings every day.

Hal stepped farther into the room. "I brought you something." He held out a wooden box, and I stood and took it, knowing as soon as I saw it that it was full of paints.

"Oh," I said. "Oh, no, you shouldn't have," but meanwhile I was opening the box, looking down at the tubes of oil paints arranged by color, white to black, with a few empty spaces in between. They were Winsor & Newtons, a deluxe set. "They're gorgeous," I said, and it was true, the tubes expensive, plump, unopened, each marked with a smear of color and a name: Vermilion Green, Ochre Yellow, Titanium White. *If you knew me,* I thought. *If you only knew*—and resolved to return all the things I'd stolen from the house.

"The cadmiums are missing," he said. "I hope you don't mind, it's just they're carcinogens; you can replace them with naphthols. I meant to do it, but I didn't have time."

"It doesn't matter."

I shut the lid, put the box on Max's bed, and sat down next to it. It's all toxic, I almost said. The oils, the mediums, the thinners. For Max and Alida especially, the whole world is a carcinogen—water, air and sun. Didn't he know it as well as I? Fragile planet, fragile ravaging people, wanting and wanting what they wanted *now*. Suddenly I didn't care. I wanted the cadmiums, color so powerful the smell of it could change the structure of your cells.

"Thank you," I said. "I don't even remember telling you I painted, I mean, did I? How did you know—?"

"You bring up colors a lot," he said, "and you got really into doing crafts with the kids, and I've seen you sketching quite a bit." He shrugged.

"Well, you were right. I . . . I majored in studio art in college."

I won the senior art prize, I wanted to tell him. In my twenties, I was in a few juried shows, a gifted imitator, though perhaps without much of a style of my own. Or the other, truer parts of it: how time used to bend and shimmer when I was lost inside a painting. How the world's shifting shapes became lines to follow, curves to hold. How I *saw* things clearly, apart from all the muddle, saw and held them, for once I'd painted something it was never lost to me, even as the light kept changing before my eyes. When I first met Ian, I had tried to explain it to him, but it always came out sounding wrong, too many words for a wordless act, and eventually I'd more or less given up.

"Actually," Hal said, taking a step back, "I can't take credit. I knew you were an art major. Max told me."

"Really? How did that come up?"

"I think we were talking about school."

"Well." I patted the box and stood. "I wish I had something for you. You're the one who's given us this time here, and we should be giving you, I mean—"

"Anna. Stop. It's okay."

"All right." My face felt hot. "Thank you."

"You're welcome. Thank you, too, for helping out here, and for spending time with Alida. She really likes you, you know. She'll miss you."

"Oh, she's wonderful, you're doing a great job raising her—" Alone, I nearly said.

"The paints, actually they were Robin's," Hal told me. "I got them for her with a book on how to paint from nature photographs. It was when she couldn't go out anymore. I thought she could paint in her room, but she wasn't the type. She wanted to be *in* the woods, not painting them, and then . . ." He held up his hands. "Anyway, better not to waste them, right? She always hated waste."

Suddenly the gift felt like a charge, even a burden. "Thank you," I repeated, and then I was moving across the room, leaning up, kissing Hal—sweetly, simply, chastely—on the cheek.

"No problem," he said gruffly, almost rudely, backing away from me.

I nodded. The awkwardness was terrible, nearly unbearable. I wanted to go back, start again, but what would I do? No kiss at all, a simple thank-you? Or something more, for now that I'd felt the scratch of his cheek with my lips, it would be so easy to turn my head and find more of him, hard click of teeth, soft seeking tongue. He's waiting, I thought. Part of him is waiting. A voice came to me, then, stern and sure, not quite my own. *Not for you. Unsafe.* I dropped to my knees and rummaged in the duffel, and when I looked up, he was gone.

Around three in the morning, Ian pulled up the van and we loaded our suitcases, the boys' crafts projects, a bag of pinecones and pebbles Max had collected, a walking stick Ian had peeled and carved, snacks for the road, my paints, Max's owl. The boys went inside to say their good-byes. Ian did, too. I made some excuse about needing to check on how the car was loaded and so managed to part without a scene.

Something ripped inside me as I climbed into the van and put my seat belt on. Something tore. At the time, I managed to tell myself it was over leaving this abundant place, these people I had quickly grown to love, for the tight and solitary corners of our house. I have, I thought, been spoiled. In the back of the van our souvenirs were piled high, but it wasn't enough. I wanted the lake, the mountains, the sun on my closed lids, all the nooks and crannies of the lodge. I wanted Hal singing about the world turned upside down and giving me gifts because he'd noticed, in these three short weeks, who I was and what I lacked. My child healthy—most of all, I wanted that, but if not healthy, then here where he belonged. In the backseat were Max's ski mask, sunglasses, blanket cape, gloves, long socks. In my jacket pocket, the checker piece, the key and photograph. I'd put them there after Hal left me to my packing so that I might return them, but in the end I took them anyway. Greedy, you might say. Grasping. Yes.

Our van on the dirt road that night was part of a caravan of other minivans and station wagons, their headlights pushing through the dark. The boys were quiet. Ian drove, and I placed my hand on his knee. Thank god, I thought. Thank god that I have you and you and you. But at the same time, I felt far from my family, as if I no longer quite knew who they were, or was it me? When we got to the highway we picked up speed, and first there was one van behind us and another in front, and then the first van turned onto an exit ramp, honking its good-bye, and then a truck got between us and the other van, and finally, of course, we were alone.

FIVE

Home was two places then: the house where I'd lived for nearly thirteen years and Camp Luna, where we'd spent three short weeks. It happened so quickly, so easily, as if I were a fickle friend. Once we were home, camp seemed almost unfathomably far away, but at the same time, our old life felt oddly unfamiliar, out of whack. Here we are, I kept telling myself as I sat with Max by the computer, or bundled him up for a doctor's appointment, or listened to him complain, for he, too, was more restless and ornery than before. Here we are, as I talked to Adam about school, sorted laundry, paid bills, cooked dinner, half woke from sleep to find Ian lying next to me during the hours when our sleeping overlapped. Here we are, when I raked leaves with Max in the backyard, noticing how the smell *contained* light even when it was too dark out to actually see the leaves—a red smell, burned and moist, like heated soil. This, our backyard, our porch steps, our rake. Here, where we live. A good, a fine, an okay place.

Is it possible to be unhappy for a long time and never know it? Or is unhappiness a distorting lens you train back on your life once you're standing in a whole new place? The camp, I knew, was supposed to have given us a respite from the real world. It was meant to be a sanctuary, an adventure, a break. *I feel so rested and refreshed*, a better, a more grateful, graceful person might have written to a friend. *Camp Luna was a gift.*

How small and tacky our house seemed after the lodge. How low its ceilings, how grimy the cabinets and brittle its linoleum, nothing built to last. The jungle murals I'd painted years before on the boys' bedroom walls seemed almost grotesque, the monkeys like wizened, starving babies, the lion a swollen yellow dog. Even our pots and pans seemed toylike, tinny, unsuited for actual food.

I e-mailed my college roommate Sophie in Chicago and complained a little, and, obligingly, she complained back—about how she was too old to have the energy for toddler twins, about budget cuts at the city hospital where she worked. She told me about the weekend cottage she and her psychiatrist husband had bought on Lake Michigan. I wasn't jealous of Sophie, not exactly. It had taken her years to get pregnant. She worked hard at being a good doctor and still found time for play—delighting in her kids and making eerie collages from discarded X rays and ultrasound pictures. Every year around my birthday, she sent me one—this year, a spiked EKG report embroidered with my name and surrounded by flecks of gold leaf. She would have (I was sure of it) handled my own life, had it been hers, with more aplomb. For a week or so, the fall after I got back, we sent e-mails back and forth, a friendly flurry. Then one of us dropped the ball. Probably it was me.

All the little efforts I'd made to brighten up the house—the glossy red woodwork in the kitchen, the white lights winding up the banister—seemed pathetic now, flimsy as a theater set. One night when Ian was at a movie with the boys, I took the lights down and stuffed them into a grocery bag, and then I did a mad sweep of the house, throwing away old take-out menus, soccer schedules, expired prescriptions, torn underwear, congealed skin lotion, bent hangers, single socks. I took a stack of the boys' drawings and schoolwork up to the attic, where we kept big plastic tubs marked with each of their names. Usually, when I went to put things in these boxes, I'd stop and look inside at the birth hospital bracelets and homemade cards, the handprints, the milk teeth nested in cotton inside film canisters. Now I just dropped the drawings in, and if I felt something like sorrow, I couldn't have said if it came from a sense of time moving too fast or moving not at all. Later, in the middle of purging the bathroom, I stepped on the scale and saw that I'd lost close to eight pounds since we'd been back. I didn't look good so thin, my elbows too sharp, the hollows under my cheekbones like charcoal stains on my face.

Somehow, through it all, I still sketched, but in a driven, irritable way, as if my hand couldn't stop, pushed by some sort of tic, almost a compulsion. In my blue art notebooks, I drew people—embracing, slumped or running; children asleep on mothers' laps; a crowd of women waiting by a door. I drew pine trees and bushes, the corners of rooftops, abstract doodles like dead-end mazes, covering a page but going nowhere. I drew rooms and houses, wandering, elaborate structures—follies, really—that kept expanding, spreading from one page to the next. In the morning hours when Max was sleeping and Adam and Ian were off at school, I drew naked people—a woman with her legs wrapped around a man's torso, a man's penis, rising like a mushroom from a blur of hair. These drawings I made not in my notebooks but on scraps of cheap newsprint paper. And though I liked some of them, I always tore them up when I was done.

As I drew, I remembered. The water, the mountains, Alida in my lap, Max running, Hal making loon calls by the lake. One night I drew a man seen from behind, facing the water, his shoulders hunched. I liked the ambiguity of the sketch, how hard it was to tell who he was or what he was doing—the intake and release of breath, the sad, sad sound.

I worked in the brief snatches of time when I was alone or when Max was doing homework. I stored the notebooks in a file box on the highest shelf in my closet and showed them to no one. They were filled with flaws—wrong proportions, bad perspective, sloppiness, impatience, nostalgia. In one way, they felt like a poor imitation of what I'd once thought myself capable of; in another, they presented too accurate a picture of my brain.

As I was drawing, I'd often find myself thinking not just about the previous summer but about other things as well, from further back. My mother, how she used to call me every Saturday, *Hello, morning glory*. How disbelieving she'd been when I told her about Max's disease, all her years of caution suddenly, bizarrely, gone now that real danger had arrived. I remembered my father's spilling-over briefcase, his Japanese-language tapes, his wristwatch, so much like the man himself, five dials going at once—urgent, urgent, but measuring who knows what. They had moved from New Jersey to California two years after Max was born. For the climate, they said, but there was my brother Matthew just a few miles down the road with his healthy children, his perky wife, fruit trees and a pool in his backyard. I'm the *daughter*, I remember thinking, as if that should have made a difference. But at the same time, I was relieved to have them far away, for the geography provided a concrete excuse for the distances between us, already so wide.

I remembered Ian when we first met, the ropy muscles on his arms, his level gaze, the way he often thought for a beat before he spoke. We used to drive down back roads outside of Boston, stopping to look at sheep or horses or, once, a llama spitting at a goat. One afternoon we pitched our new tent in a meadow full of milkweed, just to try it out. It was still light out, but we crawled inside with fistfuls of milkweed pods, stripped, and painted each other with fluff and milk. A trip to Quebec province, I remembered. We went dogsledding. It was our honeymoon. When the malamutes were taken out of harness, they pounced on us and licked our faces with sandpapery tongues.

I'd given Ian an atlas, and when we got home we sat with it and planned future trips. India, Bali, Portugal. The Alps and Pyrenees. Iceland, Morocco, Rome. With a red pen, we dotted each place we'd visit. *For my fellow traveler*, I wrote inside the atlas's front cover. I liked the term better than *husband*. Ian's shelves were full of travel books. He'd taken time off from college to work on a fishing boat in Alaska; after graduation, he'd gone on an anthropological dig in Turkey for six months. The units he created for his social studies classes were intricate and beautifully done. Sometimes, that first year after we got married, I would open one of his folders at random and read his notes: *The Incas believed in reincarnation and saved nail clippings, hair cuttings, and teeth in case the returning spirit needed them. . . .*

"Ayllus"—a clan of families supervised by a "curaca," or chief. . . . Inca legend: the original Inca people were flood survivors who, by hiding in a hollow up on a very high mountain peak, were saved and repopulated the whole earth. Though the notes were usually not much more than lists of facts, I had found them moving, almost private, like some kind of coded language of desire.

Then Adam. Max. Day by day, we lived our lives. We didn't complain much, not out loud. How could we? Max was the one, after all, who was shouldering the burden. We were at once the lucky ones and part of the problem, passing on the disease while escaping it ourselves. Now my territory was clearly marked, my charge simple: *Keep him safe.* Ian and Adam went off together to school and came home late in the day after coaching and sports, sometimes together, sometimes not. Then I'd go for my little walk through the neighborhood. I might have gone farther, stayed away longer, but I never did, for I quickly grew lonely for them all, even as I'd been waiting for hours for the sensation of setting off by myself.

That fall, I designed homeschooling units for Max and found other lessons on the Web, filled with knowledge I didn't possess and had to learn along with him. More and more, he was outpacing me, remembering details I'd already forgotten and asking questions I couldn't answer. Sometimes we'd take a break from the computer, lounge on his bed and read together, from *The Wizard of Oz* or *Alice Through the Looking Glass* or *Harry Potter and the Sorceror's Stone,* stories where kids drank potions that shrunk them down or wore capes that made them invisible so they could travel, undetected, through the night. There's no place like home. In the book, Dorothy's aunt and uncle are dour, pinched people, the house an ugly shack. Still, while she's traveling through the Land of Oz, Dorothy longs for home, though she's walked on streets paved with gold and made new friends who understand her better.

"Where would you rather live," I asked Max when we finished the book, "in Kansas or in Oz?"

He picked at an insect bite on his arm. "I don't know. Why do they wear sunglasses in Oz?"

"I think it's so they'll believe that everything is emerald green, even though it's not. It's sort of a trick the Wizard plays on them." I stilled his hand with my own.

"Oh," said Max. "I thought maybe their eyes hurt."

"Maybe that, too."

He sat up, rubbing his own eyes. "I guess I'd live in Oz. But only if it was for real."

One night we had dinner with Iris, who taught social studies with Ian at the middle school, and her husband, Joel, and their three kids. They'd spent their summer vacation with friends on a white-water rafting trip in Colorado. As we sat in their living room, they showed us photos: churning rapids, an orange float, children clinging on. It sounds, said Iris, like you had a great time this summer, too, but when she pressed me for details I couldn't come up with much. Swimming, I said. Canoes and Ping-Pong, arts and crafts. And what else? she asked. Don't pry, I thought, although I had nothing to hide and she was just trying to be nice.

Max came in from outside while we were talking. The rest of the kids were out in the yard with a gang of neighborhood children. From where we sat, their voices reached us only as inflections, punctuated by laughter or a shout. Iris and Ian were discussing the faculty's contract negotiations with the school district. Joel kept chiming in with various opinions—try for this; whatever you do, don't give in on that. Only half listening, I was making color trails in the room with my eye, something I always do when I'm bored. Red rug, red spine of book, red socks, red sweater stripe, red pen, red roof on magazine, red flowerpot. Yellow bowl, yellow pattern on pillow, yellow Post-it note, yellow house trim in a painting. . . .

Max mumbled something we couldn't hear and then repeated it, looking straight at Iris. "I want to go home now."

"Soon, buddy," Ian told him. "Go back outside for a little while more."

Max flopped onto my lap, gripping Who by the head. Usually, these days, his owl lived inside its waist pack when we were out in the world. It was Ian's idea, a move I'd initially resisted, thinking Max should be able to carry around a stuffed animal without feeling ashamed. But Max had gotten teased about Who more than once—at the doctor's office, at gym—and one night Ian came home with the black nylon waist pack and, inside, a tiny rubber rat, a pair of miniature glasses, and a typed label: *WHO'S LAIR*. Quickly, Max came to treasure the pack itself, stroking the nylon until it turned shiny, which was almost as bad as his stroking Owl in public, maybe worse, since the pack often sat over his crotch. "Out of the frying pan," Ian had said, laughing, and though I'd smiled, I'd felt real sadness at the thought of Max transferring his affections away from the toy he'd loved since he was two. Now, though, the pack was empty, Who out. I ruffled Max's hair.

"Hey, sweetie," I said. I could feel Joel and Iris watching.

Ian slid over to us and patted Max's shoulder. "What's up?" he said. "You don't get to see these guys hardly ever. This is a treat—for them, too. Why don't you go back outside?"

I gave him a look: *Don't push.* Max could be so rude when he felt like it. But also, if I were to be honest with myself, I welcomed the weight of him on my lap, the fruity smell of his shampoo. And I, too, was sapped, ready to go home.

"We were hearing about your camp earlier, Max," Iris said. "It sounds like a great place. What was the best thing about it?"

"The kids aren't stupid losers." Max flashed his teeth at her, a mockery of a smile. "Like here," he added softly, in case we'd missed his point.

I nudged him from my lap and stood. "I guess somebody's tired. We'd better go." I smiled weakly. "Sorry."

Ian stood, too. "No, you're not sorry. It's Max who should be sorry, for being so rude. How about an apology, Max?"

Max ducked his head. "I told you. I—want—to—go—home."

"Maybe something hap—" I started to say, but Ian cut me off.

"Adam!" he was calling, leaning toward the open window. "Come on in, Adam, we're going home!" He turned to Iris and Joel. "Thanks. It's always great to see you. We'll have you over soon." Then he turned to Max. "We'll go as soon as you apologize."

Max held up his owl and spoke to it, his voice high and girlish. "Sor-ry!"

"It's all right, Max," said Iris, but her mouth was pinched—whether with pity or irritation, I couldn't tell. "We're just sorry you didn't have a better time."

Max sat up, stuffed Who into his waist pack, and yanked the zipper shut.

"Okay," Ian said, and his voice was hard, almost bitter. "Get in the car. Go."

Adam listened to his Walkman on the way home. Max picked at Who's fur and sulked. Ian and I, too, were silent. I knew I should ask Max what had happened, but I couldn't seem to find the words. *I hate it here*, was all I could find to think. *I hate it here with these stupid losers*—as if it were I, not he, who was the rude, impulsive child.

It wasn't until Adam was in bed and Max was upstairs reading that Ian came down and sat with me. By that time I was calmer, settled on the couch with an afghan his mother had crocheted and a mug of mint tea.

"What do you think happened?" I asked. "I guess they must have teased him or something. It never ends, does it? It's so hard for him to fit in."

"I asked Adam." Ian sat down. "No one teased him. He just sat there without saying a word and then ran off."

"According to Adam." I cradled my tea. "But he might have missed something. He's on his own turf again, with all his friends—he gets distracted. Did you ask Max?"

"Max ain't talking."

"Well." I let the steam rise up into my face. "I'll try to talk to him later. *Something* happened. Maybe he was in the middle of one of his pretend games and they made fun of him. Or he took out Who. Kids can be so ruthless. Anyone at all different gets smashed, you know? Sometimes it's in subtle ways."

"I guess." Ian shrugged. "But they can also be generous. I see it all the time with my students, how they are with the Down's kids, often they—"

"Max isn't a Down's kid. He's . . ." I didn't know how to say it without its sounding wrong: *He's smarter, he's not as friendly, he's not retarded, he's more complicated; he's not as all-round sweet.* "For one thing," I said, "he understands all too well that he's gotten a raw deal."

"Maybe. But he's also lucky in a lot of ways. Sometimes—" Ian hesitated. "I sometimes think you enable him."

"What? Speak English, please."

"Come on, Anna. You know what I mean."

"No I don't, actually. I'm completely out of the psychobabble loop."

"He's almost ten years old. He shouldn't be sitting on his mother's lap at a party and carrying around a fetish object. He needs to interact with other people and learn to be polite. He can do no wrong in your eyes, but it's not fair to him to treat him like that, not in the long run. The two of you, it's like—" He shook his head.

"What?"

"It's not right for a kid his age. Max needs to—" He got up, his back to me, and I thought *stranger, stranger,* though that was exactly the opposite of what he was to me. "You just sit there," he went on. "Neither of you says a word, except about leaving. You tell me you want to go out more, but then we do and you just . . . I mean, you space out, like you're on drugs or something. These are my friends. It's embarrassing. Max isn't the only one who comes off as rude."

My anger startled me—how blunt it was, how ready to come out. "Oh," I said. "Is that right? Is that how it looks to you? This is about me? Why didn't you say so, instead of railing on poor Max? I guess I should apologize now—I'm *so* sorry for embarrassing you in front of your dear friends. But how do you think *I* feel, has that ever occurred to you? With you and Iris going on about school politics, and Joel bragging about his practice and . . . and soccer games, and me sitting there like some—some goddamn fifties housewife? I have"—I banged the mug down on the trunk we used as a coffee table and watched tea slop over the rim—"nothing to say. Not to these people, who don't know me at all. At least Max knows me—god knows, we spend enough time together."

"Shhh, he'll hear." Ian bent and tried to touch my arm, but I jerked away. "He does know you," he said. "And you're a great mother for him, and a great friend. I just think we need to start thinking more about what he needs to grow up—for himself, not what *we* need."

"You mean what *I* need," I said. "Don't be patronizing. Why don't you say that? Is it impossible for you to be direct?"

"All right." He sat in a chair across from me, speaking so softly that I could barely hear him. "What you need, then. Fine. We could start there. Go ahead."

"I need for him to be happy and not . . . not hurt by people. You saw him at camp. He does really well with other kids as long as they accept him—there's nothing wrong with his social skills. But you don't want him to embarrass you—that's what *you* need. You want our entire family to win the popularity contest. But—" My voice broke. "Max won't, he never will, can't you see that? He can't go *outside* during the day, and that's just not in right now. Maybe someday that'll change, but for now—"

"Lower your voice," Ian said sternly. "They can hear everything."

He stood and moved toward the door, and I felt a jolt of surprise: Would he actually leave the house, burst onto the street like people did in movies? We hadn't fought about Max this directly in a long time. Mostly our struggles over him were subtle, a well-worn, nearly wordless dance. Now I felt exhilarated, close to laughter, even. My own voice as I spoke had sounded almost foreign to me, so quick and fluent.

"I think you need to examine your own—" I started to say.

"I won't discuss this inside," Ian said, and I rose and followed him to the sidewalk in front of our neighbors' house. We were both facing the street. It was well past midnight. Up and down the block, the houses were dark, except for a purple-blue glow of a TV in one upstairs window. Above us, a streetlamp made a buzzing noise—an electrical current, perhaps, or insects drawn heedless to the light. For an odd moment, I felt filled with some kind of anticipation, a girl just come home from a date: Will he kiss me, say this was fun, let's do it again sometime?

"I want him to feel connected to other people." Ian turned toward me. "Just like you do. That's all. And for him to be healthy, of course. We don't really have a disagreement here."

"He *is* connected—he can be. You saw him at camp. He . . . he just blossomed."

"Camp isn't the world. He needs to learn how to take those skills and use them in other places, so he's not"—he sighed—"so stuck in one corner. So he can have friends when he grows up, and not just people with XP. Kids are really different when they have a chance to be out in the world. Often they're more mature. I see it all the time with my students, how they regress the minute the parents show up. He does well with a little encouragement, but he needs to control his impulses and develop a thicker skin."

He heard his own words and let out a laugh.

"Oh, you're right," I said. "Let's just buy him a new skin. That would solve all his problems, all our problems, for that matter. Why didn't we think of that before? Let's just—"

And then I was crying. I rarely cried since I'd had children, not in front of anyone, not even Ian, but here I was, my chest heaving, my breath escaping me in gasps. Tears were the wrong thing for someone in my position; I knew that. Humor was the thing. Humor and a dash of irony and one-day-at-a-time and focus-on-the-positive, and anyway we're all terminally ill in the long run, ha-ha. Confidence was the thing, and chutzpah, to stomp your tiny feet—*when he grows up*. Not this noisy, wet dissolving, anything but this.

Ian moved toward me. "Shhh," he said. "I know. If only we could."

Briefly, I leaned against him and felt my tears recede, but I couldn't let it go. "Why?" I said into his chest. "So he'd be normal? So he'd be *popular*? You make him feel like he needs to—"

Ian drew back. "Jesus, Anna, I tried to explain—"

"I'm sorry." I took his hand. "I know, I'm being unfair. I'm sorry. I am. It's just . . . it's hard coming back. I used to be okay, everything seemed manageable and under control, but now for some reason—" I coughed.

Ian waited, his hand limp inside my own.

"I don't know." I caught my breath. "Everything seems harder, things I used to accept. I *did* want to go out tonight, but then I . . . I don't know, I had nothing to say, and I started thinking why don't I have a job or at least have access to a studio or something? But then that feels so complicated, and I'm committed to Max, of course. I just keep wishing Marnie and Tommy lived here, or Hal and Alida—people like us, you know, who understand. Max and Tommy were getting so close—he's never had that with a friend. I don't think he can, here, I really don't. I just wish we could've stayed at camp, even for a few more weeks, to get more"—I shrugged—"*energy.*"

"Camp was fun for Max," he said. "I'm glad we went, and

I figure it was good for him for a little while. But it's not real life. No one has a life like that, with so much money and leisure, and all those games, and . . . and staying up all night. And Hal . . . It's almost like he thinks having XP makes you *better* or something. It's a shitty disease. It's bad, bad luck. That's all." He took his hand back. "Anyway, Max shouldn't be surrounded by other kids with XP all the time. Some of those kids won't make it. It's not a pretty picture—you idealize it. Why not try to make the best of things here? If you want to go back to teaching, we should think about that. It doesn't have to be out of the question."

"My salary would be pathetic. If I could even get a job."

"But coupled with mine."

"Yours? Who would stay with Max?"

Ian stiffened, and I girded myself, knowing what he was about to say. "I still think we should get him into school," he told me. "If they'd coat the windows in even a few classrooms, it could work, especially once he's in middle school, where I could keep an eye on things. We can push for that, other families have, but you'd have to really be behind it and be ready to work with the system. It takes faith, trusting other people. And it would involve a lot of arranging and negotiating. We'd need to start now. I wish you'd just—"

"Not now." I shook my head. "Please. I'll talk about it, but not now, okay? I'm too tired."

I didn't bother to pull out my old arguments: how it wasn't safe enough; how Max could never do field trips or recess or sit in the lunchroom under fluorescent lights; how the other parents didn't want their kids cooped up in a dark classroom—one of them had come right out and said so the last time Ian brought the issue up at a PTO meeting. The cruelty of children, the impossible-to-explain direness of the disease, the way nobody would keep track of Max the way I did, all the time, every second, like the most exquisitely tuned radar. I knew I couldn't be his teacher forever—I had almost no knowledge of high school math and science—but I also knew that school would be, for Max, a difficult, dangerous place. And then the other reason. For years now, Max and I had shaped our lives around each other, like two trees that learn to grow entwined in a narrow space. Was I ready to let him go?

"All I'm saying is there are options," said Ian. "I'm not just thinking about Max here, but you, too—how to get you out more, and back to your painting, if that's what you want. Maybe we could finally build you a studio off the garage. We could all help. It might take a while, but it wouldn't be a big deal."

I shrugged, then nodded. How thoughtful of him. He so often was, though lately I found myself suspicious, as if each considerate gesture hid some deep self-interest—or was I only responding to myself? Ian had always appreciated my quirks—my art, my tendency to fantasize—but only in small doses. We still had some of my paintings around, and the ones he liked best were the miniatures, representational, contained. Three limes on a blue plate, their shadows merging. A boy and a woman on a bus. Two eggs, smooth curves. In the attic crawl space, I'd stored other canvases, some stretched, some rolled. One of these was also of three limes, but here they were enormous and nearly abstract, a hundred greens and yellows, with the kind of pocked, close-up beauty, verging on grotesqueness, that a microscope brings. In the top right corner sat a cut-open blood orange, its color seeping toward the limes. I'd been going somewhere with this painting. It was looser, less imitative; the fruit seemed almost human, like something I'd encountered in a dream. Years ago, I'd wanted to hang the painting in the living room, but Ian had protested, saying it would give the boys nightmares. The boys, I'd asked, or you? It looks like an infected cut, he'd told me. It's *fruit,* I'd said. Instead, we had hung up a framed poster—a table with dishes, and behind it (not until months later did it even strike me as ironic), a window looking out to water, pools of light.

"You could call a friend," Ian suggested now. "Make a date for a movie or coffee. I'll stay with the kids. Or we could get a sitter and go out ourselves. There's a new Pan-Asian restaurant where Rossini's used to be."

"That'd be nice," I said, but already my mind was traveling elsewhere, to glinting copper, serving bowls heaped full, tomatoes still dusty from the vine. I didn't, for one, like the term *Pan-Asian;* I thought it covered too much ground. How difficult I was. I tried to smile. Ian looked exhausted, steadying himself against one of the skinny saplings the town had planted on our street, their trunks bound with tape. He closed his eyes, and I reached over to stroke his eyelids, his cheeks, the bridge of his nose. Kind man, gentle man, how was it that underneath my love for him, I sometimes felt a dim buzz of hatred, vibrating deep inside my bones?

"You didn't like it there, did you?" I said. I'd known he had some reservations about camp, but it was only then that I saw how strong they were, and I felt suddenly as if we'd sprung from separate species, so alien he seemed, so wrong in his response.

"I told you." He opened his eyes and stepped back from me. "It was fine. I just don't see it as a long-term solution. And no, I didn't find it heaven on earth."

"You seemed pretty involved, like you were having fun. Was that all a sham?"

"No. They're good kids. And I liked being in the woods and getting to spend more time with Max. Anyway, I'm not going to sit around and sulk—I'm a team player. But am I glad to be home? Yes."

"We'll go back, though. Next year. Right? I thought that was understood."

"If Max wants to."

"Of course he does."

"Then we will."

"And so," I said, "do I."

"Why?" He looked at me now, really looked. "It seems like it's making you sort of miserable," he said. "Having been there, I mean."

"No." I shook my head. "No, it's made me happier. It's given me a sense of wider possibilities. I just . . . I need to figure out how to—I don't know—*translate* them to here or something. It hasn't made me miserable. . . ."

"Okay." He glanced at his watch. I could tell he'd had enough. *A team player.* It was one of those expressions I found grating, like *We're on the same page* and *A level playing field.* And yet he *was* a team player, more generous than I was in many ways, less likely to complain.

"We'll figure it out," I said, as much to myself as to him, and he nodded and started walking toward the house. Then he stopped for an instant, and I thought—hoped—he might come back to me.

"Of course we will. We have no choice," he said, continuing on.

Family squabbles. We'd had them before, though not often at this pitch, and they always resolved themselves, usually fairly quickly. Someone said sorry, someone else shrugged and accepted; we moved on. But the problem now wasn't with Ian, or tempers rising, or the secret hurts lodged in the lives of our two boys. It was me. I couldn't stop crying. It happened that night after dinner with Iris and Joel, and it kept happening after that, my tears coming out of nowhere. I never cried for long. Most of the time nobody even noticed. I'd go for a short walk if Ian was home, or I'd pull Max into my lap and tell him a story to distract myself, though increasingly he squirmed away. Why don't you call a friend and go out, Ian kept saying, as if there were multiple possibilities, as if my own family couldn't possibly cheer me up.

Once, I'd had real friends in our town. I'd gotten close to a few people after we moved here—an artist named Carly whom I met at a local Life Drawing open studio; a group of mothers with children Adam's age; a guy I'd gone to college with who ended up living three blocks from us with his lover, both of them architects. As the years went by, though, it became harder and harder to keep up, no sitting by the local pond while the kids swam, or having lunch at the café on Main Street, or sharing studio space, or meeting new people through a job. For years, ever since she'd moved to the Midwest a few years after college, Sophie and I had managed an annual weekend visit, I to her or she to me. I'd last gone to Chicago a month after her twins were born. She had accused me, on that trip, of being distant. I had accused her of not being understanding. You have no idea, I'd said, about my life. So tell me, she'd answered, but wearily, distractedly, a baby at each breast. Instead, I filled her freezer with lasagna and pesto, painted a watercolor for the nursery, bathed and held her daughters, though it was their mother I ached for, our friendship, the heat of it, the endless words. That was over two years ago, and we still hadn't planned another trip.

Much of it, I knew, was my own fault. For a while, my isolation almost hadn't seemed to matter. My children, my family, kept me snug inside a circle. They consumed me. I let them, *made* them, perhaps—especially Max, who'd become, over the years, not only my son, but my best friend, too. We had a whole world together. I didn't think anyone else could ever truly understand it, the same way that, as a child, I would return from my imaginary games dazed and almost feverish, with a sense of how impossible it was to convey where I had been.

You make your own bed, so the saying goes, yet sometimes, especially lately, I also blamed Ian. Did he have to coach each season—soccer in the fall, basketball in the winter, softball in the spring—or was it that he wanted to? In his own way, Ian pursued his own desires, his need for a "normal" life, with quiet determination, even as he liked to see himself as more flexible than I was. Often he announced commitments he'd made—to teach during the summer or serve as a consultant to a new charter school—after he'd already made up his mind. We need the money, he'd point out if I protested, and since we did, it was hard to argue. Ian had his friends at work: Iris and the other teachers, the front office secretary, the varsity soccer coach. He'd mention them offhandedly—a joke they'd told him, or the fact that someone's father was having surgery. I envied him this daily interchange with people, lives intersecting in the mailroom, the lunchroom, even as I saw how tired he was, staying up late to plan his lessons and spend time with us, then rising early for work.

Go out, Ian kept saying now. Call Carly and go to a movie; I'll stay with the kids. Finally, one day in early November, I did.

I let Carly choose the film. The more foreign the better, was all I said. It was raining when I met her outside the cinema, the sidewalk plastered with wet leaves. The air smelled of fall, and I was giddy with anticipation, drunk on this little corner of the outside world. Then the movie. It was in Spanish, about a destitute woman whose only son is kidnapped by a cult. As I watched, my mood plummeted. My one night out, I kept thinking. My goddamn one night out. Afterward, we went to a café. All around us were pairs of people—men with women, women together, a mother with her teenage daughter. We talked. About her painting and teaching, about my kids. Are you seeing anyone, I asked, and she said no but that she'd started answering personal ads; it wasn't as bad as you might think if you had the right attitude. It really wasn't so bad.

"So who have you met?" I asked. "Anyone interesting?"

She wrapped her beautiful, large, paint-stained hands around her coffee cup. "Sure. Interesting and psycho. Interesting and married. Or maybe it's just me."

"No," I said. "It's not you. You're wonderful."

She looked up, and I knew I'd said the wrong thing.

"What I meant," she said, "is that I'm not sure I want it, the whole mess of another person and how much, you know, effort it is. I'm in the middle of this big series. I'm a witch when I'm working well."

"I remember that feeling," I said. "Barely, but I do. I miss it."

"Well, I miss having a pretty little family. Maybe the grass is always greener."

"But I thought you said—"

She got up, and for a moment I was afraid she might be walking out on me, but it turned out she was only going to the rest room. She ran her fingers through her hair, which was long and dyed a brilliant red. We were the same age, born within a month of each other. Old, I thought. We're getting old. Then she shrugged. "I don't know what I want. I'm sorry, Anna, I told you, I'm a witch when I'm working."

"So I shouldn't have called?"

"No, I'm glad you did. More than twice a year might be nice, but whatever, we're both busy and it's just as much my fault. It's good to see you. You look terrible, though. Are you? You look—I don't know—wiped out."

I should have been honest, then. I should have let her in. But it was almost eleven o'clock, and she'd just told me I looked terrible, and I wanted nothing more than to go home. "I'm tired," I said. "I'm always tired. But otherwise—" I smiled and felt as if my face would crack. "I'm fine."

Looking back, I might say I was depressed. Why not? An American disease, familiar as the common cold. I'd turned forty-two that fall. Things catch up with you. Sometimes you just need to sit still and let them throng. But with a child like Max, there's so little time. No time for doctors for yourself, no money for therapy or massages, no time, even, for the long musings I fed off as a girl. If I wasn't with Max, I was with Adam. If I wasn't with Adam, I was with Ian. If I wasn't with Ian . . . Sometimes when I'd finished planning Max's school lessons, I did read, I managed to do that—novels set in Sri Lanka or Brazil, a few pages at a time. Once or twice I took out the paints Hal had given me, but I only looked at them, the colors arranged in a spectrum, the untouched brushes. I thought about teaching oil painting to Max, but lately the craft projects we did seemed to bore him, and anyway, the paints were unhealthy for him and I didn't know how I'd begin.

"Everything under the sun is beautiful," wrote the Impressionist painter Charles Hawthorne. The quote sits on the front page of one of my college notebooks, written in the loopy, optimistic letters of a freshman. The way I was taught to paint, it was all about natural light: hazy or cloudy, pure or refracted, warm or cool, north or south. It was all about light and its absence, but never its total absence. Off with you, go outside, my favorite professor used to say, and we'd disperse across campus, shouldering our easels, until we found a tree, rock or wall that made us stop. Stare and stare, harder and harder. Notice the pinks underneath the grays, the tonal variations, the different values. Squint so you can see the color masses. Return in the early evening and again at dawn. This was perhaps what I loved most about painting—how it sent you out into the world, then drew that world back inside your eyes, your fingers, until you knew it as you knew a lover, or your own body, or your child's. Yes, I could turn on fans and set up lamps for Max, make some indoor shadows, show him how to mix and scrape and brush, but I knew it wouldn't be the same.

Sometimes, when the kids let me onto the computer, I roamed the Web, listening in on conversations, visiting travel sites and looking at pictures of distant places, or browsing online catalogs full of clothes I couldn't afford. I only talked to Marnie on the phone a few times that fall, and I didn't write into the Camp Luna listserv at all, though I read the messages. Occasionally, they made me feel better, but more often I ended up feeling disappointed—too much false cheer in them, coupled with too much bad news. The words were so thin compared to the people themselves, yet still I logged on every few days when I could find the time. One night on a radio call-in show, I heard some people talking about how glum they were, how they "had SAD." At first I thought they were a bunch of New Age crackpots, but eventually I figured out that SAD stood for seasonal affective disorder. Aha, I thought, almost hopefully. Perhaps I had SAD, too. Maybe I needed a light box, my years of deprivation finally catching up with me. Oh, to be the sick one for a while, tea and lozenges, honey and bed rest, baths of UV light. Meanwhile, of course, I was as healthy as a workhorse, not even a cold for over a year, and bringing home a light box would be like importing poison for Max.

In December, Max had another squamous cell carcinoma removed, this one from his right hand. We spent Hanukkah alone as a family. My parents sent a box of presents, generous gifts, carefully chosen. I sent a similar package to them, and to my brother and his family, then worried that I'd forgotten to take the price tags off, for I'd gotten nearly everything on sale. Phone calls were exchanged. Thanks, just what I wanted. Nobody bothered with *wish you were here*. For Christmas, Ian's mother and stepfather came up from Florida, where they'd moved from Boston the year before Max was born. They had a strict rotation among their collective five children, and they'd finally come around to us. They'd just been in Ireland visiting relatives. Like my parents, they had taken to traveling now that their kids were grown, though they stayed with friends or went on Elderhostels, while my parents booked nice hotels.

"I think," his mother, Sally, told me in a low voice, one night as we washed dishes, "that there was a girl in the family like Max, with XP, but of course they didn't know what it was back then. In my grandmother's generation, some kind of cousin."

"Really?" I let the frying pan sink under the suds. "How do you know?"

"My great-aunt showed me a family picture, and this girl was in it. Something was"—she put her kind, damp hand on my arm—"well, clearly wrong with her. They said she was deaf, for one thing. And her skin was full of sores. Of course, with such fair Irish skin, you never know."

"How long did she live?"

"Oh, darling, I don't know." She began drying again. "The family's had its share of trouble. I wouldn't want to make them dwell."

Sometimes she sounded exactly like Ian. "Maybe they'd want to talk about it," I said. "What was the girl's name?"

She looked blank. "How silly of me. I forgot to ask."

"I'd like to know it, when you talk to them again, if you don't mind asking."

She nodded. "The girl looked happy in the photo. I mean, her skin wasn't right, but she was smiling, a little imp. And pretty, or she would have been. I thought maybe she had something of Max's spirit. Do you think that's possible, that he could get not only the disease but some other parts of her, too?"

I tried to answer, but the tears were starting.

Sally gripped my arm. "Is Max all right, Anna? You'd tell us if—"

"Oh no, he's fine. Please don't worry. He loves having you visit."

"What about you? You don't . . . I wasn't going to say anything, but you don't seem quite yourself."

"I'm just a little tired. I love having you here too."

I gave her a reassuring hug, but for the rest of the day her words hung in my mind. *Not quite yourself.* Not quite myself, but who had I been in the first place, and if I was, these days, no longer quite that person, who had I become?

The little girl was named Anna, I decided later as I fell asleep. She had my name, though she shared no blood with me. Dear Anna, I thought, as if I were writing her a letter or smoothing lotion on her skin. Dear Irish Anna, who shares my boy's disease.

On New Year's Eve, Ian brought home sparklers and we ran around the yard at midnight as the century turned, a new millennium. For once, the whole block was up with us. We took the sparklers into the street and handed them to our neighbors. Someone produced champagne. The kids sipped and made faces, holding the drinks in their gloved hands. I drank a whole glass and felt the night sky move closer, clear and wide and harmless. Ian appeared out of the darkness and kissed me, his mouth warm, and I felt a surge of fresh desire and old love for him, and for the planet, and for all its living souls. Some people were merry; others seemed sober, trying to grasp what it meant to move from this number to that one, a shift at once meaningless and huge. The air that night was crisp and cold. The older kids, Adam among them, built a sort of bonfire in a Weber grill. Max ran by with some other children. He's lived in two centuries, I thought. Another milestone; I found them everywhere I could. For a moment, standing there in the dark, I was happy.

On January thirteenth, I read on the group e-mail that Nicole had a Stage III malignant melanoma, spread to the lymph nodes under one of her arms. She had just had multiple nodes removed and was starting biochemotherapy and interferon. The news should not have surprised me. These were highly at-risk children, after all. No matter what we did, their chances of getting skin cancer were a thousand times the normal rate. As Ian had warned, one or another of them would eventually fall. And yet somehow I didn't believe it. Briefly, I made myself feel better. Stage III was not Stage IV, after all, and she was getting treatment. Quickly, though, worse thoughts followed: that she could die within the year; that maybe, if she died, the other children at the camp would escape, by some odd twist in statistical logic; that Nicole, the prettiest, most outgoing girl, the one who so clearly should have led a normal life, would somehow be the sacrificial lamb.

Later that night, I got the bathroom ready for a skin check for Max. Adam and Ian were already asleep. I'd been withholding the news of Nicole from everyone, unsure of how to bring it up. I turned on the space heater in the bathroom, spread a towel out for Max to stand on, switched on the sink light and got a flashlight out. We did these checks once a month, and they felt, by now, like a familiar habit. And though I always feared what I might find, I loved how the checks brought me back to when the boys were babies. I went into Max's room to get him. Scuffing his feet, he following me into the bathroom, stripped to his underwear and stood there shivering, despite the heater's warmth. He was so thin. He always had been—it was just his build, like mine—but as I watched him, his knobby spine and sharp shoulder blades, I felt a surge of panic.

"Lift up your arms, okay?" I said, and, well trained, obedient, he did. I aimed the flashlight and ran my hands over his skin, which I knew better than my own or Ian's—this patch of freckles on his neck, that mole on his back, the spattering of scars and rough patches from biopsies and excisions. At first he hopped from foot to foot, impatient, but eventually my hands seemed to soothe him and he let himself grow sleepy, and when, examining his face, I bent near his temple, he pressed his face to mine and we stood there for a moment, cheek to cheek. When I got to his underwear, I pulled down first one side, then the other, to examine his bottom and hips, and he cringed but stood still enough to let me look.

"I'm sorry," I said when I was finished. I knew Ian should probably be taking over these checks, but I couldn't quite give them up. "You do your penis, okay, and also let Daddy take a look tomorrow. You look good, no changes."

"I know. I was at the doctor's, like, last week."

"Three weeks ago." I handed him his shirt and sweatpants. "They can miss things. They want us to check too, remember? And I've got an eagle eye."

He got dressed. As I was turning to leave, he wrapped me in a tight hug.

"You look great." I smoothed his back. "I can't believe how tall you're getting. We have to mark the growth chart. Soon you'll be taller than I am."

Max stepped away and glanced at himself in the bathroom mirror. "So guess what? Nicole's got cancer, the spreading kind, in her lymph nodes."

Inside me, something crashed. "Who told you that?"

"Dad."

"He did? When?" I realized Ian must have read the e-mail at school, but why had he spoken to Max about it and not to me? "She—" I searched for the right words. "She's got excellent doctors to help her get better. Did he tell Adam, too?"

He nodded. "Will she die?"

"No." I said it forcefully. I knew it might be a mistake to gloss over things, but I couldn't think of another way.

He stuck his tongue out at himself in the mirror. It was deep purple, and for a moment I was startled, but then I remembered he'd had a grape Popsicle for dessert.

"What about me?" he asked.

"You? No. I told you, sweetie, you're doing great."

He pulled at the sides of his mouth with his hands, making a monster face. "Never?"

"Oh, Max." He was standing too close to the heater, and I bent to turn it off. "Someday, of course. Everyone dies eventually, except for maybe the Greek gods, and they're myths. Remember them, how they live forever? It caused them all sorts of problems."

He lowered his hands. "If I was a Greek god, I'd make it so everyone died at the exact same second, or else make it just another thing, like, you know, waking up or going to sleep. So you'd say, 'Okay, I'm tired, I think I'll go die now,' and the next day, you'd say, 'Okay, I'm gonna go, um, live now'—whatever you felt like—but you'd have to get passes or tickets, they'd sell them at bank machines, maybe with watermarks, like on money. I could design them on Quickdraw. Wouldn't that be cool?"

I reached to stroke his arm. "Very."

"Who will die first," he asked, "me or you?"

"Parents almost always die first, since we're older." I meant it as a reassuring answer, but the minute I said it, I realized it was not. "But not for ages and ages—when you're really old and I'm even older, like a hundred, or even older than that. My parents are still alive, right, and I'm a grown-up. So are Daddy's. Grandpa Mike still goes running. Let's go to your room and do some school. Sometimes"—was there a less insipid way to say it?—"it's good to focus on just living."

"When Nicole dies, will she go to heaven?"

"If you believe in that. A lot of people do. Her family does—remember how they prayed at camp? So do Jess and Amy."

"But not you."

"I—" The air in the bathroom was too warm, too close. I opened the window a crack. "I don't know, Maxie. I'd like to. I believe that people live on in a thousand different ways in . . . in pictures and memories and a sort of spirit. . . ." I shook my head. "Sometimes I dream about my grandmother, and she died when I was eight. Maybe she's visiting me, I don't know. There's not one answer to any of this, I don't think. You'll figure it out for yourself as you get older—it'll just happen."

"Nicole was Adam's girlfriend," Max told me. "And now he's got another one, Michaela, but he also sort of likes this other girl, who's new. I forget the new one's name. I guess Adam must be *hot*."

I laughed. "You know a lot more about his personal life than I do. He might not want you spilling his secrets. We'd better go do your history lesson."

"I'm sick sick sick of history."

"Math, then. For half an hour or so. Then free time, then bed. We're falling way behind."

"In a few years, they'll have a computer chip to implant in your brain that's got all that stuff on it. It'll make everything so easy. Download! Delete! Download!"

"Maybe. I hope not. That's spooky to me. Anyway, for now we have to keep up," I told him. "It's part of our contract. We owe Julie a report next week."

"If we're all going to die"—he met my eyes in the mirror—"then who cares?"

I nodded. "You have a point there. We could study philosophy, the Existentialists. They might agree with you."

"Or we could study nothing."

"True. Carpe diem. That's Latin for *seize the day*. Or we could seize the night. Say we didn't do school tonight? What would you want to do, if you could do anything?"

"Camp."

Snowdrifts on the steps of the lodge, the living room dark, sheets draped over the couches, a mouse running like a wayward thought across the kitchen floor. "Me too," I said, "but we can't. It's all closed up. What about around here?"

"Maybe . . . how about bowling?"

"That'd be fun, but they're not open this late on weekdays."

He slammed his fist down on the sink.

"Max." I took his hand, still balled up, in my own. "Try not to get so frustrated, okay, baby? There are other options. You can think of something else."

"I can't."

"You can."

He rolled his eyes. "McDonald's."

"They've got too many fluorescent lights, you know that. We could do drive-through, if you want. Or something inside the house maybe. Or how about a mysterious place we could drive to, like . . . like the water tower or the monument? How about that? We could go to the monument and get take-out fries on the way."

"There's just garbage and graffiti at the monument."

"Then try to think"—I knew I should come up with something inventive, but my mind was emptied out—"of something we haven't done before."

"I have to pee," he said. Since we'd returned from camp, he'd stopped doing it in front of me.

I left him there and tiptoed into Adam's bedroom, half expecting to find him awake—crying, perhaps, or staring into the dark. But he was sleeping, his face peaceful, his schoolbooks piled on the floor.

In the end, Max and I went downstairs, made chocolate-chip cookies and played a cooking show game we called Mixer Max and Mom. Max cracked the eggs, poured in the flour, stirred. "Be sure to stir all the lumps out," he told his TV audience in a squeaky chipmunk voice, "or your kids will vomit on the rug." My accent was exaggerated British, mixed with some gravelly Julia Child. "Chocolate," I declared, "is more temperamental than you might expect." While the cookies baked, we licked the bowl and spoons.

Lucky, I thought for the first time in a while, watching Max work at a wooden spoon—his lowered gaze, his strong pink tongue. Lucky that Max had a "good" strain of XP and was diagnosed early. Lucky to be playing cooking show in our kitchen, with its red table and blue nesting bowls and the radio playing jazz. Lucky to have one another, the boy in front of me, and Adam and Ian asleep upstairs. To have camp. Did it take Nicole's cancer to bring me to such thoughts—there but for the grace of god go I? It might have been guilt that made me suggest we send the cookies to Nicole. It might have been something better, wanting our food to travel, sweet, into her blood and bring her strength. If I've learned anything lately, it's that motives are tricky things and always mixed. Max and I ate four cookies each, and then, when they were cool enough, we put the rest in a tin to go south, to Alabama and Nicole.

I went into therapy that spring—with myself. It sounds like a joke, and in a way it was, but it was also both serious and oddly effective, like something you've paid a lot of money for and are determined not to waste. Once or twice a week when the boys were doing their homework or spending time with Ian, I'd complain of a neckache (this wasn't quite a lie, I'd had a chronic tight spot for years) and retreat to the bathroom for a soak. I'd run the water so hot I could barely stand it, pour in bath salts and climb in. Within minutes, the room would get so steamed up you could hardly see. Then they would begin, my *conversations*. That was how I thought of them at first, conversations between myself and some vague other, a calm, inquiring presence—hi there, how are you, what was the day like, and the night, why do you think you need to make excuses to take a simple bath?

A breath of air inside my lungs, my stomach rising, the water lapping. I don't know, I don't know. Shhh, I'd tell myself. Not a thought in your head, not a care in the world. I shut my eyes. I sank.

These were times to drift, at first, to roll my neck from side to side and flex my feet. I liked the sound of water, first the tub filling, then the quiet splashing as I moved. But after the first few times, something shifted, and I started talking. In my mind, of course, never out loud; somebody would hear. *I found four gray hairs today. Max yelled at me again. I cried at a commercial for cell phones, my moods are so up and down.* I talked to myself, at first, but after a week or so that changed, too, and then there was another person with me, seated on the edge of the tub. I'd been in real therapy twice, once in college and once for six months after Max was diagnosed. In college I'd found it helpful, but the second time, the psychiatrist kept trying to put me on anti-depressants, and I kept saying no, afraid the pills would dull my judgment and blur my ability to keep Max safe—and anyway I was still nursing. One day, she suggested that Max's disease was a rich metaphor for my ambivalence about having a second child and another boy.

"It's not a metaphor," I said evenly. "It's real."

"Of course, I understand that, but could it not also function as a metaphor?"

"It's our life," I said. And then—surprising even myself—"You've got some fucking nerve."

I left then, feeling strangely better, and never paid the bill.

This was different. The people at the other end of the tub knew me inside out—my thoughts, my skin, my genes, my kids. Of course they did—I know, I know—but my visitors didn't *feel* like me, but rather like friends who knew me well. I fell right into it. I spoke. Sometimes the therapist was Marnie. I'd see her as if she were really there, sitting in running shorts and a tank top, her eyes direct. Sometimes it was Daniel, a lover I'd had many years ago in France. Ah, here you are, *minou*, he'd say, delighted. How did you arrive here, at this particular house, this particular life? Oh god, it's a long story. Tell me, *dis-moi tout*. I was naked, of course, in the bath, and the person at the end of the tub was always clothed, but it didn't matter, it didn't seem strange. It was like the nakedness of a child, as if I *were* a child there, floating, babbling, and sometimes the person was my father or my mother, but always understanding, always unblinking, and sometimes it was Sophie or Carly, and they called me Annie, as if I were a girl still. What is it, Annie, what?

Death, I said, to her, to him, to them. How it was with me all the time, even when I wasn't consciously thinking of it. How when I woke, I was often surprised that one of my people hadn't stopped breathing while I slept. It was a low background noise, this fear—a scrape, a chafe, chalk on blackboard, bone to bone. So you're afraid of dying? No, not exactly, except as it would affect my family—otherwise I don't think about my own death much; I figure I wouldn't have to be there afterward. Then whose? I can't . . . I can't say, I'd admit, as if naming would make the thing come true. But try. And so I'd try. Nicole's—she's so young, such an energetic, lovely girl—but also . . . also her getting sick; it makes it really hard not to wonder. . . . Marnie might nod. My mother might nod. Yours, I'd say to her. And Dad's. I know we're not close anymore but still, I won't be able to stand it, I think about you every day, I wish— Yes. My mother leaning toward me, her hands gnarled but still elegant, and there, her wedding ring, jammed below her swollen knuckle. Yes, I know. And who else's death do you fear? Ian's. Adam's . . . But both of them are healthy, vibrant. I still worry. And who else's? I don't like to think about it. But you can't help it, of course you can't. No. I can't, I can't. Can't help.

Born 1990, died 2002. Born 1990, died 2010. Born 1990—May I never know. His name too short, its X like the X in the disease, as if we had anticipated what was to come. Say it. No. Say it. No. Say it. Max. So you think about Max's death a lot? Constantly and never—I believe it will happen and believe it's impossible at the same time—I can't explain, it's . . . it's like I had trouble believing in birth when I had my kids. There they were, because we'd done this *act*, we'd started them in this moment months before and so there they were, but *how*? I can't get my head around certain basic tenets of life on earth, I know it sounds ridiculous. No, Anna, it doesn't; these are life's mysteries. But they stop me, stall me. And what if you try to plow through them, surrender to them, even embrace them? Now it was no longer my mother speaking. It was a man, his jeans rolled up, his pale feet soaking in the water, toes clenched. Anna, he called me; he was the only one. Surrender? Yes, just let yourself imagine it. I can't, not until it happens, not even then. I can't. He shrugged, and I thought, *You pretend to be mellow but your feet give you away*. How was it for you, I asked. I mean, when Robin died? Impossible, he said. And then not entirely impossible, though in a certain way I still don't believe it. There was Alida to care for—that helped. Alida, I said, means wren. My two birds, he said, nodding, and I remembered a round he'd taught us: *Ah poor bird, take your flight, far above the sorrows of this sad night.* But Alida's also sick, I blurted. You could lose her too. Hal stared at me, wordless, and suddenly I felt my nakedness, my nipples rising above the water, pointing to the blunt cruelty of what I'd just said.

I sat up, relieved to be alone in the bathroom, and crossed my arms over my chest. *You're crazy*, I muttered to myself. You're out of your fucking mind.

It was a game, of course. I knew that. I never entirely lost track of the real world, just loosened my grip on it for a while, then pulled the plug and stepped out as the water spiraled down. Those nights, I slept better than on the nights I didn't bathe. Ian noticed it. Take a bath, he'd suggest, instead of call a friend. Never did he say, talk to me, Anna, tell me, what is it? Nor did I offer up my thoughts or coax him into sharing his own. Life at close quarters demands such privacy, I guess, or was it laziness that made us keep our own counsel, or tiredness, or fear? If anyone had asked, I would have said that Ian and I were so close we didn't need to talk. After this many years, I'd have gone on (merrily, wearily, an expert on the art of marriage), you get so you can read the other person's mind.

In late January, I sent an e-mail to the Camp Luna list, but despite my efforts, it felt like the sort of mass-mailing holiday letter we sometimes got from old friends, full of cheer and obvious gaps. *Adam made the honor roll. Max is learning French.* Still, I sent it, for I knew I'd stayed away too long. A few days later, Hal wrote me back. He hadn't replied to the whole group, just to me. I was a little surprised by this at first, but then I reminded myself that people wrote to each other directly all the time. My message to the group had barely skimmed the surface of our lives, and Hal had seen that and wanted, as my friend, a clearer view. "You used the word 'busy' five times," he wrote. "And the word 'worried' four. But you barely mention yourself. How ARE you, Anna?"

Busy? Worried? Had I used those words? It took me a few weeks to answer him. I'd start a message, delete it, start another, the words too flat, too full, too flat. Sometimes the mere thought of Hal overwhelmed me. He wanted something from me—already I could sense it. To talk and talk, I told myself. To crack me open like a nut. Finally I did answer him, and so began our correspondence. We'd volley back and forth for a few days, then fall into silence for a week or two until someone, usually Hal, started up again. Jupiter@earthlink.net to Annasimon356@aol.com. Annasimon356@aol.com to Jupiter@earthlink.net. Subject (always): hi.

Sometimes Hal wrote about Alida, or a hike he'd taken, or a book he'd read, or his ideas about next year's camp. I wrote to him about what I was sketching; I reported funny or worrisome things the kids had said. I wrote about my mother, and he wrote back about his own. She lived near him in an assisted living complex, he said. She was losing her memory. Each week, he tape-recorded her so he could play it back to her later, so he could play it to Alida, and himself. Sometimes when I was done writing to him, I'd e-mail Sophie. "I have a new friend—I think you'd like him," I remember writing once. I might have wanted to make her a little jealous. I might have wanted her to ask me more about him, probe—a friend, what kind of friend? But she didn't ask. We were no longer in college. We were married. In a hurry. And if she'd pressed, I probably would have stuck by my story, for at the time I mostly believed it myself.

Meanwhile, Ian and I lived side by side. Kisses, we shared, each morning when he left, each evening when he returned. A checkbook. Sips of tea. Reports of days and nights. Shopping lists and schedules, doctors' appointments and school curriculum packets, the familiar sight of each other stepping in and out of clothes, in and out of rooms. Now and then, which is to say rarely, when time and circumstance allowed, we made love, but always with an odd sense of déjà-vu, at least for me, as if we were repeating an act whose true version resided in the past. Somewhere in there, of course, were two inner lives, two gel-soft brains and working hearts. If I missed him that spring, it was not in any way I could name.

Still, we each tried, in our way, to do small kindnesses. I bought him new running shoes for his birthday and cleared out a study area in the basement so he'd have a place to retreat. He rubbed my neck and brought me sketchbooks and oatmeal soap smelling of breakfast and babies. The soap started out oval, but I wore it to a nub, running it over myself during my baths until everything was slippery and slick. Sometimes I'd stop talking and simply wash myself, stroke myself. Touch. Once or twice I came in the bathtub. No audience, then, no therapist, just me and a gasping openness and—again—a rush of tears. It wasn't me crying, not exactly. I was nobody, nowhere, pure breath.

I always felt different after those baths, drained but also frightened in a way I couldn't explain. I'd wrap myself in my old terry-cloth robe, sponge out the tub and return the bath salts to the cupboard. I'd open the window to let the steam escape, and then the mirror would clear, and there, of course, I'd be.

SIX

Hal had extended the session to run for the full month of August the following summer, and though I knew it was impractical, knew Ian had reservations, I wanted us to go for the whole time. "Next year at camp," I'd say, like *next year in Jerusalem.* "Soon you'll see Tommy again," I'd tell Max when he seemed down. "Soon you'll be swimming in the lake." Most New Englanders looked forward to the coming of spring, but for us it meant longer days and shorter nights, more time stuck inside, a fiercer sun. The boys always squabbled more in summer, their differences accentuated, and since Ian taught summer school each July and early August, we had only a sliver of time for a vacation before he had to start preparing for the new school year. But this year when the crocus tips pushed through—a faint, hopeful shade of green—I felt better than I usually did. One night, Max and I cleared out around the bulbs, tossing the layers of leaves onto the lawn. After we had raked and bagged the piles, we went inside for school, a unit on photosynthesis. We read about how the light from the sun travels 150 million kilometers to the earth, how the green plants capture its energy with chlorophyll and use it to build carbohydrates. We found a Web site that depicted each plant as a bustling factory: the little lens-shaped chloroplasts, the veins like burbling rivers carrying water, the lacy web of roots. It's pretty amazing when you stop to think about it, I said to Max, and he said, Yeah, it's cool. For a moment, then, we let ourselves admire the sun.

One Saturday, I went through the boys' summer clothes, boxing up Max's outgrown items to give away and putting aside Adam's hand-me-downs for Max. Late that afternoon, while Ian took the kids swimming at the indoor pool at the Y, I made a trip to the Salvation Army to drop off our discards and pick up some things. The clothes I found there were fine, barely worn. One T-shirt was covered with planets. Another, which I got for Adam, had NORTH ADAMS STATE COLLEGE printed on it. Usually I enjoyed these expeditions, but this time I felt slightly sour, standing at the register with a pile of $1.49 shirts draped over my arm. Hal, I found myself thinking, would never be here, for though his own clothes were faded and worn, he bought most of Alida's at a children's shop in Berkeley—owned by a friend, he'd told me, and I'd pictured a tall, tanned woman with short hair and jingly bangles on her arm; perhaps she'd been his lover at some point. The clothes were all organic cotton, bright and playful, deep purples, turquoises and blues, with big buttons shaped like turtles and sunflowers. They were exactly how I would have dressed my daughter—if I had a daughter, if I had the money. On impulse, I stopped at the Gap on the way back and charged two new sweatshirts—red for Adam, purple for

Max—and, from the clearance rack, a flannel shirt for Ian and a pine-green hooded sweatshirt for myself.

Now and then, I returned to the things I'd taken from camp—the stencil, the checker piece, the key. Twice, when everyone was asleep, I set up my oil paints in the basement, turned on a fan and went so far as to dip a brush and make a mark. If you're painting from memory or from inside your head, I told myself, you don't need light, and for the first time in years, my mind—that wide, that narrow space—felt like enough for me, though once I made a mark on the canvas, I had to stop. Still, I didn't mind so much. I could feel myself on the brink, so what was the rush? If having children had taught me anything, it was that things often happen slowly, in their own time. The tooth emerges, the word forms, the apology comes sidelong, buried in another subject, weeks after the fight. Later, I told myself, I'll paint. Later. At camp. And each time one of the boys whined or snapped, or Ian was late getting home, or I let a glass slip through my fingers to shatter on the kitchen floor, I'd say it to myself again: At camp.

Looking back, I can see how I wasn't all there that spring, too many long baths, perhaps, too much talking to myself. Oh, there were moments when I came forward, times when I lived inside my family, right there with them all. Adam went to his first prom, and while I'd never been a prom kind of girl myself, I found him beautifully, sweetly awkward in his tan suit, posing in our front hallway with Michaela, who had pearly-pink bitten-down nails and laughing eyes. Max turned ten in March. A double digit. We gave him a mini-trampoline for the backyard, and he received a flood of cards and e-mails from his camp friends. That spring, he made a friend in gym class, a girl named Judy who was new to town. She'd been born with a cleft palate and had a scar now and a slightly lopsided mouth fixed in a permanent half-smile. She could twirl on those rings and scramble up the rope, fist over fist. Do you want to have her over, I asked Max one day, and first he hesitated, but then he said okay.

Judy came for dinner one Friday night and stayed until close to ten, when her father arrived to pick her up. I kept waiting for something to go wrong—for Max to bristle over an unseen slight, for Adam to disapprove of Max's choice of friends, for the wrong words to fly out of my own mouth. It was Ian, of course, who kept things afloat at first, asking the girl questions, joking, ever the relaxed, interested teacher; I'd forgotten how good he was. Everything went fine, better than fine. Everything went well. At dinner, Judy was polite and quiet, but afterward she and Max went into the backyard; through the open window I could hear them playing one of his space alien games. "State your business on my planet," he said in his robot's voice. Judy giggled. "State your business," Max repeated. "I'm, uh, looking for my frog," she said, or was it dog, or clog? "Follow me to Trampoline Headquarters," said Max. I stood at the kitchen window listening, trying not to listen, until Ian called my name.

Behind our days, like a murmur, like a wound, was Nicole. She was a subject of e-mail conversation that spring, though her family rarely wrote in and the news was never good. The rest of us did what we could—discussed, worried, stayed in touch—but never too much, never at great length. The superstitious among us knocked on wood and crossed our fingers—for Nicole, for our own kids, for Nicole's parents, for ourselves. The hopeful hoped. The fatalists waited. The true believers prayed. I was all of these by turn, all except a true believer, for though I sometimes longed for a god to cup me in his palm, I couldn't seem to summon anything that felt like faith.

Max and I baked. We sent Nicole butterscotch and chocolate brownies, meringue drops and hermit bars. We made fudge, wrapping each cube in wax paper and arranging the pieces in a plaid tin. We were careful bakers, and though we chatted or played Cooking Show as we worked, we never lost track of measurements or left lumps in the batter. I loved our expertise in the kitchen and sometimes found myself fantasizing that it wasn't desserts we were concocting, but medicine. Scientists, we were, then, and our wooden spoons were eyedroppers, our mixer an autoclave, the dough under our rolling pin a length of healthy skin.

One evening, I stopped in the middle of packing a batch of cookies, found Adam in his room, and asked if he wanted to include a note for Nicole.

"That's okay." He was sprawled on his bed with his homework and didn't look up.

"Are you sure?" I stepped farther in. "I bet she'd like to hear from you, even more than from us, or maybe you've been e-mailing her—"

He gave me a withering look, but I forged on.

"Listen, Adam, I know what's happening to her is really hard, and that you were—" What, attracted to her? In love? Going out? They'd seemed like lovers when I interrupted them by the water—that solitary, that self-enclosed, two people of whatever age clasping hands. Might they have slept together, she thirteen, he fourteen? I doubted it. I didn't want to know. "I realize you were special friends." As soon as I said the words, I regretted them. "And now—"

Adam pulled his textbook closer. "Mom, I've got a test tomorrow. Sign my name if you want, okay?"

"Sure. I will. Or I could run down and get the card up for you to sign."

He flipped a page and spoke into his book. "Just sign it for me. Anyway, we weren't *special friends.*" His voice was steely. Why don't you find a career writing Hallmark cards, he might as well have said. Or better yet, go drop dead, you and Nicole.

As I turned to leave, more words escaped my mouth. "I . . . I just find all this . . . it's . . . sometimes it's a lot to handle." My eyes stung, though whether at Nicole's cancer, or Adam's coldness, or my own sense of having failed him, I wasn't sure. "And I thought maybe it was for you, too, and that sending her something might, you know, be a way. . . . It's just that holing up inside yourself isn't necessarily the best—"

"I'm not holing up. I'm studying. For a huge history test. It's almost half our grade."

I stared at his door frame. "Okay, but if you ever want to talk—"

"I have a *test.* Most parents want their kids to study. Can't you just leave me alone?"

I turned back to him. In the instant that I'd moved toward the door, he had tucked his legs under his body and clamped his hands over his ears. For a tall boy, he had made himself tiny, folding his limbs into a ball. I had a memory of myself around his age, how each month the orthodontist would tighten my braces and I'd feel myself shrink down, tighten, welcoming the pain. Slow down, I used to want to tell my body. It had been my biggest secret, since all around me girls were bragging about their periods and buying training bras.

I probably should have gone back in and sat there quietly with him until he was ready to uncurl. Or stood in the doorway, just stood, neither in nor out, until he turned his head. Then again, he had a test. He was aiming toward his future, deliberate and focused; I could see it already. Didn't every parent want this, as he'd said? He would return to his book after I left—Kristallnacht or Pearl Harbor or Hiroshima, for they were doing World War II. Big history, vast violence, sorrow deep enough to drown the world, but the point here was to get the facts right, to get the dates. December 7, 1941. August 6, 1945. *A*. What did I expect, for him to sob and beat his breast over all the trouble—past, present, future—in the world? Adam, like his father, didn't often stop to keen or wail. It might have been his best quality, and his worst. Or maybe he wasn't upset about Nicole, not even underneath. Perhaps he had held hands with her in the most casual way, or maybe I'd imagined even that. Maybe he was too young, still, to think about death as something that could happen to a girl you'd had a fleeting crush on, or to your brother, or yourself. Or maybe he was more mature than I, his mother, was. Who knew? We were all leaning away from one another that spring, nursing our private pains, our private plans.

Everything in its own time. Sometimes I didn't have the patience, not for their slow unfurlings, which seemed even more halting and inscrutable than my own. Leave me alone, said Adam. Good luck on your test, I said—and shut the door.

I suppose it shouldn't have surprised me when, a few weeks later, he told me he wasn't going back to Camp Luna. We'd been talking about waterskiing, and I'd said maybe he could try it at camp.

"I'm not going," he announced, just like that, as if we were acquaintances sharing summer plans in the checkout line.

"What did you say?" I asked.

"I'm not going this year. You should all go, though. I mean, I figured you would."

"Oh, I see. And what will you do while we're away, if you don't mind my asking?"

"Soccer camp," he said. He had gone several times in the past, to a day camp held at Dobney Academy, a private school a few towns away. Ian drove him in the morning and picked him up at three-thirty. Afternoons, he'd worked at an ice-cream stand, putting half the money he earned toward the camp fee.

"That's not an option." Now my words spilled fast. "Not while we're away. You can't stay alone, Adam, you're not remotely old enough. And how would you get there? Anyway, we do things as a family in the summer. It's the only time we really get to be together, and it's important that we all go to Camp Luna, for Max. We can look into soccer camp for part of July if we can afford it, but you'll be coming with us when we go. I've already signed us up, and it means a lot to Max to have you there."

Adam shook his head. "Max doesn't care if I go. He has all his little buddies. I'll stay with someone here. Somebody'll let me, like Roy or the Morans or somebody. Don't worry, Mom, okay?" He flung his arms back as if he were lying on a beach and exhaled. "It's really not a problem."

I sat beside him on the couch and tried to ignore the panic that was coming over me. "Is it because of Nicole that you don't want to go?"

"What?" He shot me a look of deep disgust. "No."

"Then why?"

He shrugged. "All the best players practice in the summer, and you fall way behind if you don't. It's kind of obligatory these days, if you want even a chance at making varsity. Anyway, the kids at Camp Lunatic are mostly younger than me and—"

Not normal, I expected him to say. Weird, sick, dying. Just say it. I might have slapped him if he had. Sitting there, I almost didn't recognize him, this half-grown son, this confident, smug boy posing as a man. If he had his own exigencies, his own deep needs, I couldn't see them. But then he surprised me.

"The camp," he said, "is great for Max, but I think it might be even better for him without me, so it can be his own thing and I'm not, like, the big brother all the time. He never got to be an only child. I got that for years, like the way we have so many more baby pictures of me, you know?"

I nodded, remembering how singular my affection for Adam was before Max was born, how I couldn't imagine expanding my heart enough to hold another child, so full it was with my first-born, so packed with steady joy. Did he remember too? The long gazes, the babbling nonsense conversations, the ground we covered, wandering about? Adam described his early days as a gift denied his brother, but he might just as easily have presented a different story—how the new baby arrived and suddenly the whole world changed shape: sick boy, Mama's boy, bye-bye. How none of Adam's childhood troubles could ever seem anything but paltry next to the weight of Max's disease. How, if there were fewer baby pictures of Max, it was mostly because we spent so much time at the hospital, leaving Adam with a neighbor who had her own three children under six. Even then, he had borne it all so stoically, offering me his cheek for a good-bye kiss before he turned, his face tight with concentration, to the neighbor's children's toys.

"The Morans told me I can stay there anytime," he said.

"What? You already asked them?" My voice was shrill. "You can't go making summer plans by yourself. For god's sake, Adam—"

"No, I mean in general, they said I could stay over whenever

I wanted. Nick has two beds in his room, and his own bathroom. It's a huge house. I could help with yardwork for, whatchamacallit, room and board."

"Room and board?" I laughed, despite myself, and reached to muss his hair. "You're not an orphan. You have your own family. And we hardly know them. I've seen them maybe twice in three years."

"*I* know them. I see them all the time."

"Well, I don't. And you're not moving in with strangers."

"Why not? Everyone at Max's camp was a stranger, and then—*whoops!*—they croak."

Suddenly I had no words. "She's not—" I finally managed to say. "She hasn't . . . oh, Adam—"

We heard a noise and looked up. Max was coming down the stairs in a red bathrobe, peering forward at us. He'd been playing with leftover Halloween face paint and had made himself white with bright red spots of rouge and a pink nose. He intended, I imagine, to look like a clown or mime, but with his curly hair and fine features, he looked more like a pretty, blushing girl.

Adam saw him and laughed. "Hey, Maxipad. Excellent makeup!" He made a kissing noise.

Max touched his own cheek as if he'd forgotten what he'd done. "What're you guys talking about?"

"Nothing," I said. "Adam, don't call him stupid names."

Max met Adam's eyes. I don't care, I could feel him thinking. Call me whatever you want. Then he turned to me. "Why's he moving in with strangers?"

"He's not."

"But you said—"

"I said he *wasn't* moving in with strangers."

"But why—"

I stood up. "You both have homework, and Max, that stuff is very drying, you need to wash your face and put on moisturizer. I'm making lasagna, we'll eat at nine. Bring your stuff up to your rooms when you go up and put it *away*. There's a pile for each of you on the stairs. Don't just stand there." I flicked my wrist at them. "*Go.*"

They were both staring at me, and for a moment I saw myself through their eyes: as irritable, humorless, mired in details. I turned first to one boy, then the other. "No one's moving in with anybody. This"—I laughed, trying to sound lighthearted, but the sound came out thin—"is where we all belong."

It was Adam, finally, who had the idea of sleep-away soccer camp. His friend Trevor was signed up for three weeks in August at a program an hour or so away from us, on a college campus in the northwest corner of the state. Trevor's brother had gone the year before. Even ten-year-olds could go there, Adam told us. Eight-year-olds. Fourteen was practically too old. Pros did the teaching. We could drop him off on our way to Max's camp. He fished around in his backpack and produced a shiny brochure. Ian scanned it first, then passed to me. I folded it in half and told Adam we'd discuss it and report back.

Really, I thought, there was nothing to discuss. We couldn't afford it. It was that simple. Max's camp was largely paid for by the Luna Foundation—meaning Hal's inheritance plus some donations—but when we went, it meant that Ian taught one fewer session of summer school, and we were stretched to the limit financially.

"It's not possible," I told Ian much later that night, when I got into bed and found him awake.

I could see him nodding in the dark. "I know. I wish it were, though. He wants it so badly. They have a couple of scholarships, but I doubt he's good enough."

"Why? I thought he was really good." I'd only seen Adam play twice that year, and I'd enjoyed watching him dodge and kick his way across the field—intent and red-faced, quick.

"No." Ian sat up. "I mean, he's decent and he's gotten a lot better, but he'll have to work like a dog to make varsity in high school."

"Oh."

"We could—" Ian hesitated. "We could maybe go to camp with Max for just two weeks, so Adam could have two weeks of soccer camp at the same time. We could drop him off and pick him up on our way."

"Where would the money come from?" I asked. "Anyway, we're already signed up—a month for me and Max, three weeks for you and Adam. We need to be consistent—we've promised Max. Couldn't Adam do camp at Dobney again when you're back the last week of August? And play soccer at Camp Luna?"

"Dobney's over by then. He wants to really *play*. We could charge it and pay it off later."

"No," I said. "We're not going further into debt. He'll be in college before we know it. Then we'll go into more debt." I got up to make sure our door was shut tightly. When I returned to bed, I lowered my voice to a whisper. "Anyway, this isn't just about money. Max deserves to be on his own schedule for a month out of the year, with his family and his friends. Adam gets that all year, plus a whole fall of soccer practice. I mean, let's be fair here."

Ian lay back down. "I'm trying to be fair. Everyone has different needs."

I lay down too, but rigidly, not touching him. "I know, but I just don't think we can shorten Max's camp time. He's been looking forward to it all year."

"You have two kids," Ian muttered.

"What?" I sat up and turned on the light. "What did you say? Jesus, Ian—"

Suddenly, though, I was deflated, exhausted. Two kids, of course I did, one in each arm, and their faces were dirty and their diapers full, and though my arms ached so hard they trembled, the night was cold and the bridge narrow, and there was nowhere safe to set my babies down. I switched the light back off and sank into the dark. "I'm really pissed now," I announced over the drumming of my thoughts, but I said it weakly, and he didn't bother to answer. It was close to three in the morning. Outside, the moon was full, but we couldn't see it through the window film. I had my period—a heavy, achy one—and for an illogical moment, as my belly cramped, I yearned for the pinprick egg I was shedding, for the child it might have been. Once, my life with Ian had been all looking forward, the bright lure of potential. Now we were deep inside our lives; soon, we'd be looking back. Would we grow old together? Briefly, I allowed myself to wonder if we might not and felt my anger turn to sadness—a wide, white blanket—and my sadness turn to emptiness, then sleep.

I had no choice. The next day, with Max still asleep and Ian and Adam at school, I called my parents to beg for money. Fortunately, my mother answered the phone.

"He's awfully young to be going off like that for so long, isn't he?" she asked.

"Adam? I don't think so. Anyway, he could try it for two

weeks, and if he liked it, he could stay on for a third week—or else join us at Max's camp. He's not so young. He's fourteen."

"Yes," she said, but I could tell she'd lost track. "We didn't send you off at fourteen."

"Nobody's sending him off. He wants to go. Desperately. But the thing is, it's just—" I stalled here, my words stumbled. "Ian can't teach a second summer-school session this year since we'll be at Max's camp, and—" I waited for her to jump in, but she was silent. "The soccer camp is quite expensive. We're not sure how—"

"Oh," said my mother. I pictured her plucking dead foliage off a plant as she spoke, or aligning a pile of index cards in a neat stack. "I see."

"I mean, depending on how you're doing, of course, and only if you could—"

"I'll ask your father," my mother said. "I'll ask him—I'm happy to do that for you. But you know we need to watch our budget in retirement, and you know how he worries, it's practically a phobia with him and it's gotten worse as he's gotten older, he's not exactly logical about it. I mean, if I buy a fancy *shampoo* . . . so you need to understand if it turns out we can't—"

"I know, I know, of course. Only if it seems right. I'd never want to take—"

"Shhh," she said. "Darling, please." She sighed. "You sound so stressed out. Is something wrong?"

I drew myself together. It was a ridiculous question, at the same time that nothing new *was* wrong. "No," I said. "We're just trying to make our summer plans. It's complicated to figure them out, that's all."

"But the kids are fine. Nothing's wrong." She said it declaratively, wanting only one answer.

"Yes. Everyone's fine."

"Good. Julia was in the school play last week. She played a talking pine tree. Oh, she was proud! It was very well done—they hired a professional set designer. Have you talked to your brother lately? You know we'd all love a visit. I could take you to my yoga class. I've found it really helps with stress."

Listen! I wanted to yell. *Money. Money and airplanes and fluorescent lights in the airport and houses without film and you saying, Oh, let the boy get five minutes of fresh air, Annie, it's cloudy out, it's almost dusk, children need to be outside, don't you remember everything I taught you about the garden?* Never *Don't you also remember how scared I made you, how I taught you that the world would sting, bite, scald?* Never *I'm so sorry about what you all have to live with.* Never *Anna, Annie, grown girl, baby, I am scared.*

"Or you could come see us," I said, knowing she would not.

The check for Adam's soccer camp arrived a few days later, folded inside a card with a photo of a wolf on it, its eyes yellow, its silver fur glossy in the light. I turned the card over. ENDANGERED SPECIES, it said on the back. My parents must have given money. "For our dear Adam," my mother had written on the inside. "So you can run as fast as this handsome wolf and win every game."

And so we returned. Our new plan was that Adam would stay at soccer camp for three weeks, as long as he liked it; then he and Ian would come home together so Ian could prepare for the new school year and Adam could see his friends. Max and I would stay at Camp Luna for the whole month of August. One twelfth of a year; it seemed luxurious, on the one hand, and too long to go without seeing Adam on the other. We dropped him off at the soccer camp in the Berkshires on the way, a quaint green campus filled with brick buildings and ivy. At the drop-off site, the boys formed a boisterous, jostling crowd. Adam let first Ian and then me hug him, and he promised to call and e-mail, and so did we. He dove inside the van one last time to whisper something that made Max laugh, and then he was gone, dragging his bag behind him.

Something felt wrong, unbalanced, then, as the three of us continued on, a triangle and not a square. He's *not* old enough, I found myself thinking, and I resolved to call that night and remind him that if he didn't like camp, we would come get him right away. When we pulled back onto the highway, it was just getting dark. The route this time was one we knew, and we didn't get lost, and no deer stepped into the road. Max prattled in the backseat: Will there be new kids? Can I share a room with Tommy? Did you remember to pack my baseball hat? Do you think we'll put on a play this year? I want another pretzel stick. Ian answered, passed him snacks, fiddled with the radio. I drove. I'd been waiting and waiting for this night to arrive, but now that it was here, I half wanted to turn back. Partly it was leaving Adam; I had a sense of things dissolving, of having left a bit of myself behind. But also I suddenly wasn't sure I really wanted to go. Maybe, I kept thinking, I'd only imagined how wonderful the camp was. Perhaps the place, when we drove up, would be smaller or shabbier than before, a trick of perception, trick of memory. The e-mails had felt like a sanctuary during the long winter months, but what were they really? Bulk mailings, that was all—flat words from near strangers on a screen, smiley faces made from colons and parentheses. Maybe Max would hate camp this year. Maybe Ian would step forward and tear the curtain down, revealing an elaborate sham.

A logging truck passed us, honking, and I tightened my grip on the wheel. Ian handed me a pretzel and I ate it, the salt stinging my chapped lips. As I chewed and swallowed, another vision came to me—the camp as a place not of falsehood, not of refuge, but of cure. Someone passes around a copper cup filled with clear liquid. The children drink. The potion passes through their blood, their genes; it mends. The sores on their skin disappear. Their moles shrink down and become beauty marks. Day breaks, and the children get up to greet the sun.

Or not cure, but cure's opposite. Someone drowns in the lake at night. I didn't want to picture it. I did. A girl going under—her lungs, heart, mind. A search team, dogs and helicopters, boats dragging the bottom to find a shirt and sneaker. Or a boy wanders out into the sunlight, his mother made dreamy by the pleasures of the place. He walks from the woods to a meadow where there is no shade, and even when he finds a bush and creeps under it, waiting, the sun fingers its way through to find him hunched and hurt. Burned skin, I saw—not the regular sunburned kind we knew as children—the whipped cream of Noxzema, pink turning overnight to brown. This skin was puckered, weeping, no boundary left between the body and the world.

No fair, I thought. No fair no fair, and it was as if I were thirty-two again, the age I was when Max was diagnosed, when I'd spent months banging my head against the injustice of it all.

I took an exit ramp and flicked the blinker off. Ian and Max were talking, but their words sounded small and far away. I saw Nicole, her scalp bald, her arm belly up on a clean white sheet, receiving a tangle of IVs. "She won't be able to attend camp this year, please send her your prayers." And if you believed in nothing—no afterlife, no power of thought, no children of the

Lord—what then? We hadn't given our boys any religion to speak of, just a few Hanukkah candles, a small Christmas tree, a chocolate egg, matzoh spread with jam. Dross. "She's started chemotherapy and we're hoping for the best." Adam holding hands with Nicole by the water, the secret life they grasped between them, two kids playing at adults. They had jerked apart when they saw me. I had turned away and tried to melt into the dark. A thought had occurred to me, then: that they couldn't marry, not if they wanted healthy kids, since Nicole was a carrier and Adam had a fifty percent chance of being one too. Now the thought seemed hopeful, ludicrous.

My mind was flying as I drove that night, swinging first here, then there. Let's play a game, I finally said to Max and Ian. Mineral? Vegetable? Bigger than? Smaller than? Yellow? Red? Can I drink you? Are you poisonous? Are you sweet? Chocolate. Al Gore. Arno, our gerbil. We played three rounds, then three more, and their voices were the ones I knew, and the questions stilled me, and soon we were on the dirt road, and there was the driveway, and behind it the lodge, and we were parking, opening doors, getting out.

It was only then, as I stepped out of the van, that the thought came to me so solidly it might have been another person at my side—how I'd been waiting not for camp, exactly, but for the sight of that unruly hair, those keen eyes that managed to see me as separate from my family, my life. How I'd been waiting and waiting, really, for that voice, those songs and stories, those actual, unvirtual hands offering me a stalk of rosemary, a box of paints. Is it odd that it took me so long to acknowledge the feeling for what it was—more than a flutter, more than a fancy? Some things, I suppose, seem unthinkable, until they don't.

Hal wasn't in the front hall, and he wasn't in the living room or dining room. Turn around, I told myself. Find a suitcase or duffel bag, Ian or Max, all the weighty, worthy ballast of your life. Turn around. Hold on. I looked in this room and that, waving to people but not stopping to talk, not even to Marnie, whom I greeted with a sidelong, hurried hug. I found him in the kitchen, one hand in a green oven mitt, trying to coax a loaf of bread from a pan. Hi, I said, almost speechless. Hi—more sound than word, more sigh than sound—and he looked up and I knew I'd crossed a border, perhaps had crossed it months before. He feels it, too, I realized, and a happy bubble rose inside my throat, even as I thought I might be sick. Hal took off the oven mitt and stepped forward.

And then Max was behind me, Hal and Ian were clapping shoulders, the bread was steaming, the kettle shrilling on the stove.

SEVEN

Once, in college, I worked for months on a painting of a girl and a man sitting together, sort of Milton Avery–like but without the peacefulness. In my painting, the shapes were more jagged, the feeling less settled, the figures perched so that you couldn't tell if they were about to lean closer or break apart. It was me and my father—I see that now. It was my father sitting with me, paying attention, if only for an instant. My father sitting still. I couldn't get the colors right, the reds too red, then too muddy, the light cast on the figures too stark. One day, in a fit of frustration, I took a fat housepainting brush and glazed the entire canvas with a transparent cobalt yellow wash. Suddenly the figures were aquiver, the space between them charged. They were bathed—that's what I remember thinking. Bathed and blessed.

I showed my professor, awaiting his praise. He squinted and took a step backward, then another, until he bumped into an easel. "Well," he said finally, "I think you probably got what you were after, but it's a bit of a cheap trick." He was British, an early success, painting car wrecking yards and subway stations in acrylics, the details sharp as photographs. Though I didn't much like his work, I had a painful little crush on him. What exactly, I forced myself to ask him, did he mean by cheap? "It had more complexity before," he said. "Things don't just change color like that. Not in one sweep of the brush."

Our second summer at Camp Luna, everything was the same as the first summer, more or less. The lodge, the furniture, most of the people, the room we stayed in, the food, the lake—they were all the same. The long hallways, the rust stains in the sinks, the copper in the dining room, the worn staircase, the photographs of mustached men and slung dead deer. We were no longer newcomers and we didn't have Adam with us this time around, but other than that, nothing much had changed. Except. A yellow wash, the air rippling, as if it had turned to liquid. I felt it in front of me, behind me, even in the dark, even in the middle of the night. I still loved my husband. I still loved my children. I was who I'd been for some time now—a woman in the middle of her life, the pieces set firmly in place. And yet. A sweep of the brush, a realization, as sudden as, on some other level, it was gradual. This, I thought as I walked across the lawn and felt each blade of grass press between my toes or flatten down, is how lives change. Or how they don't.

Everybody has crushes. The married have them and the unmarried, the young and the old. I knew that. I wasn't an idiot. I'd had them myself before, little spasms of fantasy, a flash of desire for the biology teacher at Ian's school, for a few of Max's doctors, even for the young woman who supervised our home-schooling, with her rows of hoop earrings and quick smile. Not very often, but then I didn't get out as much as most people.

Still, I knew what it felt like: the charge, the sense of possibility, the way you suddenly imagined the silky undersides, the creased and private—a body lowering into sleep, a catlike way of staring into space. Maybe a glance would pass between you, or you'd hand over a piece of paper and your fingertips would brush. More often, nothing happened, not even the smallest innuendo—no slip or gaze, no gasp. This was all right with me. Imagining was the best part, how you could go anywhere and come back unharming, unharmed. As I moved through a day or night, I'd picture the person now and then, but never for long, for I had—didn't I?—my own partner full of intricate particularities, my own family, at once solid and in need of my protection. And I'd not been one to court danger, at least not since Max was born and danger moved in with us for good. A real crush, had I allowed myself to act it out, might have behaved just like its name. A cookie on the kitchen floor in bits and pieces, a soda can smashed beneath a foot.

This was different. For one thing, we were in the safest place we'd been in years. I suppose it freed me. It wasn't meant to do that; it was meant to free the kids and maybe let the parents relax a little, but the point wasn't to let yourself run wild. If I were a different sort of person, this would be the story of my son and the sanctuary we found for him. It would be the story of a family coming together around a child's illness, finding a community, one another, maybe even God. It would be a tale of healing—if not of the body, then of the soul. Other parents could listen and find hope. I read these stories before Max was born. I needed to, at the same time that they often left me feeling chipped and out of sorts. The parents were always heroes, taking on the medical establishment, raising money and inventing new equipment, working for larger change at the same time that they shlepped their kids to doctors, wiped noses and countertops, stitched handmade dolls. The mothers were at once spunky and filled with a steely kind of faith. Parents didn't sneak around in these stories, or complain about how tired they were, or imagine other, prettier lives. If these tales had a villain, it was the illness itself. The families—the mothers, the fathers, the children—were pure good.

But what if the mother gets an itch, a yen? What if she tires of the tending, loses faith in the healing, needs a break? People in the paid workforce get vacations. Day-care providers get them, and nurses. Teachers take sabbaticals and leaves. What if the mother, who for years has checked and checked and checked her sick boy's skin, watches the boy run off with his new friends and starts to notice her own skin again, the way it keens for something, wants? What if she finds herself split down the middle? Now she is two people, or even more—two mothers, two women in love with two men and with solitude itself, a person at once meshed and floating, coming and going, here and there. It should be disturbing, but it isn't, not at first. She's too happy. Brimming. Her love is wide and generous; she's got more than enough to go around. This, too, isn't a new story, but it was new for me.

I didn't, of course, know any of this yet. We arrived that night. I found Hal in the kitchen. And then they were all around us, our friends from the year before. Hi, I called out. Oh, hi, you, scooping up children, drawing parents close. Alida was taller, her hair shorter, cut to just below her shoulders. Tommy had new glasses. Marnie had grown bangs. Anil's face was slick with ointment, and he was leaning on a cane. Jess and Amy were back again, their crucifixes dangling from their necks. I sought them all out, somehow free to do so now that I had greeted Hal and let my thoughts cross over. I mixed and mingled, hugged.

The year before, I'd been so hovering and watchful at first. Who are these people, I remember thinking. Who are these children? Now I poured juice into pitchers and put bread in baskets, carried a tray of food into the dining room and came back for another. A pot of chili was bubbling on the stove, and I stirred it and tested its spice. I put on an apron, emptied the dishwasher, washed bowls, wiped the counters clean. Marnie worked with me, and as we moved about, we talked. How was the trip, have you been swimming yet, isn't it great that the boys will share a room, did Adam's soccer camp seem nice? Small things, nothing really. Everything. I heard my own voice galloping, tripping over itself. Do you want some wine? Oh, I'd love some. God, it's good to see you. Her hand in mine, her eyes creasing at the edges when she smiled. The children, as we wove through them on our way to and from the dining room, were bare-legged, without helmets, masks or hats. Some of them had on the new camp shirt—pine-green background, yellow moon. I opened a bag of chips and the kids flocked around me until I gave it up.

Through all this, of course, I was moving past Ian, past Hal. Though I didn't speak to either of them, I felt them like force fields—bristling with invisible static, lit by invisible light. Ian talking to Étienne, to Françoise, to Libby and Mike. Hal bent over a clipboard, reaching for a bread knife, catching up Tommy in his arms. "Who's hungry?" I called out in the kitchen at one point, and I looked up and caught Ian watching me. This, I remember thinking angrily, is me. This—is—me, though the Anna he knew was skittish in a crowd, more comfortable one-on-one. The worst thing about marriage, I think, is how it can freeze you, over the course of years, inside a place, a role. It's nobody's fault; it just happens. You know each other too well, then not at all. Ian—calm and steady, funny and friendly, sports cheerer, runner, mixer, mensch. Anna—inward and fretful, quirky and moody, quiet until you knew her, funny only in a slanted way. Careful, prodding, death-obsessed.

"Who's hungry?" I called out gaily. My stride was long, my voice theatrical, my hair coming loose from its ponytail.

It was me, of course it was. What was wrong with him? He should have recognized me, the girl who'd just returned from Europe when she'd met him, who'd taken his face between her hands and kissed him in a parking lot. Then, I wore paint-splashed jeans and spent weekends roaming Boston with my sketchbook or half-box French easel. I led Ian to places neither of us had ever been before, talking to strangers we met along the way—fishermen by a pier, a Chinese grandmother, a short-order cook. My painting was my ticket, allowing me to observe and enter at the same time. When Ian and I led a summer youth group together, I taught the kids to paint with wide gestures and a sense of play. He had loved that girl, her energy, her spark, just as I had loved the cautious way he sometimes let me in—brief snippets of the year his father left, the childhood photos he showed me of an awkward boy who aimed to please. We saw both sides of each other then—I think we did—both sides, all sides, for each of us could do anything in those early days without the other one saying, *How unlike you, I never would have thought*. Now he should have said, *Welcome back, Anna*, as if we were meeting again after too much time apart.

"Go easy on that wine," he said, as I poured myself a third glass.

I put the glass down on the counter. "Don't tell me what to do," I said, and took another sip. I saw Hal and Marnie exchange a glance. I saw Max look up.

"Whoa." Ian laughed uncertainly and looked around.

"What? It's not like I'm pregnant," I said. How, I might have inquired of the room, might I be pregnant when I can't remember the last time I had sex? This, I might have said, is my roommate Ian—the moral majority, the alcohol police. This is Ian; once I knew him. Instead, I raised my glass in a toast. "I'm celebrating," I said. "We should all be celebrating. We're back!"

Marnie lifted her water glass, Françoise her wineglass. The kids stopped talking and looked up, and the whole room fell silent, waiting, though I had nothing left to say.

"*L'chaim*," said Hal after a moment, and then he smiled at all of us but somehow mostly at me—a radiant, childlike smile—and I knew that everything would be all right.

Ian put his arm around Max. A line in the sand, perhaps. I see that now, though I couldn't see it then. He toasted the air with an invisible glass. "Who can argue with that?" he said. "To life."

When I think back on the next few weeks, it is mostly to try to locate a before and after. Here, a woman with wandering thoughts; here, with wandering hands. One body curled next to another. Or another. A shirt rising. New skin, new yet so familiar, the selfsame X and P, flung neck and seeking tongue. Did it begin the instant I allowed myself to think it? Was there a time—a week, a day, a second—when it might easily have gone another way?

What you might expect: a troubled, tortured time. To act or not to act. A measuring of consequences. Weighty words like *betrayal*, *guilt*, or *torn asunder*. Glances exchanged. Journal entries written and torn up. Defenses and offenses, meditations on marriage as a flawed patriarchal institution, on communal living, on the way the best long-term relationships should be able to accommodate some swerve, some change. Doubts in all directions—is it all in my head, does he feel it too, is it worth the risk, the children, Ian—as all around me camp played out its bubbling life.

But no. Not yet. Nothing so heady or vexed. I was thoughtless that week; I was nearly without thoughts. I started to paint again, and that is what I remember most: the smells of sun-cured linseed oil and Liquin, the thin curve of palette, the way the feel of the paint returned to me, hued memory, as if I'd never stopped. I found a hillside one morning when Max and Ian were asleep. It was a fifteen-minute walk from the lodge, near the abandoned hangar where the summer people used to keep their planes. I'd never been inside. I didn't yet know about the rows of oilcans, the broken white airplane, the wicker lawn furniture whose cushions smelled of mold and light and sex. The sun was rising onto a hot day. I faced a row of straggly pine trees, a long sloped rock, ground that went from pine needles to chartreuse grass to taller grass the color of dried wheat. The rock had lichen on it, silvery-white with a hint of blue, and a dark crack down its center. A shadow covered half of it, purple blue fading down to purple greenish-gray.

I didn't sketch first, or stop to plan. For years I'd been talking about trying to paint again, of moving beyond the doodles in my notebooks and returning to color, texture, light. For years, sometimes to Ian, more often to myself, I'd been complaining. Mourning. A lost vocation, sundered talent, blah blah. For god's sake, Anna, it's not like someone chopped your fingers off. Now I just started, no big deal. I painted *alla prima*, fast, thick and goopy, one landscape and then another, not good, not even remotely finished, but I didn't care, it didn't matter, the smell, the touch of the paint was heady and I breathed it in. I didn't wear gloves to protect my hands. I'd ordered the more toxic colors—cobalt violet, Naples yellow—to fill in the gaps in the box, and a tube of alizarin crimson, though it always fades and cracks. First I painted literally, but then, on the same canvas, I moved closer to abstraction, the shapes so close it was as if they were pressing from inside against my eyes. Puzzle pieces—the blue-green of shadow, the gash of crack, the light at the top of the rock, so saturated, like nothing you'd see with a lightbulb. The longer I stood, the more I saw, and the order there was comforting, and the disorder thrilling, even as, beneath it all, I felt something close to fear, or was it rage? This, I realized, was partly why I'd been afraid to paint—the way it distilled things, moved them close, laid them bare. The rock, how it would be there long after we were gone. The light, how it wouldn't stay still.

One boy was sleeping nearby, the other was far away, eating breakfast or doing soccer drills. One man was sleeping, the other was. . . . At first, I only thought of Hal in snippets, in small moments. How he'd given me the paints. How he'd suggested that I order more art supplies on-line, scribbled down a credit card number; get whatever you need, Anna, for you or the campers, carte blanche. I'd gone overboard, clicked and clicked—sure, one of these, a few of those, cost no obstacle, though somewhere in the back of my head was the bumper sticker stuck to the door of the lodge's laundry room: LIVE SIMPLY THAT OTHERS MAY SIMPLY LIVE. The boxes had arrived two days later, and I'd unpacked them in the basement, at once excited and ashamed at the sight of so many new toys.

This morning, perhaps, Hal had stood at his window and watched me heading off, a restless, longing man who couldn't sleep. Through the window film, which turned things soft and blurry, he might have seen me stooped under the weight of the easel and paint box. I hadn't looked, I hadn't turned around. And later, by the hillside, did I feel a hand on the back of my neck, eyes on my canvas, a heat urging me on? Of course I did—the sun, my long-lost friend. I wore no sunscreen, no hat. It wasn't my disease, after all. I carried it, but I didn't have it; sometimes I almost forgot. Partway through the second painting, I took off my shirt and stood in my running bra and jeans. I took off my sneakers, and though the flies and mosquitoes found me, it seemed a small price to pay. The sweat on my hands ran off blue and purple, red and yellow, and I returned that morning bitten, paint-smeared, burned.

If before Max my family was a triangle and after Max a square, that week we were something else. Exploded, dispersed. To say that we had no relation to one another, no discernible shape, would be going too far, but it felt a bit like that. Sure, I slept next to Ian, made sure Max took his medicine and vitamins, did all our laundry, but these things were so habitual I didn't need to think about them. I e-mailed Adam every day, and every few days, an answer came back: "Hi everyone. Camp sounds fun. I'm getting better at soccer but some of the other kids are like pros so it's still pretty hard. The library is cool with a big dome in the middle and a staircase up to a catwalk. Some famous actress was here yesterday but I never heard of her. Gotta go, A."

At home, Ian had tried to fit in a short daily jog during his lunch hour, but now he started running distances, as he had before the kids were born. He'd leave at dusk, when the light was grainy and the deer ventured into the fields, starting off down the dirt road in front of the lodge. Sometimes I'd notice him stretching against the porch railing before his run, his legs shiny with bug spray, a baseball cap on his head, or I'd see him after he returned, his color high, his expression distant or else pained, as if he'd pushed himself too far. I'd be sitting on the porch, or reading in a corner, or standing talking to someone on the lawn, and I'd see him and think what a nice body he had—the curve of back, the strong, long legs—at the same time that he seemed more like a photo of an attractive husband than the thing itself.

Ian had always had an air of privacy about him, but in the past this largely seemed a calm, simple sort of thing: Here I am, here you are, no need to push and prod. It was, I think, part of what drew me to him in the first place. Someone I could live with, who wouldn't take up all the oxygen in the room. Now it felt different—or was I looking for excuses? When we first met, he was curious about my life, though never in a pushy way. Now he asked me few questions, and his answers to the ones I asked him were often so brief as to remind me of Adam, who had the excuse of adolescence. Live and let live. He knew I was painting again, but he didn't ask to see what I had done, and when I undressed in front of him, I felt as unremarkable as an old night table or chair. Now I pictured him running and running—down the dirt road, onto the highway, through a patch of woods, across a brook, onto another road. In my mind, he ran until he got to a place where a whole different life awaited him. Two healthy kids.

A wife who taught art and painted on the side. Weekends spent backpacking in the mountains. Vacations in far-off lands where ancient civilizations showed their traces. Sex—with whom? A woman more athletic than I was, less thorny, more able to turn to him and say, I'm missing you, let's make love. Or maybe he ran the way I painted—to enter the world he was passing through, to feel his breath inside it, the muscle of his heart. To live in it more fully, knowing it would pass, we would all pass. Or he ran to pound the anger from his limbs.

Of course this was all in my head. Ian was not given to extremes, and he never disappeared for long. After an hour or so, he always came back, took a shower or swam, and joined in. Both of us led activities for the kids—Hal expected it of all the parents—and Ian's were ambitious and successful. He got the Adirondack Museum to stay open one night and give the campers a special guided tour. He built a tree house with a group of children, and afterward, when they came up with a secret password and handshake, Ian was the only adult they'd let into their club. He made friends with the other parents too, with an ease I envied. Not so much with Marnie—I suppose I'd marked her as mine. Not so much with Hal. He spent time with Josh and Angela, with Françoise and Henri. He and Étienne hit it off; I'd see them throwing a glow-in-the-dark Frisbee across the lawn and feel a surge of missing Adam.

Ian went canoeing and fishing, played horseshoes and Ping-Pong. He did repairs around the camp with an eagerness that irked me, since at home, broken shades and rattling doorknobs sat for years unless I fixed them myself. Sometimes I'd find him alone in a corner, reading books on the history of the Adirondacks.

"You could teach a unit on it," I said once as I stopped to peer over his shoulder at a photograph of draft horses hauling logs. He looked up at me, his eyes weary.

"Or just read about it," he said.

He returned to his book and I walked away, at once chastened and annoyed, though when I snuck a glance back at him from across the room, it was tenderness I felt. His head was lowered, his feet tucked under him. He was lost in the pages; he was trying to be lost. Later, I picked up the book, which he'd brought up to our room. *Six thousand miles of rivers,* I read on the first page. *Two thousand lakes and ponds. . . . No one knows all of it.*

Now and then it occurred to me that with all this new free time we should have more time for each other. It seemed to be happening to some of the other couples at the camp. You'd run into them holding hands or looking rumpled, as if they'd just come from bed. I suggested it to him once—do you maybe want to pick a night to do something together? Did I really want this? Maybe, maybe not. Reel me in, is perhaps what I actually meant. Hold me, quickly, or I might just slip away. Perhaps he sensed this. I felt oddly nervous as I spoke, and as a result, I think my voice came out a little whiny, with a faint edge of complaint. We were on our way downstairs. He stopped, I remember. He sighed, and I immediately wished I hadn't spoken.

"I'm not the one," he said, "who keeps disappearing."

"What? Who ever said you . . . ? I just meant—"

"I'm glad you're painting, I know it means a lot to you, but you *are* gone for hours on end, like you think this is an art retreat or something."

I turned to go back upstairs. "Forget I said anything. Why don't you just"—in my own clipped tone, I heard my father's—"go about your business."

He saluted me and clicked his heels. "Yes, Chief."

My temples throbbed. "What's your problem? I was trying to be nice."

"Maybe what we both need right now is some time alone. There's nothing wrong with that. I'm not opposed to that, for you or for myself."

I nodded, though I was hurt. "You mean," I said, "in order to come back together more—" What was the word? More fully? More passionately? Or was he granting me some kind of leave? How much did he see already? *Nothing has happened,* I wanted to say. For a second I wondered if he had a lover at the camp, or if he'd set his sights on someone, perhaps Françoise, who was pretty in a severe, French sort of way—high cheekbones, hair pulled tightly back. But of course not. We were all here with our families. I ran my hands over the banister, which felt suddenly greasy, as if too many people had run their hands over it.

"In order to—" I repeated, but just then the dinner gong sounded and Hal's voice rang out.

"Come and get it, folks!"

"Dinner," I said. Already my resolve had weakened. I knew we should set a date, tomorrow or the next day. Time slipped away from us without such planning; it had happened again and again. So how about tonight, why not? Max was signed up for an African drumming workshop led by a former Peace Corps volunteer, an old friend of Hal's. But no, I couldn't, I was busy; tonight wouldn't work. I'd promised to help Hal sort through boxes in the crafts room and start making costumes for the new play he was doing with the kids. How I loved a good costume, sequins and glitter, the swing of a cape. Masks. And something else, a whole new person to talk to—no gnarled history, no sense, with each word spoken, that ten more lay underneath, like layers of cracking leaded paint. Tabula rasa. And it was Hal.

Okay, so maybe tomorrow. If Ian really wanted to. But he'd hardly greeted my suggestion with open arms.

By then we were at the bottom of the stairs. Through the doorway I could see Hal in the dining room, and when he caught my eye, I tried to smile. He kept looking. Stop it, I thought, just as Alida tugged on my shirt and asked if I'd sit next to her.

And so it went—Alida, Hal and I down at one end of the table, Max somewhere in the middle, Ian at the other end. Did a leg touch mine, then? A child's leg? A man's? Hal filled my wineglass. I helped Alida cut a piece of quiche. Some of the kids had made candles, and now the table was covered with them—crooked and lumpy, shaped like clovers, lighthouses and Mickey Mouse. I was wearing a tank top that night, and a light summer skirt. I could smell my own sweat and see the paint specks on my arms. I could smell Hal's sweat, too, and the stale, almost imperceptible odor of his secret cigarettes. He was quieter than usual, but I felt his attention on me even as he ate his dinner and asked the children questions. See, I wanted to call out to Ian. See how he notices my arm on the table, how he takes in when my plate is empty and passes me more food? The children all looked beautiful in the candlelight—reaching for serving bowls, jostling one another, eating. At one point, Alida yawned and rested her head against me, her hair tickling my arm. When I drained my glass, I held it out to Hal without a word, and he filled it up again.

Ian, of course, might have set a date for a romantic rendezvous. Ian might have said yes from the beginning, or put his arm around my waist, or kissed me on the stairwell before we joined the group. That was just one moment, there on the stairs. There were others like it, small corrosions. There are, I suppose, thousands in a marriage, times when you might go forward, come together, and instead something stalls or stumbles, and without exactly deciding to, you move inside yourselves, apart.

The crafts room was in the old stable up the hill from the lodge. Though it had been redone, a few of the stalls had been left standing and you could still feel the presence of the horses—a stomp of hoof, a nervous whinny as, outside, thunder sounded or snow slid off the roof. Now the stalls were lined with shelves stacked with boxes of pipe cleaners, egg cartons, tin cans, empty baby-food jars. A cardboard box sat unpacked on one corner—tempera paint, felt, glow-in-the-dark Popsicle sticks, and glue-on eyes I'd ordered for a finger-puppet project with the kids. When I arrived that night, Hal was already there, sitting on the floor next to a brown paper grocery bag. I'd almost brought Marnie. I'd almost not come. I'd changed from my skirt into a pair of baggy jeans and thrown on one of Ian's sweatshirts over my tank top. I'd pulled my hair into a ponytail, taken it down again, put it back up, unsure if I was trying to make myself prettier or uglier. "I'll be in the crafts room if you want to help out with the costumes," Hal had said to me over his shoulder when he got up after dinner. "I might sit in on that drumming workshop for a while," I'd answered. "Oh, you should," he'd said. Already we were doing a dance, the movements so familiar to me from years earlier but also oddly alien, for wasn't I a different person now and not quite in a position to do this pas de deux?

The floor was strewn with fabric, and with old shirts and discarded costumes that a local community theater company had donated to the camp. I sat down a good four feet from Hal and picked up a blousy beige shirt that might have belonged on a Civil War soldier, or perhaps in a Shakespeare play.

"You came," Hal said.

Outside, the drumming had started. Ever since he'd woken up that day, Max had been anticipating the workshop, beating his fingers on tabletops and pretending with Tommy that they lived in the jungle. I'd passed the workshop on the way to the stable—a circle of kids and a few parents, each with a drum, and in the center, the teacher, who looked, with his stringy blond hair and scraggly beard, like a Renaissance painting of Christ. I had, in fact, been tempted to sit cross-legged next to Max and watch him play his drum. "Let's call in the rain gods," I might have whispered to him, "so that this drought comes to an end and our crops can grow." At home, he would've said yes, let's, but since we'd arrived at camp, Max was much less interested in pretending with me. At the time, I chalked this up to his newfound independence; finally, he was getting a chance to go forth on his own.

"Costumes over drumming?" Hal said. "I can see why. It's loud, even from here."

I started sifting through clothes. "So tell me about the play," I said quickly. "I mean, I know Max is some sort of gatekeeper, but I don't know what the other parts are or where the story is set. I hope I remember how to use a sewing machine, I haven't used one in years—"

I cleared my throat. My own voice sounded dithering to me, all the pleasant tension at the dinner table shifting, now that we were alone, into plain awkwardness. The cloth on the floor looked garish, cheap costumes that would tear if you raised your arm to wave hello, good-bye. A loneliness swept over me. I didn't know this man; I didn't care about his play. I stood up to go, and as I did, Hal stood, too.

"Okay," he said.

"Sorry?"

"Sit," he commanded, but gently, using his foot to nudge a pile of clothes into a heap. "And I'll—" He hesitated. Later, he would tell me he was trembling. "I'll tell you the story, okay? Of the play. Like you asked. It won't take long. Just sit. And close your eyes."

"Why?" I asked, though already I was obeying, lowering myself onto the costumes, leaning back against a beam. With my eyes shut, I could be anywhere; the whole thing could be a mere thought.

"You'll see it better that way," he said. "You'll visualize it. Sometimes I ask the kids to do this during rehearsals. Maybe you'll even see the costumes and save us a few steps."

"All right, if you shut yours, too."

I opened my eyes. He had moved farther away to sit on the edge of a table. His head was tipped to one side; he was watching me. He had left his sandals by the door, and I saw—as if it were happening, as if it had happened—my hand reaching out to touch his foot.

"But I already know the story," he said. "I don't need—"

"Please." I sounded harsh. Don't look at me that way. Do, don't. I was about to leave; I could feel my body taking me. A headache, I'd tell him. A sudden stomach cramp. My period, a bloody mess. I'd find Ian, bring him upstairs, guide his hand to the wetness that was gathering, now, between my legs. I stood, stepping on a piece of fabric. "Listen, I've got to—"

"I'll shut my eyes," Hal said.

I sat back down.

"Once," he said, "there was a tribe of children who lived by the light of the moon. One day a storm came over the land, and the wind blew, and the leaves blew across the paths. . . ."

I only remember parts of the story—an eclipse, a spell—but I remember that the room became his voice, which went from low to high to low again, and that the play was whimsical but also full of grief. A child gets lost. It isn't a boy and it isn't a girl. A child. It gets lost when the sun is blotted out by the eclipse, and the XP children find it with their sonar, and there are no parents around, just toads with golden warts, and singing bats, and a gatekeeper—this would be Max—who invites the lost child into the kingdom of XP. Though my own eyes were shut—the whole time, I didn't open them—I could feel Hal's eyes on me, and I knew he was cheating but I didn't care. I couldn't remember the last time someone had sat me down and told me a story like this—so detailed, so patient, and spun out just for me. I might have been a girl again, wanting, even as I was afraid of it, to be lost myself, to push far into the woods until I could no longer hear my mother. I might have been a child, or I might have been a mother led steadily, gently, toward her greatest fear, for if Max played the gatekeeper, who played the child who got lost, and where were the parents, and what would happen when the sun came out again and the kingdom turned from night to day?

Finally, Hal stopped talking, and I opened my eyes to find him kneeling beside me, and then, briefly, his hand was on my cheek, which was (how hadn't I noticed?) damp with tears. The light in the room seemed too bright. I ducked away from his hand, and he backed up and squatted a few feet away.

"I'm sorry," he said. "I've upset you."

"No, I just—"

"I get carried away. I went way beyond the play here. You looked so absorbed, I guess it encouraged me."

"It's a good story." Suddenly my tears felt far off, his story too, as if I'd been jolted from a dream. "You should add in the new parts. The costumes—" I tried to focus on them, but when I pictured the children in the story, they were naked, their bodies slipping through the night. "Maybe they should be sort of fairy costumes, in earth tones, or—"

"I didn't shut my eyes," he said.

I nodded. From outside came the sound of drumming, hollow beats.

"I wanted to watch—"

I shook my head. "Come on, Hal. Let's be reasonable, okay? Please."

He started folding pieces of fabric and dropping them into the bag. "Okay, but then you'd better go, because I've never been good at keeping quiet when I feel strongly about something or . . . you know, someone, though I've tried, I really have, but then you came here tonight—" He sounded furious. He took a deep breath and put the cloth down.

This is a man who's quick to flare, I remember noting, as if we were on a date and I was trying to figure out if he'd be a viable long-term prospect, a good mate. This, before me, is a man of gale winds, strong and sudden moods. It might have been a description of myself lately, except that beside him I felt oddly unruffled, even as part of me was moving toward the edge of his shirt, the rim of his shorts, everywhere hems ended and skin began. I *had* come here. He was right about that. All winter, I'd been slowly coming here, even when I couldn't admit it to myself. To help with the costumes, I told myself again, knowing it wasn't true.

"What is it you want, Anna?" he asked.

"I don't know. I—I'd like a good friend." It sounded right. Safe, reasonable, true. "Someone I can really talk to—about Max, and . . . and everything. . . ."

"You have that. Of course I'll be that."

I nodded. "And me, too. For you, I mean."

"So that's all?"

"It's no small thing. I haven't had it, really, not for years. It's mostly my own fault—I've let things run away with me, I've stopped making enough efforts. Sometimes I worry I'm too overwhelming as a friend, too—" I stopped; the only word I could come up with was *full*.

"I think I can probably handle you," he said. "But what else do you want—in your life, I mean—if you stop to take stock?"

"I'd like—" I took a breath. "I do think it's important to be satisfied—with everything I have, all the lucky things."

"But you're not."

"No, I am. In lots of ways, I am."

I looked up. Now his hands were fidgeting, and for the first time, I sensed impatience. He was waiting. For me to stop spouting clichés. For me to run through all the other stuff and get to him.

"It's been a hard year," I said. "I don't even quite know why, since the kids are okay, everyone is fine, it's almost like we're *not* in constant crisis anymore, we know what we're living with, and it's—" I held up my hands.

"It goes on," Hal said. "And on and on."

I nodded. "I mean, thank god it does, but still, I think it wears away at all of us in different ways. Except for here. Here it goes away. For me, anyway."

"Does it? Really? Just"—he blew into the air—"gone?"

"No, but it's transformed, it's made okay, even beautiful. You do that, somehow, without negating any of it. It's a gift you have. I've never seen anything like it. You make another world."

"Oh, Anna," he said. "That's the nicest thing anyone has said to me in years."

We sat without speaking then, for a long minute, maybe two. I felt the darkness gathering around the stable, pooling inside me. I looked at Hal, away, and back. He watched me steadily, and for a moment it was as if I could see myself through his eyes—so much desire, so much confusion crossing on my face.

"I'd better go," I said finally. "I wanted to help with the costumes, but whatever you do will be fine, it doesn't really matter, the play is great and I shouldn't—"

"All winter," he said, "I've been thinking about you, and now you're here, with Ian, of course—I like him, I do, very much—and I told myself it'd be enough, just to see you all and . . . and, you know, get the kids together, but—"

"Shhh." I meant my voice to come out definitive, but instead it sounded soothing, a lullaby. I tried again. "It has to be enough."

"I know."

"I mean, it's not that I don't also . . ." I shook my head. "Our lives are so complicated. I don't think they could take any more pressure."

I stood up. The drumming had stopped. The workshop was over, or maybe they were taking a break. I had no idea how much time had passed.

"I'm sorry," I said.

Alone, he'd been (had he?) all winter. He'd put Alida to bed, sat somewhere and thought of me. And I in my bathtub—and I in my kitchen, my minivan, my married-mother bed. Dreaming of camp. For Max, I'd told myself, fooled myself. A place where he can be safe, free, less lonely.

"I shouldn't have come," I said.

Hal was standing between me and the door. The door was behind him; I had to move toward it in order to leave. Background, midground, foreground. Fill up the whole space. I had to touch him. A necessity, a luxury. An expansiveness, a blow.

I stepped toward him, and he brought his hands to my face, and for one instant, and then another and another, I didn't move away. Lightly, cautiously, we traced each other's faces. His mouth, his cheek, the tumble of hair over his forehead; my mouth, my jaw, the slope of my nose, one cheek and then the other. I blinked, and he let my lashes beat against his palm. We didn't kiss, didn't even look at each other, and after a time he shut his eyes, and this time I kept mine open, trying to hold on to the particular translucence of his eyelids, the lines around his eyes, the way his eyebrows arched, his scruff of day-old beard. This, I told myself, is it. Enough. For the longest time, I managed to believe that we were, at each precise instant, going exactly as far as we would go.

Outside, something brushed against the window. A twig, perhaps. A person looking in. I stepped away and glanced toward the door, half expecting to see Max standing there, or Ian, come to find me—hurry, Anna, it's an emergency, something's happened!

"Oh, god," I said. "This is all my fault."

Hal traced the inside of my wrist. "It feels like you're painting me," he murmured. "How can that be wrong?"

"How?" My voice was sharp. "Because there are other people involved, who depend on us—me—not to mess up."

He took his hand away. "All right. If that's how you see it. The last thing I want is to mess up your life."

"My life," I said, "is already a mess," though even as I spoke, I was not sure it was true.

And then we were holding each other, holding and rocking, and now it wasn't desire I felt, exactly, but desire turned to grief—the gash of it, the flow, seeping out between us, not shared, exactly, but known, but understood. It was grief in its obvious forms—his dead wife, each of our sick children—but also in its quieter, slower incarnations. My mother, my father and brother, how far away they were. All the friends I'd lost touch with over the years. Adam, how I often wasn't the mother he deserved. Ian, yes, Ian, too, maybe even mostly Ian—how I was failing him, not just at this moment but for a long, long time. How he was failing me, something gone awry when we weren't paying attention, turned slowly, subtly, wrong. It shouldn't have been possible, I know, for Hal to soothe that particular pain—he was, as we stood there, swiftly becoming part of the problem, just as I was part of it myself. But Hal was on my side. He saw the world as tipping toward extinction and still he loved it. Nothing was too dark for him, nothing too light. Use the whole spectrum, my art teacher used to say. Excavate. Explore.

The windows in the crafts room were tinted, of course. The door that led outside was shut. No one could see in. The drumming started again. Now the kids were chanting, too, and I couldn't pick out Max's voice from all the others. Hal and I held each other by the blind windows, and eventually my grief changed color, and then it was joy I felt—nothing complicated about it, joy and pleasure—and then we kissed and kissed. Two people. A fine hunger. Mouths. We didn't have sex. We did what we used to call making out in high school—hands on fabric, zippers zipped, his erection pressing up against my crotch.

I left before Hal did. The workshop was over. I hadn't noticed when the noise stopped for the second time. The lawn was empty of people, the dock by the boathouse, too. On the porch, the rocking chairs faced the water. A Monopoly board was still set out, and I had an urge to stuff my pockets with play money as I passed by—a safeguard, insurance, but for whom and from what? Soon it would be dawn, our backward call to rest. I went upstairs. Max and Tommy were asleep in their room, shirtless but still wearing shorts. I pulled blankets over them and pushed their sneakers into a corner so they wouldn't trip on them if they got up to pee. In the bathroom, I scrubbed my hands and face, my neck, between my legs. I brushed and flossed my teeth. We're animals, I remember thinking as I caught sight of myself in the mirror. I looked feral, smudged. We're just animals with noisy minds.

Barefoot, I went down the hall to our room, undressed and pulled on the oversized shirt I slept in. Ian was asleep, his face turned toward the wall. I got in next to him and settled down, and he stirred and rubbed his foot against mine. Hi, I whispered, patting his back. Hi, stranger, hi, Ian. I'm sorry, I thought, but was I really? He felt more like my roommate than my lover at that moment—perhaps we'd met through an ad in the paper: compatible, similar values, let's raise some kids together. A good man, a good father. And more than that, of course. A person with a past, with a present—once a boy whose father had left him, now a father who would never leave his boys. Once a climber of mountains, a builder of cabins, a traveler. Now he traveled only in the classroom with his students, and their dioramas were imaginative and detailed, their maps accurate and true. What would have happened if I'd stopped right there, roused him from sleep, confessed—a small thing, still, a smallish, forgivable, fleeting thing—a few kisses in a stable, so ridiculous, I didn't mean to, let me hold you now, please, here where I really live, with you in our life, with our children. With you.

I curled up and shut my eyes, and as I did, Ian receded, and it might have been Hal next to me, sleeping soundly because I was beside him, his breath made steady by the regular, consoling rhythm of my own.

EIGHT

"I don't think so," said Ian.

He stood up as he spoke, and everyone turned to look.

"I mean, the play itself is a great thing for the kids," he said, "but why do we have to make it public? Why do we need the *media* here?" He looked around the room. "I think we should tell them no. Interviewing the researchers or doing a short piece on the camp is one thing, but if they plant themselves here for days, it'll change everything. The kids just want to have fun. Can't anything"—he shrugged—"be private anymore?" The word *private* sounded louder than the others, and I stiffened. "They've had enough people staring at them," Ian said more quietly. "This is their vacation. Anyway, that's"—again he shrugged—"what I think."

He sat back down next to me on the slick cracked-leather couch, and I put my hand on his arm, aware that everyone was still looking. His arm was warm, and it jumped a little under my touch. Nobody spoke; they were all waiting for something. For me? I agree, says the wife. I agree with what he just said. Everyone sat next to his or her spouse at these weekly parents' meetings, each couple leaning in, leaving a small gap on either side. Françoise and Henri, Josh and Angela, Libby and Mike, Ian and me, all the others. Only Hal and Marnie sat alone. XP families seemed to have an abnormally low divorce rate—at least here, at least so far, the kids mostly still young.

Once, after Max was diagnosed, Ian and I went to a support group for the parents of chronically ill children, only to be told by the facilitator that the strain on such families was tremendous and that many of us would end up splitting up. That afternoon, we wrote a letter of complaint to the hospital, and for the next few nights we slept clutched in each other's arms, Max beside us in his bassinet, Adam right next door. So bound, we were, so sure. I even remember thinking how the genetic fluke—the rare, rare fact that we both were XP carriers—was a signal that we were intertwined as tightly as the two strands of a gene. A romantic, even twisted notion. I see that now, just as I understand how splitting up can take place in so many different ways. A sharp, clean break. A jagged split. A series of slow, almost invisible hairline fractures until—for no reason in particular, for no reason at all—a break occurs.

"I don't know." It was Marnie who spoke up now, from where she knelt on a pillow on the floor, halfway between us and Hal. The kids were all in the boathouse with the counselors and a stack of games and prizes, lured away so we could talk. The BBC wanted to come for several days to film the play, interview us all, and produce an hour-long documentary special on XP and the camp. Marnie looked from Hal to Ian. "I see what you mean, Ian," she said. "But on the other hand, every time there's an article or news show or whatever, it raises awareness, plus the donations come piling in. We have proof of that. And it's the BBC. They're probably pretty good. Isn't it better to go into depth than to do some cheesy little sound bite? Anyway, a play is *meant* to be seen." She snorted. "It's not like we're letting them into our bedrooms or something."

Everyone laughed except for me and Hal. He was leaning back, but his face was focused and intent. Two days had passed since we'd met in the crafts room. Since then, we'd barely spoken, though we'd brushed arms a few times as we passed each other. Sometimes I'd look up and find him watching me. Other times I'd come across him deep in conversation with someone else—a woman, often—and I'd be compelled to keep looking until he sensed my presence and caught, with a flickering glance, my eye. We were waiting. For something to pass. Or something to change.

"So there's a logic to letting them come," Marnie said. "Not to mention that Tommy thinks cameras are cool, and I doubt if he's the only one. I just don't think he gets traumatized by the media, and he's pretty shy. He asked me to frame that *Parade* article with the photo of him and Nicole. It made him feel important."

"For having XP?" Ian said. "Tommy has real talents."

"I agree. All our children have talents." Françoise nodded. "They're not just—how do you say it?—*les pauvres malades.*"

Hal muttered something inaudible, and we all turned toward him. He had that ability, and not just with me. He could clear his throat, and the room's attention would swivel toward him and stay there, rapt.

"What?" Marnie asked. "What is it, Hal?"

He leaned forward. "I won't pretend I can't see Ian's point," he said. "It's very tricky—god knows, it's a situation we wish we weren't in. But we *are* in it, and in the end, when I really think it through, I disagree with Ian." His voice grew louder. He leaned farther forward and, just as he did, Ian did, too. A picture crossed my mind: two horned rams locked in battle, butting heads.

"For one thing, the play," Hal said, "*does* showcase everyone's talents. That's the whole point isn't it? Drama, spectacle. But also, why not let the kids be proud of having XP? It's part of who they are, it informs every second of their lives. It—I really think it gives them a particular set of gifts, as well as particular problems. They're wise old souls. They just are. They're lovely and . . . and vulnerable, but also strong in a way that's informed by this disease, whether we like it or not. And the play's going to be good—they've been working their butts off and we've got some really gifted actors here. Étienne and Anil and Helen are designing a set, and Anna"—he turned toward me, and everyone looked over—"is doing the costumes."

He stopped talking, then, and I felt a spark of anger that he'd directed the group's attention to me.

"So what do you think, Anna?" asked Françoise.

"I—I don't know," I said slowly. "I'm not sure. . . ."

Lights going on, a stage set: trees, a rock, a child. A toad hops by, the moon comes out. Meanwhile, scaffolding, microphones, strangers. Meanwhile, hands on my hips, a mouth on my mouth, a whole new night country. Drama. I wanted it (was it that simple, for a time?) in all its many forms. "Cut!" barks a British voice. "We need to adjust the volume." And Alida, who is about to deliver a line, lets out a little sigh that is amplified tenfold by the mike. Later, the show, first aired in England, then here. An hour on the kids, on XP. A ten-minute clip of the play, and the children are great, the costumes gorgeous. "An orphan disease," says the narrator. "Brave children of the night. Difficult, courageous lives." Max is funny in the play; he's confident and good. My parents call to congratulate us. The show also features Anil with his cane, Tommy with his round moon face and owl glasses. Back in England, they've filmed an XP girl with Type D of the disease. Briefly, they show her wheelchair, her blind and broken body. Then it's back to camp, Alida jumping off the dock. After the show airs, we're flooded with donations. We give a grant to the radiologist in Seattle who is working on new ways to deliver genes to the skin. We set up more scholarships for camp and hire extra nursing care for Nicole. We buy more window film. I mean, let's be practical here; these are our children. Yes, Hal has an inheritance, but it's not enough to save the world, our world.

"I think," I found myself saying, "that we should let them come."

I saw Hal smile at me. I felt Ian stiffen at my side.

"Or maybe"—I exhaled—"not. I don't know . . ."

Everyone stared. I must have been pale, blanching. My breath, in my ears, was loud. It was a simple question and demanded a simple answer, but inside me something was crumbling and I wanted to cover my eyes, as if that would make all these people, all these watchers, go away, leaving me alone to sort things out. I needed to find Max, to check on him and make sure he was all right. He wasn't a strong swimmer, and they were down by the boathouse. And I needed to call Adam. Are you flossing? I'd ask. Are you using sunscreen and not wearing yourself out? The simple, soothing questions of motherhood; I'd had years to get them straight. Or no, maybe what I needed was to get up, walk outside, and stand alone in the dark. After a time, I'd feel a hand on my neck, and without knowing who it was, I'd turn and we'd touch—the man who found me first and I.

And if no one came? Then it would be up to me and up to me and up to me.

"It's . . . it's pretty complicated," I said finally, since I had to say something. "Maybe we need more time to figure it out?"

"Okay." Josh clapped his hands together. "So can we table this and talk about the Lipisome lotion trial? I have some encouraging things to report. I tried to make sense of the early findings. I put it on the Web site, but I know people have lots of questions, so I thought—"

"Hold on, Josh. That's great, but we have to wrap this up first," said Hal. "The BBC needs an answer. They've been calling and e-mailing five times a day. This is very last-minute for them. We'll lose the chance if we don't move fast."

Marnie nodded. "Let's vote, then. Let's just vote and get to the other things, and then go swimming with the kids. We're on vacation, in case you've all forgotten."

Nobody answered. Something was wrong in the room, that much was clear, but did anyone know what it was?

"Or jeez, let's"—Marnie looked around—"vote on whether to vote. Okay?" She laughed. "You guys are as bad as the people at my clinic. Don't you just love meetings? Raise your hand if you're ready to vote."

She lifted her arm first. Other people followed, until everyone had raised a hand.

"Okay," said Marnie. "Now. Should we give the BBC permission to come film the play? Hands up if you want the BBC to come."

"Excuse me." Ian spoke quietly this time and stayed seated. "If nobody objects, I'd prefer a paper vote."

Oh, love, I thought. Oh, Ian. His voice sounded lonely and somehow unfamiliar, and abruptly I wondered if he knew everything—not just the few kisses but, worse, the course of my thoughts over these past few days, how small he'd become in them, how tight, wooden and remote. A paper vote, as small and flimsy as a paper ship. Can't anything be private, he'd asked. But everyone knew what Ian thought, so what did he have to hide? My vote?

I reached for his hand but he moved away, and as he did, my sympathy did too. Why couldn't I disagree with him in public—if, in fact, I disagreed, which I might not? He was always so worried about presentation, approval, passing in the eyes of the world. Whenever he gave me a present—a necklace, a scarf—he managed to find out if other people liked it. Did you show it to Carly, he'd ask casually, predictably. Did you tell her it was from me? He liked Max and Adam to have frequent haircuts so they'd blend in with the other boys. He didn't want a red minivan; cops stopped you, he claimed, if you stood out—this from someone who had never gotten a speeding ticket in his life. And so our van was dark green, like the fleet of others in suburbia. And so I chopped off Max's lavish curls while Adam and Ian went together to the barbershop. I was sick of it all. I would vote how I wanted to. We weren't joined at the hip, and I had nothing (or only a little, and not about this) to hide.

"Fine." Hal nodded. "A paper vote it is."

Somebody gathered paper and pens from the porch, and someone else offered up a baseball cap. Scraps were passed, and pens. In my mind, I wrote *yes, no, yes*. In the end, I left the paper blank, folding it in half and then again. Josh fished the scraps from the hat and made two piles, one on each knee. When he finished, he looked up. "Nineteen yesses," he announced. "Five nos. One abstention."

"Bring in the clowns," muttered Ian.

"So—" Hal managed to sound neither jubilant nor contrite, but I could hear the pleasure in his voice. "I guess that means we're on."

I examined the pen in my hand, the one I'd only pretended to use. Someone had gnawed on it, leaving toothmarks up and down its spine. Josh was already passing out handouts on the Lipisome trial, which was far more important than any play. He would recite elaborate statistics—curves, means, probabilities—that Ian and I would try to decipher later. A cure, perhaps, a remedy at least. Maybe. Don't get excited, folks; early phases, trial studies, limited funding, take the long view, too early to tell. The flare, in all of us, of hope, well hidden as a shiver of desire. After the meeting was over, we'd disperse, down toward our children, up toward each other. The husbands and wives, the mamas and papas. It was early still. The night, as they say, was young.

Later, when Ian asked, I said I'd voted no. And when Hal asked, I said I'd voted yes. Covering all my bases, I suppose, but then again, maybe they shouldn't have asked. Can't anything be private? A blank, like an empty canvas sitting in a corner of the basement, uncommitted, left in peace. Still later, I told the truth to both of them, but by then too much else had happened and nobody much cared how I'd voted on the play.

It was close to dawn when Hal found me sitting near the airplane hangar. He unlocked the padlock on the side door, and when I followed, he closed the door from inside with an eye hook, pulled a musty cushion from a deck chair to the floor and flicked on a dim light. We stripped in silence and had sex quietly, fiercely. He'd brought a pack of ribbed condoms in his pocket, a high school boy plotting his big night. We didn't speak, hardly at all. No stories, no real tenderness. We were crossing over, and it wasn't a comfortable feeling or even a pleasant one. He was bigger than Ian, and I was dry inside. He moved too fast, too hard.

Afterward, he rolled off me, sighed and took my hand. "I want you to come too," he said, and I said, No, no, that's okay, I don't want to, cringing at the sound of the word *come* in his mouth and at the acid feeling of having already been disappointing, disappointed. I don't want to, I said again. And it was true, I didn't want to; this was too much already—too much gaping, too much wanting, and now a thud of disbelief, this is it, this is *all*? Two bodies rolling, two beasts rutting, and meanwhile my brain was on overdrive, ticking on and on. But next time, he said. Next time, then, when we're less nervous. He kissed me on the forehead. I sat up. For the first time, I noticed the old seaplane in the middle of the hangar—its white bird body and broken wing—and the red oilcans lined up like sentries against the pleated metal walls.

"I don't think," I said, and my voice sounded deliberate, strangely formal, "that there should be a next time."

"Oh, Anna," he said, and then he was holding me. "Don't say that."

"My situation," I told him coldly, "is not the same as yours. I'm not free."

His hands were moving over me as if I hadn't spoken, and if part of me felt disregarded, another part was swinging toward a silent place, all nameless, necessary urge. And we were touching again, but differently now. This time was gradual, almost sleepy, Hal moving slowly down my body as I sat on the cushion, my legs in front of me, my ankles crossed. At first I touched him, too, leaning over him as he traveled along me, feeling the nape of his neck, the knobs of his hips—so finely put together, so delicate, like an antique music box or violin. He eased my legs apart, his fingers, then his tongue coaxing me open with a flickering, rhythmic pressure, and I lay back and felt my thoughts grow smooth and disappear.

So the next time was right then; that's how much self-control I had. The next time was right after the first time, and I couldn't help thinking that he did pretty well for a man approaching fifty, and then I was on top, easing him in as I touched his face—the fine mouth, dark brows and clever eyes, the skin that felt, somehow, so young, so good against mine. Above us, the early light came in through gaps in the hangar's metal shell, tattooing our skin with stripes that joined us crookedly, thighs to abdomen, hands to shoulders. As I rocked on top of him, he arched up and touched the roof of me, and I gasped.

It was Hal who thought to slip out long enough to get another condom. Would it have occurred to me? Ian got a vasectomy when Max was five; it had been years since I'd considered birth control at all. As for safe sex, I was, at that moment, beyond all thoughts of safety. Hal put the condom on and slid back underneath me, and as I bent over him, he pulled me closer and reached for my breast with his mouth. He suckled there, then, in that place where my boys, my three boys, had all put their mouths in different kinds of hunger. I shut my eyes, and for a moment I saw them—Ian, Max and Adam—and I remembered the thin, sugary taste of the milk I'd made and knew it was not a choice, the way we were joined, all four of us, but a fact, hard and empirical, their bodies forever linked to mine.

"Anna?" Hal whispered, knowing I'd left, calling me back. "Anna?"—my name in his mouth somehow foreign and familiar at the same time, Russian, maybe, and Jewish, a song that belonged to my ancestors but not quite to me. I opened my eyes and he pulled me closer, and I let myself drop down until my face was flat against his neck, his hair. Faster, we moved, harder. It hurt a little. I let it hurt. Something might split in two, and there—a geode packed with prisms, crystals formed in darkness, waiting for light.

And then we had turned, he was on top. A heartbeat, breathe in, breathe out. A seeping, inky wash. And they were nowhere in my mind, Max, Adam and Ian. They were nowhere at all, and I wasn't looking for them. For the first time in years, I wasn't looking or attending, protecting, feeding, prodding or keeping track. Gone. It was my greatest fear, but at that moment it meant nothing to me. I was no longer a mother, scarcely a human. I knew nothing of family or love or sickness or death or the long, hard work it takes to live even the most ordinary life. I knew nothing.

We were bone to bone, Hal and I, bone to bone and blood to blood, a double-stranded helix with its own mute code. And I was spinning and unspinning and undone.

NINE

Two lives, I lived, after that, like our little camper Helen, who was nearly blind by day but could see up to the stars at night. Two lives, or maybe three, for I've always lived in several places at once: the known and the imagined, what I have and what I long for. A dreamer, perhaps—or is that just a dressed-up word for a malcontent? I often scan the real estate pages; I look at travel guides and maps. I'll spot a girl in the street, a man in a door, a house with lit windows, a bus, and for a moment, my life twists out of its normal shape; I leap. It's how I'm like Hal and Max. How I'm not like Ian or Adam, who seem so tethered to the real world.

Until that moment, my little leaps had never really been a problem. One life was real, the other wasn't, and I could find solace both in how my daydreams lifted me high above the daily, and in how my real life called me back to it, so particular, so *mine*. A nightscape—it suited me in a certain way, despite my love of light. It gave me an otherness, shadow-gray and stocked with hiding places. Max, it gave me, still and serious, laughing and beckoning—come on, Mom, over here. The windows on our block gone dark, and there we are, Max and his mother, and he's a prince and she's a queen, or she's a mole and he's a possum, and the houses are castles or mountains or battleships or foxes' dens.

But now. I wasn't playing games with Max or reading about foreign countries or talking in the bathtub to myself. I wasn't squatting in the woods as a small girl, telling my name to the bearded gnomes who stood around me in a ring. This, this was actual, happening, not in my head. This was real enough to touch. In the beginning, what struck me was how easy it all was—to split yourself like that, to be two places, two people. To have it all. A breeze. Part of it, of course, was the camp with its three hundred acres, its outbuildings, Max and Ian busy with activities and friends. Hours could pass where no one looked for me. How strange, after all these years. How unreal.

But it wasn't just the camp, of course; it was also me. Some parents stuck by their children all night long or sat on the porch in large groups, playing Scrabble, bridge and backgammon until it was time for bed. Some parents weren't looking for excuses to run off. *See you in a couple hours, sweetie—I'm going to paint, I'm taking a walk. I think I'll go work on the costumes.* There was a gracefulness, an ease with which I slid into my double life that both frightened and impressed me. My painting was my alibi—the easel on my shoulder, the paint box in my hand, not a backward glance. Then to the hangar. I had a key now, stuffed inside a latex painting glove in my paint box. Once a night, sometimes twice. Or to the crafts room, where I really would work on the costumes with the fancy new sewing machine Hal had ordered on-line. That machine could do buttonholes, criss-cross stitch, blanket stitch. It could embroider clover leaves and butterflies, birds and bees. The door to the crafts house didn't lock from the inside—until, one night, it did. A shiny brass dead bolt, installed when I wasn't looking. And all that fabric. Cotton and taffeta, nylon, muslin, silk. A gatekeeper's uniform. A child's tunic. A bed.

I've always told small lies, here and there, like most people, I suppose, or maybe a little worse. My mother was a prober. Where are you going, Annie? What time will you be back? She didn't see diaries as private, or dresser drawers, or phone conversations. If she picked up the extension while you were talking, she'd listen, sometimes even chime in to say hello. And if I approached her directly, told her to get off or leave me alone, she would withdraw into herself with a ferocity that left me withered. From early on, then, I developed a system of subterfuge. I had a code word to let my friends know my mother was on the phone. At one point, I had a plan to keep two diaries—one for my mother's eyes, the other for real—though in the end it was too much work. I'm going into town for ice cream, I'd tell her as a teenager, when really I was going to the woods to smoke pot. I'm applying to Harvard, Brown, Yale and a few safeties, when in truth I was only interested in experimental schools with no requirements and lots of art classes. Oddly, my mother never pushed very far—happy to hear what she wanted to, despite her need to ask. This was the part of her that would come out when Max was born sick, the side that could block things out when they clashed too radically with her necessary understanding of the world. As for my father, I could have announced that I was on my way to Mars, and he'd have murmured good idea and turned back to his stocks or language tapes.

With Ian, as a grown-up, I'd turned more honest. Ian was always truthful—I thought he was, at least—and he left me plenty of room. Anyway, I didn't have much to lie about. Little things, only. My neck hurts, I need a bath, when actually it was my mind that hurt, my soul. Or I'd pretend not to notice that we'd almost run out of toilet paper, peeved at being the only one to keep the house well stocked. Where do we keep the extra toilet paper, Ian would ask cheerfully, as if he'd just, that very day, moved in. I'd look up. Huh? Have we run out?

Now lying came back to me in all its finer forms—how to keep your voice flat and disinterested; how to slip a false destination into the middle of a conversation or invite the other person along, knowing they'd decline. How to announce that you were going off to sketch, and then actually sketching a little when you got there, so that it wasn't a lie, exactly, more like a partial truth. How to shower and scour and rub your body clean—this the hardest thing, the way I could feel Hal's hands on me even when he wasn't there. With Max as my child, I thought about skin more than most people—the way it mends or doesn't mend itself, the way it holds imprints, from light or from another person's touch. A toad loses its skin every four months and swallows it, recycling. Humans lose all their cells in six short months and knit themselves anew. The skin is, as every schoolchild knows, the largest organ in the human body. The cells in its outer layer, the epidermis, are all dead.

That summer, I wanted two skins. It would have made things so much easier. Just as I sometimes pictured a suit of new healthy skin for Max, I imagined myself, now, as a quick and slippery animal, slipping into this skin, then that, moving into those arms, then these. No traces, no squirming sense of carrying an invisible residue that rubbed off on Ian without his even realizing it. Instead, I showered and swam a lot and didn't reach for him in bed. Nor did he reach for me, so it wasn't too hard to pull off. Somebody *wants* me, I'd find myself thinking. Somebody watches how I move, comes toward me, trembling, can't help himself. Don't you notice *anything*, I half wanted to ask, for I knew I was coated with leftover desire, sticky as glitter, and yet Ian looked right through me, over my shoulder, good night, good night. The anger in our room was like a thick fog, but at the same time it was as if we had come to a tacit agreement: don't ask, don't tell, just get used to this air, so stale and uncomfortable to breathe.

Sometimes, in my sleep, I'd move toward Ian despite myself—out of long habit, or rising love, or because I thought he was Hal. Once I woke to find him flung on top of me, both of us sweat-drenched, groggy. For a second I thought we'd been touching in our sleep, but then I realized he was snoring, his body heavy, lifeless, on my own. I rolled him off me and faced the wall.

Like sleeping with a dead person, I thought. Like living with a dead person. That passive, he seemed to me, that impervious, bending to take off his sandals, falling asleep in his boxer shorts, his limbs like weights. The sleep of the innocent, perhaps, or the sleep of the oblivious, the unfeeling. Certainly not the sleep of the jealous, or the aching, or the wronged. Once upon a time, I'd seen him stirred, found him stirring. Now he seemed like a boy, someone else's not-quite-grown son—taciturn and thick, smoldering with resentment at the adult world. Like Adam. Like Adam and Max, all three of them turned away from me, when once I'd been so central. Or was I the one doing the turning? But because they drove me to it. *Take some responsibility, Anna*, I could hear Ian saying—a man again suddenly, but oh so public, no dark root there, no blind grasping, a middle-aged man at a PTO meeting, standing up to speak. Take some responsibility. *I'm not in love with you,* I thought, trying it on, but I couldn't bear to picture how his face might change—or, worse, stay calm and clear—and the words sounded too clean and simple for what we had, and I wasn't even sure if they were true.

Then I pictured telling him I needed a break; hadn't he more or less said the same thing? After fifteen years, after so much grief and worry, so much cooperation, participation, negotiation. It had worn us out. A mini-vacation, like a scuba-diving lesson or a day spent baking in the sun. Or I might say nothing, just go upstairs and climb into bed with Hal, who would want me purely and without hesitation, the way my babies, sleeping, used to reach for my breast if I was near. Mormons moved around between lovers, at least they used to, and Chinese kings did too, though always, of course, just the men. A red lantern by the door of Wife Number Three or Wife Number Four. Ian could take up with someone too—one of the mothers or one of the volunteers. I'd let him. I'd understand. I pictured him with Jess, though she was only sixteen—her long braid come undone, sweat trickling over the crucifix between her plump breasts, and Ian with his hands made younger, faster, by this just-ripe object of desire. Even as I laughed at the porn-shop tackiness of my vision, my hand was slipping down between my legs. Meanwhile, Hal awake somewhere, asleep somewhere. Meanwhile, Ian, his eyelids twitching as he dreamed.

Looking back, I have to wonder what he saw during this time, what he suspected, wondered. Did he trust me too much to think I might sleep with another man? Did he care? Or was it too hard for him to see what was right in front of him, just as it had taken him so long to accept that Max was sick? In this way, he reminded me of my mother, though I'd never thought of them as being much alike. Had my father had affairs, the long evenings at work really a cover for something else, the sober, self-made man unbuttoned, his office a place where longing showed its wide, unguarded face? It would explain something of my mother's tight-lipped anger and her ceaseless ineffectual monitoring of her children. And me—perhaps it would explain me a little, how well I snuck about, how seamlessly, even as I couldn't have imagined actually doing it just weeks before.

If I learned anything during that time, it was how little I knew about anyone, myself included. Ian and I had so many habits together. My toothbrush was always translucent green, his translucent blue. I slept on the right side of the bed, he on the left. I ate the olives from his salad; he ate the ends of my asparagus, the woody parts I found too tough. We both loved Schubert. We both loved camping. It might have looked like knowledge, this shared compendium, but it was not. It might have looked like intimacy, but it was more like the residue of what had once been intimacy, a snail's pale trace along a path. When I stopped to think about it, it made me terribly sad, but mostly I wasn't stopping, wasn't thinking. Reach for the olive. Pick up your toothbrush, squirt the toothpaste out and wash your lover from your mouth.

Hal liked a festival. He liked a good, elaborate ritual, with candles, music and some chants. It wasn't that he didn't have a sense of humor about it—"I feel a need for some gobbledygook," he'd say—but he also took his projects seriously, making them ambitious and elaborate, planning out unfolding layers of details. As a boy in Brooklyn, he told me once, he'd been taken to synagogue each Saturday, and he'd loved the velvet-wrapped Torah scrolls, how you were allowed to touch them only with the spine of your prayer book or the fringe of your father's prayer shawl, and then you'd kiss the spine, kiss the prayer book, and be blessed. He'd loved the cantor's singing, the Hebrew prayers, even as he'd never quite felt the presence of the God they summoned. Our culture, he thought, was sadly lacking in rituals outside of religion. And so the drumming workshop, the camp shirts, the songs, the dinner gong, the plays. To give the kids something to remember, he'd say, and though he liked to think of himself as living fully in the present, I could see how it wasn't exactly true, each moment already being shaped and polished, turned to relic—as if without such attention, it would disappear.

I don't know how far ahead he had been planning the Skin Festival. Hal was full of surprises, even once I began to know him better. One evening at dinner, he announced it: a Skin Festival, to take place two nights later. Rub-on tattoos and face painting, a fortune-teller, skinny-dipping in the lake. I could see some parents roll their eyes. Others laughed.

"You're too much, Hal," said Marnie, but Hal shook his head.

"We're happy in our skins. We want to throw our skins a party, right, kids? I mean, why not? *Vive la peau!*"

From around the table, some children said yes but others looked unsure.

"You can get pretty sick of scalpels and tests and always thinking of your skin as trouble," Hal said. "I know Alida does. I know I do."

"Me too," said Max.

"Me too," said Sara.

"Okay, so start thinking about what kind of tattoo you want."

He paused. "I mean, between rub-on and—you know—the real kind."

"He's joking," Helen's mother said. "Tell me you're joking, Hal, right?"

"Can I get my nose pierced?" asked Étienne's sister, Natalie, who was sounding more American by the day.

Hal looked thoughtful. "I hadn't considered piercings."

"Nose pierce! Nose pierce!" the kids started chanting.

"Butt pierce!" Carl called out, and the children erupted into laughter.

"Yikes," I said to Hal, but I was smiling despite myself. "See what you've unleashed."

He froze, just for an instant, before busying himself with his food. My words felt too loud, and for a moment I could feel it all collapsing, moving toward chaos—not just Hal and me, but also the kids and other parents, family units splintering, clothes being cast aside, the lodge burning—suddenly I saw it—great timbers falling, all of us moving, naked, painted, for the cover of the woods. I saw burrows and twig huts, blankets made of animal pelts. We would carry torches, wake when the sun came down, catch fish from the lake and skin their hides. Like a game I'd play with Max. Or a game I'd play with Hal. It might be magical. Or brutal. Or not a game at all.

The Skin Festival itself turned out to be tame enough. Rub-on butterfly tattoos on the girls' arms and ankles, an inch-long dragon for Max. The children found unscarred places on their bodies to decorate. Some parents fussed a little—will it itch, will it irritate?—but no one went so far as to say no. After they were painted and tattooed, the kids all posed for a picture holding a sign they'd made: WE MISS YOU NICOLE. It was raining that night, the air outside smelling of fall. The fortune-teller was a friend of Hal's from town, Yvonne. One of the city hippies who'd settled in these parts in the sixties and seventies, she helped run the area food co-op and was into tarot cards. She arrived in a ruffled skirt and peasant blouse, reminding me, with her red hair and gray roots, of a plump, exotic pet. Hal handed each child a chocolate coin, and they lined up by the army tent he'd set up in the piano room. Each time I passed by, I could hear her saying the same thing—long lifeline, good health, love—and then adding a few predictable variations: a trip to a far-off country, a good deed, a reward. Had Hal, I wondered, instructed her on what to say? Was it cruel to promise long lifelines to these kids?

What, I wondered, would she say if I appeared inside the tent and presented her with my open palm? Love, she'd promise me. What kind of love? Sex. With whom? Lies, she might promise me. You're full of them too, I'd fling back, as if this canceled something out. Her voice passing through the tent was falsely mysterious and put on, and I found myself distrusting not only her but also Hal, the camp and, of course (in a floaty moment that took me far outside my body, looking down at my own limbs), myself.

Max didn't line up at the tent. He was, as far as I knew, in the basement with Ian, who had organized a game of Murder in the Dark. From the living room, you could hear shouts now and then, rising muffled through the floor—the shriek of someone tapped, bumped or taken by surprise. Ian and Max weren't there when Marnie and I cleaned up the face paints and set out snacks, or when Alida came to sit in my lap for a time, as she did, now, almost every night. They weren't there, either, when Hal appeared in the living room and asked who wanted to skinny-dip, and the kids giggled and groaned and said forget it, Hal, it was yucky out, too cold.

He looked around the room. "Oh, come on, guys. The moon's out, the rain's stopped. Show some Skin Festival spirit!"

Marnie was lying on the floor by the couch, her head propped on a pillow. She half opened her eyes, murmured, "Gimme an S, gimme a K, gimme an I, gimme an N!" and shut her eyes again.

"Atta girl, come on, Marnie." Hal prodded her with his foot. "You're no chicken."

Marnie rolled over and yawned. "No spring chicken, and no polar bear. I'm a slug. A rare tropical slug."

"Fine." He sighed. "I'll go alone."

Marnie tipped her head back and spoke from upside down. "Anna will go."

"Why do you say that?" I asked, not meaning for my words to sound so pointed.

She swiveled around. "You love to swim. More than anybody here, except for maybe Hal."

Her gaze seemed frank, uncomplicated, but I wasn't sure it really was. Should I say no, I wondered. Should I say it's too cold out, I have to find my family?

"I'll get a stack of towels," I said instead. "There might be people already down there, or someone might—"

Hal shook his head. "It's okay. There are towels in the boat-house."

"Well, then, I'll"—I glanced at Marnie, glanced away—"I'll just run upstairs to get my suit."

"For a Skin Festival?" Hal asked. "If you want to. Suit your-self."

The water was too cold that night, a chill inside my bones. My bathing suit stuck to me like seaweed. Hal wore one, too. I insisted. Anyone, I whispered as we were getting ready to leave the lodge, could see. Afterward, in the boathouse, we peeled off our suits and changed into dry clothes, each in a separate corner, as quiet and abashed as teenagers. In my balled-up suit, on my sticky skin, in the air between us, I felt the rising of a palpable, dense panic. In a few days, Ian would leave to pick up Adam, and Max and I would stay on for the final week of camp. Then we would leave too. Of course we would. In another ten days. A few swims more or less, a few fucks more or less, what difference did it make? We would go back to our lives. I would go back to my marriage, not knowing how badly I'd damaged it or what I'd find. Max would go back to having only his mother for nighttime company, and she—and I—no longer a soul mate, an honest soul.

Hal sat on one overturned canoe, I sat on another. Ian's sweatshirt, which I'd adopted as my own, was soft, worn in by him, the cuffs frayed to a whitish pale green. Nearly unconsciously, I started tapping on the hull of the canoe with my knuckles.

Hal looked over. "What are you doing?"

"What?" I stopped. "Oh, sorry. Drumming, I guess. Tapping. I used to get in trouble in grade school for doing that—I'd forget other people could hear." I shook my head. "It's a nervous tic, I guess. I'd almost forgotten."

"Someone *might* hear," he said.

"We're just sitting. We're not doing anything wrong."

"Except I'd rather be sitting *with* you. If you don't mind. Just for a second?"

He came over to my canoe and sat behind me, and I shut my eyes and leaned into him. Suddenly, I couldn't stop shaking, my teeth chattering and shoulders heaving, though I was no longer cold.

"Oh, Anna." He reached for a towel and draped it over my shoulders. "You're trembling. What's going on?"

"I don't know." I pulled his arms around me. "I'm . . . I'm just losing my cool, maybe. I've been so abnormally calm these past . . . with, you know, what we've been doing. It's not like me at all, to just slip away like this, to—" I shrugged. "It scares me. It's not a good quality in a person, in a parent, I mean, Jesus, my kids—and now—" I started shaking again, so hard I couldn't talk.

"Your kids are fine."

I shook my head. "Adam's not even here. I can't tell a thing, really, from his e-mails or from talking to him on the phone. Max is okay, I guess, but who knows? And Ian—" I sat up straighter, moved away a little. "I'm not like this. I'm not impulsive or . . . dishonest." As soon as I said it, I knew I was both. "Or maybe I am. I used to be, sometimes. I guess I'm regressing—"

I reached over my shoulder and found his hand, its shapes already so familiar to me, etched in my mind along with the other bodies—of lovers, children—that I'd known almost as my own.

"This should feel wrong," I said, "but it doesn't, quite. It feels *normal*."

He raised my hand, laced with his, to his mouth. "There's inside of time and outside of time, inside our lives and outside." He kissed my knuckles. "Outside, our hands have always been touching."

"Have they? That's a nice thought. How do you know?"

"I remember. When we were three. And seventeen. And twenty-eight."

"When you were three, I wasn't even born."

"It doesn't matter." He put down my hand, and I thought, he's said this same thing before, to Robin. He's said it before and she didn't question it, and now the words have come back to him, but stale, but secondhand, and with me tugging on their logic.

"Outside of time. That's nice," I tried again.

"What were you like before?" Hal asked suddenly.

"Before what?"

"All"—his hand made an arch—"this. When you were on your own. Before you had kids. And when you were little. I try to picture you but I don't get very far."

"I don't know." I knew I should be able to remember, to describe, but it all felt too long ago. "Not so different," I said. "Or maybe that's not true. I think I expected a different life, an easier one, I guess. I was spoiled in a lot of ways. I was . . . I painted all the time—in college and right afterward, anyway. I thought I wanted to be a painter. As a kid, I was alone a lot, or with my best friend—I always had a best friend I was half in love with. We'd play imaginary games. I loved that part. What about you? What were you like as a kid?"

"Fearless. A scrappy little hellion, except I got straight A's. Bossy. Sweet, too, though, at least to my mama anyway, she says I was. And lonely, underneath it all. Like most people, probably."

"Are you still lonely?"

As he nodded, I heard how stupid my question was, Robin—the lack of Robin—everywhere around us, so I could almost feel her sitting behind him on the canoe, which was, after all, her canoe, just as this was her boathouse, her lawn, her lodge. Anyway, Hal wore his loneliness; it was impossible to miss. Perhaps this, more than anything else, was what drew me to him—how obvious, even childlike his yearnings were; they made my own step forward. Now he pulled me closer, and I turned and kissed him—steady kisses that fell into an easy rhythm with the water lapping on the dock.

"This," he said, as we paused for breath, "helps. You help. Not since Robin have I felt—I mean there've been other people, but until you I never . . . but maybe there's really no point, because soon—"

"We're leaving," I said, more harshly than I meant to.

"Yes. But not quite yet. Ian's still getting Adam and going home, right, and you and Max are staying for the last week?" His voice was anxious. He thinks, I realized, that I'll say no.

I nodded, though suddenly the plan Ian and I had worked out in the spring seemed premeditated and cruel. *Would* Ian leave, I found myself wondering. Would he insist I come with him? Should I insist on it myself? So much remained unspoken between us, and I had no idea how much Ian knew, or let himself know, or wanted to know. Anyway, part of me wanted to leave. I missed Adam. I even missed not knowing, or only half knowing, how I felt about Hal—the simmer of that earlier state gone, now that we had let in actual desire and, with it, actual guilt.

"I think we need to stop things now." I hadn't planned on saying this. "It's getting too complicated. We need to stop before it gets any more—"

"I know," he said, but his hands were moving underneath my

sweatshirt, one on each breast, teasing me in playful pinches. I pushed closer on the canoe until we were pressed against each other, legs entwined.

"Or you could stay a little longer," he said.

"What?"

"With Max. Into the fall, for another month. We could see at the end of next week. I'm staying on with Alida for a little while. We did it last year, too. The lodge needs so much work—I want the wheelchair ramps finished so I can run a session for the sickest kids next year, and there's all the paperwork and closing down. . . . I'm not ready to go back, and Jess and Amy can babysit. I can do my consulting from here. You could paint—"

"I haven't seen Adam in weeks. Anyway, Ian would never—how could I explain? It would mean—"

He kissed me on my nose, brow, hair. I let my hands move over his belly, inside his pants to the tip of his penis, tender as an earlobe.

"I know. It was just a crazy thought," Hal said. "Crazy."

"In another life, of course I'd stay—in a second."

Get up, I told myself, but my hands thought otherwise. "Let's just," I whispered, "let's go to the crafts room for a few minutes, if you—"

Suddenly Hal stood and zipped his jeans. "No, Anna. Not like this." He shook his head. "I agree with you—it's getting too complicated. Maybe you should leave with Ian on Sunday. It's probably the best thing. We need to stop."

I nodded, though I hated the sound of my own words in his mouth.

"Anyway," he said, as if we were in the middle of an unfinished argument I'd forgotten about, "in another life, we wouldn't have our kids, and so"—now he smiled sadly, calmly—"we never would have met."

We stayed on there for five minutes, perhaps ten. He stood. I sat. We didn't speak. When, finally, we left the boathouse, we were so tired, so depleted, that we leaned on each other's arms as we walked up across the lawn. Someone might see, I thought for the hundredth time, and still I held his arm, and still he didn't move away.

Looking back, I have to wonder if my body already understood, that night, what my mind couldn't yet grasp—that through a series of accumulating acts, a series of accumulating thoughts, I had already gone to a whole new place. It would be a matter of mere hours before Hal and I found each other again and had quick, almost violent sex, his hands leaving faint scratch marks on my skin and mine on his. It would be three days before Ian drove away and Max and I stayed behind.

It was close to dawn when Hal and I went into the lodge. Everyone was in bed. The living room was tidy. Hal went up first, with me following half a flight behind. When he reached the second floor, he turned off. The stairwell and hallway were dark, lit only by the weak glow of a night-light.

I stood on the stairs and shut my eyes, letting everything fall away until the world became pure sound. His feet on bare wood as he went down the hall. A floorboard creaking under his weight. His breath, his heartbeat, too. The slow whistle of valves. The clicks and gurgles, hums and rumbles of another person's inner, bodied life. I don't know how these sounds came to me. Maybe in the grip of exhaustion, or leaving, or love, my jangled senses found another way. It was the most private thing I'd ever heard, and one of the most beautiful. It felt like a blessing. Maybe enough.

And then he was gone. Still I stood, until I was sure I couldn't hear him anymore.

TEN

What was I like before? It was not just for Hal that I needed to remember; it was for Ian, for Adam. It was for Max when he was old enough, since I wanted him to know the world as a place to wander through, eyes open, hands reaching. It was for myself, too, for it seemed to me that if I could summon up that girl, that young woman, I might begin to understand—a cracked code, a theorem solved—the person she had become.

When I was younger, I told myself that when I had kids, if I had kids, I'd let them run free. I'd watch them taste dirt, stand back as they climbed high into a tree, not warn them about falling. I would not, I vowed, be the kind of mother who lined public toilet seats with toilet paper, who spit on napkins and wiped her daughter's face. On walks, I'd let my children lead the way, through backyards and empty lots, down the alley behind the supermarket, where they might stoop to pick up a muddy piece of twine or a rusty bottle top.

And I did—I did this with Adam, before Max was born. Within a month of his birth, I had him strapped to my front; we were walking, moving. I remember discussing it with Sophie before I got pregnant—if having a baby means staying inside for the next five years, then it's not for me. I used to take Adam on the train to Boston. We'd walk through Haymarket, stand by the pool outside the aquarium, and watch the seals come up for breath, meet our gazes with unreadable damp eyes, then swivel around and take their leave. I took him to bookstores, thrift stores, cafés. I could *think* on those sojourns. I could dream and wander and feel, always, the warmth of this new body against mine, a mild sort of presence until he grew hungry. Then he turned fierce, a rooting monkey, and I'd stop to nurse him under a tree, or once, when it was raining, inside the front entrance of an apartment complex, where I sat on a bench and read the names on the bank of brass mailboxes while he gulped and swallowed, his breath like shakes of salt.

By the time Adam learned to walk, we'd moved to our small town, into our house, a good hour and a half from Boston in the middle of the state, where Ian had a new job teaching junior high. We didn't go into the city anymore, we stayed close to home, but now that Adam was mobile, I could let him lead. I remember how set he was, eyes fixed firmly ahead, how sure of where he wanted to go, turning left, then right, stopping to examine a glint of metal, charging after a dog, each detour not so much a digression as a sudden, necessary new path. I remember his glossy bangs, his sturdy legs, his hands—mostly his hands, which never stopped turning objects around, the whole world an astonishment. I kept him, of course, from picking up shards of glass or darting into the street or sinking his fingers into fresh dog turds, though he'd try. I was not careless, but neither was I exactly vigilant, still young myself, then, looking, really, for a playmate during those long strange days in this quiet new town. Mornings and afternoons, after lunch, between naps, we roamed the neighborhood and nearby woods, and still I let him go first, watching the deep attention he paid to the smallest moments, how entitled he was, how absorbed, in the unblinking way of a toddler. *Mine*, he might have been calling out to the bushes and trash cans, car doors and fire hydrants, pinecones and pebbles, fistfuls of dirt. *Mine* to the sun, which browned his skin in summer and reflected off the snow in winter, tossing back its daily, unextraordinary light.

Now, looking back, I have to wonder. Didn't I know about lead paint in backyard soil, about the pesticides on apple skins, the perils of a sunburn for even a healthy child, the way a toddler can choke on a popped balloon or bottle cap or drown in a wading pool? Of course I knew; how could I not? My mother had taught me to spot the danger lurking in the smallest things. Maybe this is why I refused to fret over my firstborn, my own small gesture of rebellion: yes, I've returned from Europe, gotten married, had a baby, but I'll be damned if I turn into a worrywart and let nervousness creep inside my child like a worm. "Oh, it's not that hard," I remember telling a pregnant friend. "They're incredibly hardy," I said, in a moment that still haunts me. "They might bonk their heads, but it's not going to kill them."

And before Adam? Before Ian, even? Who was I back then, stripped of my family, a single being in the world? Once I was . . . what? Someone who loved to travel, to turn into an alleyway, stop at a flea market and rummage through boxes: a dusty tobacco tin, a doll without legs, a hammer, a wooden clog. After college, I moved to New York. I didn't particularly want to; it overwhelmed me as a city, too expensive and crowded, and the buildings blocked the light. But Sophie was moving there to take the few extra courses she needed to apply for medical school. And some of my aspiring artist friends were going as well. We could share a place, waitress at the same restaurants. What else, after graduating with a BFA in studio art, was I to do? The apartment I shared with Sophie and three other friends in Brooklyn was dank, dark and overpriced, but it didn't matter. We cooked good cheap meals when we weren't waitressing or, in Sophie's case, studying and going to class. We danced and talked, had occasional lovers, smoked pot a few times a week and drank cheap wine. We went to free concerts and readings, to free Hare Krishna dinners. We bought our clothes secondhand and found furniture on the street. We talked and talked, just as we had in college, except even longer, later. Where will we be, we wondered, as we sat snacking on the kitchen floor, in ten years? In twenty? In thirty? Where, anyway, are we right *now*?

All that was fine, better than fine, like having a new family, but one that knew me better than my own. The rest of it was not. During the day, I tried to paint, often taking my supplies out onto the street, but suddenly I had no style, no sense of what to do, and I grew to dread the hours stacked in front of me before my evening job. Oil paints were too expensive; I panicked when I used them. My parents had not offered me money to float my bohemian lifestyle, and I would not ask. Sometimes I tried acrylics, but the results were too shiny, flat. I seemed to be losing all capacity to experiment or play. Mostly, instead of painting, I sketched or read or took sodden naps in the middle of the day. On my free nights, I trailed after my friends to openings, the gallery walls hung with art that left me cold and confused—blank sheets of mirror, color palettes like the paint chips in the hardware store, a target with a fish eye at its center and, below it, in reverse writing, the words DROP DEAD. Neo-Expressionism, postmodernism, nihilism: the terms made me want to scream. At the openings were dealers, collectors and rich patrons. You could spot them right away. A few of my friends—the most talented and the best self-promoters—sold work. One hit it big, a wunderkind whose mother happened to be an art critic and whose grandparents happened to be rich. I had a piece in a juried show at a tiny SoHo gallery. I sold a few paintings to friends of my parents and parents of my friends. Mostly, at the openings, I sulked in a corner, possessed by a toxic mix of self-loathing and disdain.

At home, at work in my tiny room, I tried to remember why I had liked to paint. It had something to do with a love of the world and the objects of the world, with color and the ever-changing qualities of light. And with time—that was part of it too—how fast it passed, how it never stayed still. Even then, I knew this as a daily fact. It had nothing to do with waitressing, which I hated more and more, or with galleries, or with the high-concept art that was all around me, puffed so it would sell. *New York will undo me*, I remember thinking, in the dramatic way of a recent college graduate.

The year we turned twenty-four, Sophie got into medical school and made plans to move back to Illinois, where she'd grown up. I was accepted into a teaching exchange program and moved to the north of France to teach in a public junior high school in a suburb of Lille. The school looked like a military barracks, grim and squat. Inside it, and on its concrete slab of a playground, swarmed the children of immigrants—Turks and

Portuguese, Algerians and Moroccans—transplants, as I was, to this gray northern city, this foggy, rainy air.

I am always tempted, thinking back, to remember the good parts, the ones I've lost now. The snug apartment above a patisserie, with its two-burner gas range and cot beds, doves cooing in the eaves, slabs of sunlight on the walls. There was no fridge so I kept my yogurt, fruit and milk on the windowsill outside, propped against the iron grille. I had two spoons, two forks, two white bowls from the flea market in Lille. I had a radio—the neighbors left it for me when they moved—and a rag rug from the Arab discount store. I hung postcards on my walls: a Rodin sculpture of a woman emerging, sleepy, from a rock; a Modigliani portrait of a long-faced boy. An oboist lived upstairs, and I woke, most mornings, to his music—the deep, full sound of an instrument you almost never hear played alone, but which felt like a voice speaking my native language, coaxing me from sleep. I am tempted to remember the children I liked best: the Turkish girl with the knowing smile, the twins from Portugal with golden skin and golden hair, who picked up English as if they'd been speaking it from birth.

Of course there were other things: the clang of my own loneliness; the way I'd pretend to need something—a screwdriver, a corkscrew—so I could knock on a neighbor's door; the way I'd trudge to the pay phone down the street and call home collect, wanting a conversation that filled me up, held me down like ballast, but fighting, always, as I spoke to my parents, our age-old distances, as well as the noises of the passing cars and the time tick of an international call. Once every two weeks, I saved up for a calling card so I could talk to Sophie, and though our conversations were brief, I'd hang up feeling better, but never for long. Even that loneliness I can remember, now, as something valuable, the sweet urgency of my need for people, the wide lap of my solitude, nights spent reading or sitting alone in a movie theater where each seat was like an easy chair, deep and padded.

It wasn't, actually, a very pretty picture, if you looked closely—if you looked, really, at all. I was lonely almost all the time that fall, in a gaunt, vibrating way that made me stare too hard at people in the street. I started smoking that year, and my clothes smelled stale, of cigarettes. The children I taught were poor and often came to school hungry. Many of them needed to learn French more than they needed to learn English. What English they knew came from TV and the movies and was usually accompanied with a gesture—a hand cocked like a gun, BANG BANG; a middle finger flicked out, FOCK YEW. I taught them to say *My name is Hamid.* I taught them to say *No, thank you. I am tired. I am hungry. I am happy. I am sad.* I taught them very little, for mostly they wanted to climb on tables and stomp on chalk and make kissing noises at me when I turned my back: I LOVE YOU YEAH YEAH MADAME BULLSHEET.

I must, I see now, have looked so young to them, and not at all teacherly in my long black sweaters, my gray leggings or, on a dressy day, my pleated schoolgirl skirt over a pair of pilly tights. Sometimes, in deference to being in Europe, I put on lipstick before I went to work. I was rail thin. I wore my hair long, loose or pulled back in a messy ponytail. I had two earrings in each ear, rings on most of my fingers. On weekends, I wore jeans with holes in them, my knees poking through.

The afternoon I met Daniel, I was wandering the flea market. It was early December; the day, like most in Lille, was gray and damp. I had almost no money so I never bought anything, but I liked to make my way along the booths, read old letters and look at photographs, faux-bargain with the dealers as a way to practice my French. Sometimes I stopped to sketch objects or people. This time, it was a bowl that stopped me. I bent to look. Where is it from, I tried, in French. *L'Afrique*, said the man behind the table. Nomads used it, as they wandered across the desert. Wander. *Errer.* I had learned the word just the week before and had been intrigued by the fact that it sounded like *mistake. Les nomades*, he said. *Tu comprends?* Calling me *tu*, the familiar form. Then he lifted the gourd to his lips, tipped his head back and pretended to take a drink.

Yes, I said. *Oui*, I understood. He sipped from the empty gourd again, his Adam's apple bobbing. He was tall and thin, with a kind of excited, girlish beauty—high cheekbones, flushed skin. His brown eyes sparkled when he spoke.

It was not difficult for me, in those days, to meet a stranger, catch his eye, and go home to bed with him. It was a careful dance I did, the sidelong look, the veiled question—hold your own wrist in front of him, vaguely caress it, rub your sandaled foot in the dirt. It was waiting out the silences, shrugging in just the right way at just the right moment. Okay. Maybe. I don't know. Where do you live again? I'm hungry, how about you? And then the lit refrigerator, wine from a bottle, cookies from a bag, steep stairs, a futon on an attic floor. Skin. That I possessed this power had been the oddest, most startling discovery for me when I first made it in college, since before that I'd always been the girl on the fringes, the one whose gaze was either too intense or too shy, whose hands hung heavy at her sides. In high school I was Anne or Annie, but at college I switched to Anna, and I stopped trying to subdue my curls and wore musky perfume and long earrings I'd made from colored glass. How easy sex was, I thought, back then, a secret shortcut to whisk you through the labyrinth of the social world.

Daniel offered to give me the gourd. Oh no, I said. I can't take it, not without paying you. Please, he said. I shook my head, though I wanted that gourd and wanted not to pay for it. It looked like it was made of dry, curved cardboard and bore the traces of his mouth.

"Are you a tourist?" he asked in French.

"No, I work here, I'm teaching."

"You are American?"

"Une nomade. J'erre."

"But American, yes?"

"Maybe. *Pourquoi?* You don't like us? Nobody does. I understand."

He laughed, then, tilted his head. His teeth were quite crooked, very white. *"Non, non, c'est pas ça, pas du tout."*

We stood talking for a good half hour, in English, in French, in both. I no longer remember what we said.

"You like to come to a restaurant when I finish?" he asked eventually. "To—practice my English . . . for my business?" He laughed again, a quick ironic burst.

"Oh-kay," I said, pronouncing it as if it were French. *"Mais moi, je veux parler en français."*

He bowed and handed me the gourd.

Daniel. How do you sum up a person so difficult to read, a man whose language, history and customs are not your own? We had dinner that night at a crêperie, a place so small you had to slide the table out to squeeze into your chair. The owner knew Daniel and looked at me appraisingly when we came in.

Together, they spoke so fast I couldn't understand. Then crêpes arrived, rolled and lacy—chestnuts and cream, powdered sugar and strawberries, melted cheese. Not so good tonight, Daniel said. I can make you better. Our knees kept knocking under the table. *Est-ce que tu aimes faire la cuisine*, I asked, sounding like the pert lady on my French tapes. Yes. Where did you learn? He shrugged and blew out a little puff of air in that particularly French way. Just, you know, life, he said. You want I show you? You mean, I said, *Do you want me to show you?* He nodded. Yes, you want? I wiped some sugar from my mouth. *Bah oui*, I said. I loved the *bah* and used it whenever possible. *Bah oui, oh-kay, d'accord*. I want.

Daniel lived on a modern block in a cramped, stuffy apartment filled with things he had collected on his travels and other things that he had sewn, carved and cooked. He told me he'd made them, anyway. I think I believe him; I know I did at the time. There was jam he'd made from alpine flowers, honey from bees he'd kept at his grandmother's place in Switzerland one summer, a knobby wooden stool he'd carved from apple wood. These were what drew me in—these and the simple, irreducible fact of his long body and bright eyes. Much of the room was devoted to the objects he sold at the *marché aux puces*—china that needed sorting and pricing, a box full of doorknobs and latches. These things should have lived in a cabin or an attic; they were not meant to sit piled in this white boxy room on the seventh floor. Daniel might have been wearing a peasant blouse, white and pleated. He should have channeled his unhappiness into music or walked it off during long alpine hikes. It would have made a nicer story, anyway, one that I might—in some version where I wasn't the spurned lover—have told my kids. After we went back to his place that night, he disappeared into the bathroom for a while. Then he came out and put his hands on my shoulders.

"*Petite nomade,*" he said as I raised my face to him. "But really you are a pretty American girl."

"*Merci, mais non merci.*" I drew back. "*En français.*"

"But for my English . . ."

Later, I tried to say in French, but suddenly I couldn't remember the word. I wanted to plunge into a foreign place that had no signposts, at the same time that I wanted to feel his humanness, so simple and familiar. We had sex the second time we got together, barely speaking. We used, thank god, a condom. It was in his arms, afterward, that I let myself realize how lonely I'd been in this country, and for the briefest moment I wondered if we'd gone too fast—if what I wanted, really, was not a lover, but a friend.

It was over a month before I noticed the marks on his arms. I don't know why it took that long, for though he usually wore long-sleeved shirts by day, we slept together many nights, and I thought I knew his body well. It took me even longer to notice that, yes, his eyes sparkled prettily, but also his speech slurred sometimes and his pulse raced. That he was playful and then suddenly not; that he went off to meet friends on street corners for ten minutes at a time; that he never seemed to actually *sell* antiques or even junk, yet his wallet was always stuffed with cash. Heroin. For all my bohemian ways, I was more or less an innocent as far as hard drugs were concerned. Yes, I smoked pot. Daniel and I had smoked it together a few times; he kept it in a little painted box beside his bed. I'd done mushrooms once in college and vomited before they could take effect. Never needles, never even acid. I guess I was too worried about the long-term side effects. I liked to think of myself as an adventurer, but when it came right down to it, I couldn't see pushing my luck.

Once I started suspecting, I began to snoop. It didn't take long. In the back of the cupboard under the bathroom sink was a long silver needle in a slim blue case, French and elegant, a plastic bag half full of white powder, and a shard of broken mirror. I held the mirror up and saw one of my own eyes. Sometimes he snorted, sometimes he shot up, but never in front of me. One thing about heroin is it makes erections last a long, long time. Sometimes our sex hurt me. Other times it helped me. I found the drugs and didn't say anything, not for weeks, then months, though I made sure we always had condoms. I kept waiting for him to tell me, or for him to bring the heroin to the dinner table—sugar in your coffee, lemon in your tea. Why would he hide it, after all? Why didn't he invite me in? He was such a peculiar mixture of things—the homemade jam, the drugs, the sweet face that could turn, on a dime, away from me, slammed shut. I fell in love with him. I knew it was a bad idea, but I couldn't help it. He wanted me so badly, when he wanted me. When we parted, I was always relieved for an hour or two. Then I would want him back.

Winter turned to spring. I spent two or three nights a week with Daniel, always at his place, and the other evenings I sat alone in my apartment, planning lessons, drawing, reading, memorizing words. During the day, I taught, and after school let out each afternoon, I wandered—from the Old City, to the open flower market, to the Grande Place, often finding myself at the Hospice Comtesse, a twelfth-century hospital turned into a museum. For hours, I'd stand looking at the paintings in the Salle des malades—the Van Es still life of a plate of gleaming oysters, the Jacobus Vrel of a woman reading, viewed from above and behind. Was she content in her solitude or lonely? Although I copied the painting several times, I couldn't tell. Once, that room had been filled with the ill and ailing, many of them pilgrims. They woke to the light passing through the vaulted windows and slept to shadows on the gray stone walls. Years later, sitting in a packed hospital waiting room with Max in my arms, I tried to think myself back to the austere peace of that other place. But it didn't work, for in my mind, the Salle des malades wasn't really filled with sickness, but with art.

I kept thinking I should go home and apply to graduate school in education, or maybe art, but meanwhile I was sketching every day, my students' English was improving, as was my French. I kept thinking I should end things with Daniel or at least ask him about the drugs and try to get him to stop, but meanwhile I said nothing. Looking back, I have to wonder why I wasn't more worried about AIDS, or the danger of his dealings, or the way he wasn't himself when he was high. But AIDS, back then, was still a strange new word, a far-off rumor, and anyway, something about being in a foreign country made me feel insulated from trouble, out of reach. Maybe, too, I liked circling around the danger of it all, the secrecy. "Weave a circle round him thrice," I remembered from Coleridge, the opium poet:

Weave a circle round him thrice
And close your eyes with holy dread,
For he on honeydew hath fed
And drunk the milk of Paradise.

During my Easter break, we drove Daniel's beat-up van from Lille to Geneva, where he had grown up and still had friends.

His Swiss friends were squatters, living quite nicely in an empty warehouse whose walls they had painted canary yellow and teal blue. Apparently the city, so clean and proper, let them live there, even paid for their electricity and gas. The friends were versions of Daniel, charming, brooding—a dance teacher, an actress, a musician, a few artists. After dinner on the second night, somebody took out a vial and everyone stood and gathered around. Daniel got up, and when he reached out his hand to me, I rose to join him and watched his face flicker in surprise.

The needles were disposables. There was a bag of sterile cotton balls and a bottle of rubbing alcohol. We might have been in some wartime provisional hospital, getting vaccines and tetanus shots. Everyone was silent, solemn. Daniel's friend Jean did the tying off and injecting, and somehow, without hesitating, I offered him my arm along with the others. I vomited almost instantly, barely making it to the toilet, then came back out to sit on a pillow and wonder what I'd done. The feeling when it hit was so lucid, so clean and pretty, that suddenly everything that had previously been scattered made good sense. This, I thought very slowly. This. Is. Why. I sat still for most of the evening. I might have painted the colors I kept seeing except that my hand was really someone else's, made of plastic and attached by a rubber band to my wrist.

Finally I dozed off on a sleeping bag on the floor. When I woke, it was as if I were still asleep, and for a moment I wasn't sure if what I was seeing was real—Daniel and Jean by the warehouse window, naked, Daniel behind, his hands on Jean's hips. For a moment I forgot to be betrayed, too taken with their beauty—two tall men, their stroking hands, slim hips, their necks arched back, eyes shut. I could hear their breathing, synchronized, as if they had one heart, one pair of lungs. Finally, I managed to stand, dressed only in a T-shirt and panties, the sleeping bag gathered around my legs. I coughed. They turned toward me. My arms throbbed. I was dizzy, then bending, puking again in a hot spurt. Home, I kept thinking, as my body tried to flip itself inside out. Home, as I vomited onto the sleeping bag, and gasped and coughed and threw up again, Daniel leaning over me now—part of the problem, part of the answer, *ça va, petite, ça va.*

It should have ended then, of course, a sordid little tale, but it took a few more days for things to truly unravel. It was a drug-induced mistake, I kept expecting Daniel to say, and I'm afraid I might have gone on with him for a while longer if he had. Instead, he told me sadly that he thought it was time to part ways; we'd had a great time—*vraiment, minou, c'était sympa*—but it was time to move on to other things. Like men, I said. Since when? He waved vaguely in the air. You're an addict, I said. And you sleep with men. Jesus, Daniel, why didn't you ever tell me any of this?

He looked at me, surprised. "But you knew," he said, "about the drugs. You—" He searched for the proper English word, "You explored my bathroom."

"And the men?" I said. "What about that?"

"Not men. Jean. Mostly only Jean. We're old friends, we—" He shrugged.

I winced, remembering the weekends he'd gone away, the nights we'd spent apart. "Have you been with him while we were . . . other times, I mean, or other people—"

"*Laisse tomber, chérie,*" he said. Let it go. Let it fall.

"No, I can't. You need to tell me."

"Not while I know you. He was here and I was in Lille. But from time to time, yes, since we were boys."

"Do you love him?"

"Jean? Of course. My oldest friend. And you too, I love. Neither of you . . . how do you say . . . *own* me. You see how it is?"

"That's so fucked up," I said. "That's just a screwed-up way of saying you can mistreat people whenever you feel like it, right in front of them, just like you can keep shoving this crap inside your body, you're completely crazy, I should never have—"

He spoke softly. *"Tu parles trop vite, Anna. Je ne comprends pas."*

"I hate you," I said slowly, clearly. *"Je te déteste. Tu comprends? C'est clair?"*

"Oui," he said, but it wasn't clear—not to him, not even to me. Part of me understood, that was the weird thing. Part of me wanted to go back there, to where I was just an onlooker—all right, a voyeur—or before that, to where my veins were full of poison, of pleasure. Or back further, to when I'd first met him. He'd taken me home, shown me his city, his country—a winter festival full of green dragons and men on stilts, the February ocean at Honfleur. I'd traveled and traveled, sketched and painted, which was why I'd come here in the first place. He'd taught me his language, its dips and rises, how to make an *r* sound from a new place in my throat.

Daniel gave me money to get back to Lille, and a tarnished necklace with a lock of some dead person's hair in it, and two chaste kisses, one on each cheek, and then, as I was about to board the train, a real kiss, hard and open-mouthed. Somehow, we parted friends. I can't explain that, quite. When I got back to Lille, I wrote away for information about teaching certification programs, gave up smoking, and scrubbed my apartment until it shone. No more men, I told myself. Not unless it was serious, with real potential. No more drugs. Not even art school. Certainly no more waitressing. My parents were right; it was time to be practical.

I arrived back from France exhausted, just in time to pay a brief visit to my parents and move to Boston before classes started in July. I'd chosen Boston because it was nearby but was not New York, and because it had a Masters in Education program that let me in at the last minute, and because I had some friends from college there. Nothing is forever, I told myself. Why not give this a try? Once I was well rested, I could get together a portfolio and apply to art school, or else go off on more adventures or try again to live as an artist in New York. Maybe I'd travel to some country where I could live on almost nothing and paint all day and night, or move to Chicago to be near Sophie. In fact, I think I was more scared than I admitted, more wary and tired, more insecure. Because I might have gone to art school right away, if I was so serious about my painting. I might have waitressed and painted or studied art history. I might have stayed in Europe collecting lovers. I didn't want to. I came home. I must remind myself of this if my life sometimes begins to look like a series of ever-narrower steps that fate took for me. Choices I made, many of them good ones, with my eyes wide open, each choice leading to the next. At a yard sale on my parents' street, I bought a cast-iron frying pan, four rattan place mats, and a clock. My parents sent me off with a tuition check and a floral comforter that wasn't my taste but would do the job.

"Interview the person sitting next to you," the teacher said on the first day of classes. "Find out why he or she wants to be a teacher and what he or she is most afraid of about teaching. Find out about a positive memory of being in a teaching or mentoring situation, and also a memory of being challenged in some way. Then we'll reconvene and share our impressions of each other."

I clutched inside. The fluorescent lights in the classroom

made everyone look greenish, sickly. The professor wore a short-sleeved pale blue oxford shirt and a tie strewn with red sailboats; his forehead shone with sweat. It was summer, too warm to be in school, and I felt too old. I was already a teacher, in another country; who was this American man telling me to play party games, treating me as if I were a child? I turned to face my partner. His hand was already hanging in midair.

"Hi," said the man attached to the hand. "I'm Ian."

We shook. His hand was surprisingly cool in the heat of the day, his handshake firm and friendly. My skin met his for the first time. Did my DNA tense up for a moment, coil more tightly, do a little shimmy of a dance—oh, rare recessive match, who would have thought? What if I'd been sitting next to someone else that day, the forty-five-year-old money manager who was ready for a career change, say, or the idealistic redhead just out of college? What if I'd turned to my left, not to my right, or missed the plane from Paris to Boston a week before, or not found the classroom, or gotten food poisoning that day and stayed home in bed?

Or forget about chance—what about knowledge? What if I'd known, at that moment, about the way my genes and Ian's would intersect, the one in five hundred thousand, the slim, slim chance, the boy—my Max, my weight, my love—who couldn't live in the light?

We shook. Then I took my hand back and made a face. "God, I hate these exercises."

"Me too," Ian said. "We could make things up. Why do you want to be a teacher?"

"Summers off?" I tried. "Free glue to sniff?"

He laughed a little uncomfortably, and I thought I'd gone too far.

"How about you?" I asked.

He was quiet for a long moment. When he spoke, he met my eyes. "I'm interested in history. Eventually I'd like to get a doctorate and teach college. For now, I need to pay back my loans, and I—I guess I just like kids, how they, you know, don't get all hung up on things. They just want to play outside and run around and be themselves. I guess I wish I was one still, though maybe with someone else's childhood. I find them refreshing. That's probably a lousy reason."

"No," I said. "No, that's nice, that's—" But I wasn't really listening, I was wondering if my reasons were all wrong, if I even *had* any reasons; I was looking at his hand as it lay on the table, the open palm, the fingers curved so you could see the blunt, clean nails. I was seeing Daniel's hands—on the steering wheel, prying open blue-black mussel shells, handing me a joint, threading through my hair. I looked up again, almost, somehow, on the verge of tears. Ian looked back. I wonder now what showed inside my eyes.

"You didn't tell me your name," he said gently.

"Anna . . . it's Anna Simon. I—I already forgot yours. I'm sorry."

"Ian Shea."

He put out his hand; again we shook, and I let out a little laugh.

"Try to get to all the questions," the professor called out to the group. "I'll give you a few more minutes."

"Yikes," said Ian. "All right, Anna, so why do you want to teach?"

It threw me, the way he seemed to really want an answer. I'd been living in France, after all, where, even when I could follow the conversation, the air seemed steeped in irony and indirection. "Partly it's a way to support myself," I said. "I—um, paint. I was an art major in college. I'll teach art if I can. But I guess I also—" I thought of a girl in my class in France, how she brought me a bit of lace tatting one day, told me she was making it for her dowry though she was only thirteen, just emigrated from Turkey. I thought of the secret lives behind the foreheads of the children, their growing bodies, the way they clustered in my classroom only to disperse again, like seeds. "The kids all have lives," I said. "That interests me. They've all got families, and histories, and . . . different thoughts."

He nodded. "So you want to be their teacher so you can get to know their thoughts?"

"If I could, which I can't, of course. But a little, yes."

"Why can't you?" he asked. Already, he seemed earnest, almost innocent, so different from myself.

"People are . . . complex," I said. "You think you know them, and then—"

"Then what?"

I shrugged. It was so obvious. "And then you find you don't."

You think you know them, and then you find you don't. The funny thing is that for all my speeches about complexity and secret thoughts, I was convinced I could read Ian from the start. Kind and open, playful and thoughtful, the sort of teacher any parent would seek out. He had a slight Boston accent, Irish roots, a quiet deliberateness to his every move. He was so different from Daniel, who was all steep angles, quick turns; from Sophie, who was full of words, whose eyes locked with mine and didn't let go.

None of the things I first saw in Ian turned out to be *un*true, exactly, but they were joined by so many other things, layered by a past I didn't yet know about, a present we hadn't yet had. Unbudging, I would find him later. Stony, sometimes. Difficult. Wounded (of course he was, we all were, we'd all had childhoods, we'd all had lives), but in the sulky, unattractive way of a teenager. Wanting, like a teenager, to fit in. In the second class, we sat beside each other again, and when the professor told us to partner up with someone we hadn't yet met, I felt a twinge of disappointment and caught, for the briefest moment, Ian's eye. After the third class, we went out for coffee. Hmm, maybe he likes me, I remember noting, and the feeling was a welcome one. Maybe he likes me, I seem to interest him; I wasn't sure why. And I, perhaps I liked him, too? He had sexy hands, an even gaze, such shiny, healthy hair. Here, I thought, was a man who would not push or pull or dodge.

In the end, it was I who kissed him first, after dinner one muggy August night as we stood in a lot behind a Chinese restaurant on Beacon Street, and my first real surprise with Ian was the strength, the pure inventive energy and joy and hunger, with which he met my lips and leaned in close and kissed me back, until finally it was I who broke loose, laughing, breathless.

"Come over," he said. "Will you? If you want to? I only live a few blocks away."

I nodded, though part of me was thinking *slow down*, remembering my pact.

"Only if you want to." He touched my cheek. "Or we can wait."

He was wearing, I remember, a soft purple T-shirt. His arms were brown from the sun, and bare. He was tall, solid; when I leaned against him, he could rest his chin on the top of my head. I ran my hands up his arms, inside his shirt sleeves. He had muscles—where had he gotten them—a farm? a gym?—and the smooth, hairless skin of a boy. I could say I hesitated there in that lot while people started their cars, and someone emptied trash into a Dumpster, and the smells of ginger, garlic and wilted greens passed through the restaurant's back door. I could say I stopped and considered: Wait, Anna. Think. This could be (for on some level I knew it was so) the night that leads to the rest of your life.

We kissed again. I felt myself lean forward. It was too hard to resist, this cutting through, this leaping into a strange and intimate land. I went home with him. One of his roommates, a woman, was on the phone in the kitchen and waved as we walked by. Ian's room was at the end of the hall, the bed neatly made with a bright red quilt, the pillows plumped as if he'd been expecting a guest, a map the only thing on the wall. He had a worn armchair chair set by the window and milk crates full of travel and history books. On his bureau was a little sand-colored statue—a fertility goddess, I learned later; he'd bought it in Turkey to help bring his future children into the world. Next to it was propped a framed picture of Ian as a boy, standing with his brother and sister on a dock. I picked him out right away, the oldest child, smiling, gap-toothed, his hand resting on his sister's head. Later, too, I would learn that the photo was taken by Ian's father, the summer he left the family to go dry out and never came back. Little Man, Sally started calling Ian that year. In the photo, if you look very closely, you can see the edge of Ian's father's shadow and detect something like foreknowledge in Ian's eyes. Or perhaps I'm reading too much in three kids squinting into the sun.

That night he took off his shirt, and his chest, like his arms, was sun-browned, smooth.

"I washed my sheets for you," he said as we moved toward the bed. "I hope that's not too forward, to tell you that."

I sat down and drew him to me, tracing his ribs, his sternum, the fluff of his underarm hair. "But I started it," I said. "I kissed you first."

"I know, but I was about to. You beat me to it."

"Really?" I said, pleased.

"Actually," he admitted, "I've washed them a couple times. Last Thursday, when we had dinner, and a few days before that, when we took that bike ride. They're extremely clean."

Shyly but steadily, then, with the kind of deliberateness I would later see him bring to other things, he took off my shirt and bra and looked at me so solemnly I thought he might be about to cry. What did he see? What did he want to see? A good girl with some wildness? A wild girl with some goodness? He liked my hair, I know, for how curly it was, how abundant, though he wore his own cut short. He liked that I had just come back from traveling. That I wanted to teach. That I had kissed him first.

We got into bed, our pants still on, and pulled the red quilt up. He turned off the gooseneck lamp beside the bed. The sheets smelled of sun, I remember, as if he had hung them out to dry. We didn't have sex; this was better, the pleasure protracted. His skin tasted lemony; I could feel his heart thumping in his chest. After a while, we lay back and talked a little, in that early way, about our previous relationships. I told him I'd been involved with someone in France. He said he'd seen his college girlfriend off and on since graduation but it was over now. Not then, not ever, did I tell him about trying heroin in Geneva, or about Jean and Daniel (the next year, the news was full of AIDS, and I got tested at a clinic where they knew me as a number, not a name). I can't quite say why I kept these things a secret. Maybe I worried that Ian would disapprove, or perhaps I was trying to forget. Or was it something else? Part of me wanted, I think, to *keep* what had happened, and I could only do this if I remembered it on my own terms, as troubled, frightening, yes, but also as transporting—liquid light, bodies in motion, a sense (not until Hal would I find it again) that I had left myself behind.

At dawn that first night with Ian, I told him I thought I should go home, and he said okay. The buses and subway weren't running yet. I was planning to walk home, across the river, through Central Square, into the drab neighborhood where I'd rented a place with two college friends, but Ian insisted on calling a cab. It was just getting light as I left his building, my bra stuffed in my pocket, the taste of him, still, on my lips. I didn't feel tired, didn't feel sick with longing the way I had with Daniel. I felt the way you do when you're smiling inside yourself but no one can see. I was that quiet, that secretly, cautiously happy. Safe.

ELEVEN

A child gets lost. It isn't a girl and it isn't a boy, its long hair tucked up beneath a brown cap, its legs in ballet tights, a fluted tunic made of silky tattered patchwork floating down. The child is barefoot, walking through the forest. He or she is supposed (or so I'd thought) to look anxious, sad, *lost,* but in the actual production of the play, the set was covered with colorful paper leaves and the child was Alida, who skipped and scampered as she wove her way and grinned when she caught her father's eye.

In the tower, built by Ian, stood the Gatekeeper to the Kingdom of XP. This was Max. I'd wanted him in a pale gray shimmery suit with silver buttons, but at the last minute he'd taken off my costume and now wore only a paper shield tied with string over his shirt, and a pair of rolled-up khakis. The play took place on the flat part of the lawn near the boathouse. There were blankets and folding chairs for the audience, citronella candles sputtering in tubs at the end of each row. Hal had made a backdrop from three white sheets I'd sewn together, with bright lights trained on it. It was meant to attract moths, and it worked; even before the play had started, the sheet was dotted with brown bugs, and halfway through, two luna moths landed and sat there like pale green costume jewelry before lifting off above the children's heads.

The town came to the play, at least half the town did—Jeff, who ran the local garage; the Erberts, who owned the general store; several hotel families; Yvonne the fortune-teller. Jess and Amy's family came, the parents fatter, plainer versions of their daughters. A reporter from the local newspaper showed up, and a TV crew from Albany. Hal and some other parents had worked on publicity, sending out last-minute press releases. It was partly, I knew, to make up for the BBC reporters, who'd called a few days earlier to say they weren't coming after all. I'd been sitting on the porch when Hal came out with the news. He had slammed his hand against the wall.

"Beg, beg, beg, and then they bail! After that miserable meeting and all the kids' hard work. *We need to postpone our visit*, for Christ's sake, like they'd been planning to drop in for high tea."

He looked down at his own hand as if he were surprised by what he'd done. Then he spoke in a British accent. "Sorry, wall, old chum. I seem to have lost my temp-ah."

"Are you okay?" I asked. His moods kept startling me, the way they came out of nowhere and left as quickly as they'd come. It was one of the many ways that Hal seemed childlike to me; he had a child's sense of play and wonder, a child's desire for mastery, a child's rapid flares. I was drawn to all this in him, even as it made me nervous. As for the cancellation, I would have liked to have stronger feelings about it, one way or another, but I felt only a mild relief that somehow, now, both Hal and Ian had gotten their way.

Hal nodded. "*Fuck* the BBC," he muttered, almost happily, still in a British accent. "We'll get ourselves a hometown crowd."

A child strays into the woods. Alida. She was singing as she walked, a wordless, wandering song—la-lee, la-la—making her way along a tinfoil path. First she stumbled upon Étienne, who was wearing a rubber monster's mask. She cried out, and he handed her a huge tinfoil flower and sang to her in French. Then, clutching the flower, she nearly tripped over Anil in a rubber toad's mask. He chanted in Nepalese and dusted her with silver glitter, which seemed to issue mysteriously from his cane. In my mind, these encounters should have been frightening, but they didn't come off that way. Alida tried to feign surprise, but she kept erupting into laughter, and the thin, reedy voices of the boys sounded young and harmless.

When Hal had first told me the story of the play that night in the crafts room, I'd thought it a scary, even terrifying tale. A dark forest, a missing child, strange creatures leaping out. I had listened as a mother, or perhaps as someone on the verge of crossing into dangerous territory myself. Perhaps, that night, I'd even *wanted* the fear, the descent into grief—first the brambles, then the comfort on the other side, his hand on my cheek, I'm sorry, Anna, I've upset you.

Watching now, as I sat between Marnie and Ian on a blanket, I wasn't sure if the play had metamorphosed or if I'd misunderstood it from the start. The kids were joyful, the mood merry, the journey a kind of picaresque adventure, not real lostness but a frolic through a jovial world that hid a troupe of friends. I'd gone to only a few early rehearsals, and though I'd been in charge of costumes, I'd done my job in a distracted, scattered way, ordering a whole batch of things—masks, tights, hats, felt tunics—at the last minute from an expensive on-line costume site because my own projects weren't close to being done. I *had* put effort into Alida's costume, the tunic made of layered scraps of sheer green, gray and yellow, like drooping flower petals, but when she appeared on stage I saw that it should have been more festive, less dour, covered with sequins or glow-in-the-dark designs.

Shame, I felt, then, a frothy, polluted river of it in my veins. I wasn't, oddly, feeling shameful about anything else. I screwed up the costumes, I kept thinking. I messed up. I'd forgotten that these were children, with children's energy, buoyancy and optimism, that this was a children's play, meant, above all, to entertain. I'd forgotten, even worse, that these particular children didn't need another story about fear. They needed bells, tassels and pom-poms, dances filled with flourishes and bows. It was the last night of the main three-week session. While there was technically another week of camp, many families couldn't stay that long and would be leaving, some right after the play. This would be their memory of their final night of camp.

Then, as the kids kept singing, dancing, reciting their lines, I saw that in fact the costumes didn't really matter—the children were outshining them. The play itself almost didn't matter; pushing past it, through it, were the weeks of running, whispering, shouting, telling jokes. Max hammed up his part as the Gatekeeper, speaking in a drawn-out, menacing voice. Helen was Alida's tour guide once she gained entrance to the Kingdom of XP. Natalie was the sun, first shining, then eclipsed. Tommy—who, with his round face, needed no mask—ran in front of Alida with a flashlight, playing a jocular, bossy moon.

Come on, child, hurry up!
The XP kids are having sup.
Star soup, they'll eat, and comet cake.
Run faster now, for moonness' sake.

Hal sat onstage during the play, off to one side with his guitar, his face full of pride and pleasure. Next to him was Françoise with her flute. I could sit right next to Ian and stare directly at Hal, and for a moment my shame receded and I felt surrounded, *happy*. They were both so dear to me, Hal and Ian, and so was Marnie, sitting cross-legged on the other side of me, and the children moving across the set, and couldn't love accommodate all that, and why should a person have to choose? Hal, I realized, hadn't chosen between me and the kids, me and the play. He had given the play his all, even as he was sneaking off to meet me. He was fully present right now; I could read it on his face. Somehow, Hal could do that, be multiple and, at the same time, untorn. Or did this—the kids, the play, the camp—actually matter more to him? Briefly, I allowed myself to see that. This, after all, was his vision, everything he'd worked toward, while I was—what?—a breathless, skin-soaked stop along the way? I snuck a glance at Ian. He was watching the stage intently, solemnly.

Go back with him tomorrow morning, I told myself. I started to reach for his hand, almost as an experiment, but just as I moved, Max climbed down from the tower to sing, and I folded my hands in my lap. Max stood a little awkwardly, his shoulders hunched, but his voice, unaccompanied, was clear and strong.

Welcome, lost one, don't feel fright.
We are the children of the night.

We live together on this land,
We'll take you by your outstretched hand.
We'll dance and sing, we'll leap and play.
And if you like us, you can stay.
We live by moonlight, not by sun,
Awake with us and with us run!

Alida took his hand, and then the rest of the cast appeared and joined them, dancing in a circle. Anil, who with his limp couldn't keep up, stood off to one side, beating a drum. Hal and Françoise played along on the guitar and flute. As the dance grew faster, Tommy's glasses fell off and everyone lurched to a stop while Sara ducked to retrieve them. Françoise and Hal slowed down the music, playing a threading, simple tune. Tommy put his glasses back on and waved to his mother as the dancing started up again.

Then the kids were bowing, the crowd was clapping, hooting, rising for a standing ovation. Hal stood too, without his guitar, and Alida ran to him and climbed into his arms. I looked at Ian again. He was wiping his eyes in quick swipes.

"He was great." I leaned over so he could hear me. "Wasn't he great?"

Ian nodded—I think he did—but then he stepped away from me, starting toward the set. I didn't move. I watched him hug Max, how tightly they held each other, Max's head ducked down, Ian's arms around him, both of them rocking, almost like lovers, the crowd around them blotted out.

I wanted to join them—a sandwich hug, Max in the middle. Instead, I stood. When, finally, I made my way to where the kids were, it was Alida I encountered first.

"Did you see me?" she asked. "Did you like it?"

"I loved it." I bent to hug her. Hal was offstage by then, talking to one of the reporters. Ian and Max had moved apart.

"Max was really good," Alida said.

"Yes." I straightened up. "Yes, he was. I think I'll go tell him, okay?"

When I reached Max, he was untying his shield.

"You were *fantastic*." I touched his back.

"Thanks." He let the shield drop to the ground.

"Should I save that for you, as a souvenir?" I picked it up.

"If you want."

"You're really a good actor," I said. "Maybe when we get home, we can—"

"Cast party!" somebody yelled, and before I could finish, Max was running toward the lodge.

Again, I stood, as if rooted to the spot, so that I was, in the end, the last person out there, standing among the folding chairs. Standing alone. Either way, I would be, I realized. Either way, we all were. I considered swimming, then, how I might strip, dive and take off across the lake, my body small—a speck, a tiny, motion-making ripple—and, in my thoughts, beautifully insignificant.

But Max was in the lodge. But Hal was there, and Ian. The cast party was a celebration, a culmination, a good-bye. In a few hours, Ian would drive off to pick up Adam, and Max and I would stay. I was making choices, even as I stood still. Shield in hand, I started toward the lodge.

Ian left at dawn. I wish I could remember the whole thing better: what was said, what was left unsaid. It seems important now, a clue to what lay before us. But I drank too much at the cast party. I drank red wine, white wine, a golden rum punch that tasted of mango and coconut. I danced with Ian, with Hal, with Max. I danced with Marnie, feeling her shoulder blades beneath my hands, though when I leaned in close, stumbling, she separated from me.

"Anna," she said, "are you all right? Maybe you'd better sit down."

I wasn't the only one to get drunk that night. The liquor was stored in coolers on top of the refrigerators in the kitchen, where supposedly the kids couldn't reach, but I think the older ones found it anyway and nobody seemed to care. Many of the cast members kept on their costumes, the masks circulating. Françoise disappeared upstairs and returned in a raw silk green cocktail dress, nubs of nipple showing through. Hal wore a sort of linen peasant's blouse and danced wildly but with great concentration, his shirt soaked through with sweat. The music ranged from Britney Spears to African drumming to the Rolling Stones. I hadn't been planning to change out of my shorts and T-shirt, but at one point I made my way unsteadily upstairs and started rifling through my clothes until I came upon a black rayon sundress that fell to just above my knees. I put it on, took my hair out of its ponytail. I exchanged my worn beige cotton underwear for a black bikini pair edged in lace, still just cotton but the sexiest ones I had. In the hall, I tripped, then hurried on. Back downstairs, Hal brushed by me and spoke into my ear, his breath thick with wine. "God, you're lovely, Anna."

Ian didn't drink. Neither did the other parents who were leaving. He did dance a little; I remember that. Once with me, when I pulled him out into the crowd, once with Françoise, and once with little Helen, who looked at him adoringly while he spun her in his arms. As sunrise approached, the party got louder, faster. At some point, Ian must have gone upstairs to finish packing. I don't remember seeing him leave, but I remember looking up from the dance floor and finding him standing in the doorway to the front hall, a duffel bag by his feet.

My god, I thought, in a moment of clarity. He's leaving. Leaving me. It seemed illogical, suddenly, and I had an urge to go to him and explain everything. Probably, I might tell him, this is not such a good idea. Probably I should come with you, or you should stay. There is something about Ian standing alone, Ian watching, that I've always found wrenching. It's not where he belongs; he belongs surrounded—by his students, by his children. I can't see him standing on the edge like that without thinking of his father leaving, and Ian as a stalwart ten-year-old, shoulders squared, eyes trained straight ahead.

I made my way toward him. My jaw felt numb, my brain soft and heavy. One of my straps had slipped off my shoulder and I pushed it up and held it there.

"Is the—um, rental car all set?" I asked when I reached Ian, my voice too loud in my own ears.

He nodded. "Jess's mother picked it up. It's outside."

"But do you have to go so *early*?"

"Early? I told Adam I'd be there by nine at the latest."

"I miss him!" I exclaimed, for all at once I did, terribly. "I miss him so much, it's like . . . like having a limb cut off. You know? I—I—" I tried not to sway. "I don't know if I can go another week without him."

Ian shrugged. Or turned away. Something.

"Should I come?" I asked, before I could stop to think.

He looked at me, then, but I might have been staring a stranger in the eye. This part I remember in terrible detail, the way his face was so deeply unfamiliar, like nothing I'd ever known. And cold. Almost bored. He didn't answer, just picked up his bag, so that for a moment I wondered if I'd even spoken.

"Have you already said good-bye to Max?" I asked.

He nodded.

"And everyone else?"

He nodded again.

"I'll—okay, then, I'll . . . I guess I'll walk you out."

Ian swiveled with the formal gesture of a soldier, and I followed him outside to the front steps. The light was weak but my eyes stung anyway, and as the morning world sprawled before us—gray-tinged, complicated, riddled with detail—I wanted nothing so much as to go back inside to the music, which reached us now as a sweet, insistent pulse. A red sedan was parked in the driveway, small and sporty, a getaway car. I didn't feel drunk anymore, hardly at all. My brain was my brain again. My sundress was too big.

"I'll call later," I told Ian. "After you get home. Drive carefully." I leaned to kiss him good-bye, but he backed off.

"You're drunk," he said. "You do know that, don't you? You can't even walk a straight line."

I nodded. "I think it's starting to wear off. I'm sorry."

For a moment, I was. And then my rage. I wanted to slap him. More than slap; I wanted to pummel him until he cried out—in pain beyond moralizing, in simple grief or recognition. A straight line. I didn't want one. Don't tell me tell me tell me how to walk. *Things fall apart,* I thought. I took a breath.

"Not," I said, "that it's the end of the world."

"No." Ian looked at me strangely. "I suppose not."

And then he was leaning to kiss me insistently on the mouth, and I was moving toward him, into him, feeling—or was I imagining it?—the press of his erection against my leg. I'm not sure if it was obligation or guilt, nostalgia or desire that made me open my mouth and find his tongue. For a moment he let me in; then he pulled back.

"I'll be late for Adam," he said.

"We'll see you—" I told him. I meant to add *in a week*, but the words didn't come.

Ian picked up his bag. He walked away. For a minute, I stood watching, and though his stride was steady, the bulk of duffel bag made him look unbalanced, listing slightly to the left. I heard someone calling me from inside the lodge, *Anna*, *Anna*. It might have been a child's voice, or a man's, or the voice of my own mind. It almost didn't matter; summoned, I went back inside. A glass was in my hand. Someone was filling it. No more, I tried to say. Enough. But my mouth was parched, and the punch was full and fruity, and slowly the world grew soft-edged again, porous, bathed in dark.

The way I like it, I thought as I drained my glass. The way, after all these years, I finally like it now.

TWELVE

The storeroom was on the third floor, adjoining a maid's room at the far end of the hall from where Max and I slept. Neither room had been used for a long time, and the smell there was strangely heady, a mix of mildew, old books and dust. There was a cast-iron youth bed in the storeroom, pushed into a corner behind unlabeled boxes and detritus—vacuum cleaner parts, dented lampshades, a pair of wading boots. On the slanted wall across from the bed, someone had tacked a list of animals: *15 deer, 9 pheasants, 23 ducks.* The handwriting was crude, and at first I took the note to be some kind of children's counting game—*On the first day of Christmas, my true love gave to me*—or a tally of animals spotted during play. Did you see that sweet list on the wall, I asked Hal, and he looked surprised and then amused. It's what they killed, he said.

After Ian left, Hal and I began to meet in the storeroom at eleven-thirty each morning, before the kids woke up. On the inside of the door to the maid's room, Hal installed a new brass bolt like the one in the crafts room. The storeroom door also locked from the inside, but with a hook and eye. We would meet in the hall and pass quickly through the maid's room to the storeroom, locking both locks. Once there, I always felt hidden, nested. Part of me liked the feeling, how *inside* we were, how cupped, the place as private and layered as our sex. But our hideout also led me toward punishing, guilt-induced visions: a fire in the hall, the locks fusing from the heat, Max screaming for me from his room. Or an image that was quieter but just as wrenching: Max's hand on the door—why won't it open?—and from inside, our sounds.

We kept a rotating desk fan on in the storeroom, partly for the noise it made and partly for the breeze. Hal brought along the portable part of the baby monitor he still used with Alida, since he often wandered the house while she slept. In a canvas tote bag, he brought condoms and delicious little snacks—yellow raspberries from the patch outside, pear juice in tiny cans, Jerusalem artichokes he'd dug up and cooked, chocolates shaped like shells. He brought almond-scented massage oil on the second day, blue bandannas on the third. It sounds ridiculous, but it didn't feel that way, my hands bound to the bed rails, my back arching, feet flexing as he tongued me, pink against pink, expecting nothing of me, simply that I lie there and receive. I'd never done that before—been tied like that—but it felt surprisingly familiar, even comforting, the blue cloth fluttering against my arms when the fan rotated our way.

You can't help it, I told myself. You can't help this thing that's happening to you, and I pictured him holding me hostage in the lodge, all choice removed and, with it, all guilt. I came, then, and tried to reach for him, forgetting I couldn't move. Quickly, he unbound me. Then it was his turn; he raised his arms so I could tie him down. Hovering above him, I swayed back and forth, just out of reach of his mouth. You can't have me, I thought, looking at my body grazing his. You can, you can't, you can—and as I offered him a tip of nipple, tip of tongue, his face tightened into something close to pain, and I caught a glimpse, at once moving and frightening, of what he would look like when he was very old. Liquid warmth against my leg, then, a pooling. When I untied him, he stayed there for a moment as if still bound, his face relaxed, now, and lovely in its lines. Then, abruptly, he sat up and reached into his bag.

"Here, my captor." He held up a tub of cocoa butter. "For our wrists."

"So many props," I said.

I swung my legs over the side of the bed and sat, too. All at once I felt exhausted, deflated. I pictured Ian watching us, how he would recoil not only at our coupling but also at the theatrics of it, a bad video—two middle-aged people not nearly attractive enough to be porn stars, the production values lousy, Hal directing—as always—the show. "You have it all planned out," I said.

"That's not true." He looked wounded.

"I don't mind." I patted his arm. "I like it."

"No, you don't. Or not entirely. Do you?"

I nodded. "It shows you're thinking of us. That's nice."

"And yet?"

He sounded curious, speculative. He really wants to know, I thought. He may be hurt, but still he wants to understand. Ian and I had reached a point where we let a great deal go, rarely trying to pinpoint the thought behind the thought. Had we ever, though? I didn't think so, I couldn't quite remember, knew only that before Hal's questions, I felt ill at ease, unsure of how to balance honesty with tact. And yet I liked that he was asking. "I guess," I tried, "it seems a little. . . almost like you've done it before, or like you know beforehand how it'll go." I hesitated. "I mean, what if I hadn't *wanted* to be tied up?"

He laughed. "Since when was bondage about consensus?"

"So you knew you'd tie me up?"

"Yes. And I knew you'd like it, and that your wrists would be sore afterward so I'd rub them with cocoa butter, and you'd like that too."

I was tempted to say, but I didn't like it, my wrists aren't sore, I'm allergic to cocoa butter, but none of it was true. I was tempted to tell him that I wasn't as innocent as he thought, no middle-aged ingenue, no bored housewife testing her wings. Hal made me feel young in a way I both liked and disliked, for though he was only a few years older than I was, he'd spent more time out in the world, or perhaps he just thought he had. I was tempted (each desire its own taut bubble, popping the one that came before) to tell him that his sperm on my leg made me think of babies, and that if I wasn't very careful, very prickly and quick to take offense, I'd fall in love with him—had, perhaps, already, if I could drop down to the still center of myself and block out all the background noise.

I could have said these things; Hal would have listened, heard. Instead, I was silent, too buffeted by my thoughts to speak, though later, before we went to find the children, I would try. Now I laid my hands across his lap and he dipped his finger in cocoa butter, rubbing lotion first on one wrist, then the other. When he was finished, I began on him, rubbing cocoa butter on his wrists and arms, his stomach and his nipples, which were surprisingly dark, like antique coins. Round and round I went, polishing them until they shone.

How will I hold the memory of those mornings? Pure, I'd like to keep it. Valuable. Untinged. There are certain moments in my life—the births of my children, the way I've occasionally felt while painting—that I hope I can return to as I lie near death. They are distilled moments, rare. Adam's eyes right after he was born, remarkably themselves, staring up at me from a smeared and barely human face. Max jumping on the trampoline our first night at camp, while Ian and I watched. My paintbrush—every once in a great while—with my hand. Hal and I touching, talking.

Is it possible that we only met like this for three mornings before things began to unravel? It felt like more, and for this I know I should be grateful. It felt like a life, a lifetime, and if, in a way, I may have assumed more intimacy than was really there, in another way, I'm sure I invented nothing. Yes, there was betrayal seeping in around the edges of our act, discoloring it, and some crooked thrill, perhaps, that came from secrecy and newness. And yes, those mornings, which I'd like to remember as full and glistening, cannot, in truth, exist apart from these, even fuller, facts: Three children. A husband. A wife who'd died. Nonetheless. Hal and I knew each other in that room. He knew me. I was stripped of my layers, my corrections and veneers. I was the underpainting, the skeleton beneath the sculpture. I was bare and flawed, raw and unfinished, all open seams and wire. He loved me like that. Nobody ever had, not so readily or with such open eyes. It made me bold and turned me talky. Do you like this better, I'd ask him. Or this? Kneel above me and face my feet, I'd say. So I can watch you.

I was sketching him inside my head; he knew I was. The cleft where his buttocks came together. The nape of his neck and the knobby ridge of his backbone. The slight roll of fat—thin though he was—around his hips. The veined skin on the undersides of his knees. He'd do as I asked for a while, then he'd turn around, turn me around. Come, he'd murmur. Mmmm, like this. He'd ease my legs apart, unfold me, and when his fingers came out webbed and wet, he'd bring them to his mouth and taste. Ian and I had never gone this slowly or given each other this kind of minute, clear-lit attention, and if I had moments of shame or self-consciousness at being seen in such detail, they never lasted long. Hal rarely shut his eyes, and neither did I. It was as if (we both knew it, though we didn't bring it up) we simply didn't have the time.

The children, who went to bed at dawn, woke each day in the early afternoon. On the first two days after Ian left, I managed to be back in my room by the time Max came to find me. On the third day, I was brushing my teeth in the bathroom when I heard him calling from down the hall. "One minute, sweetie!" I answered, leaning out from the doorway. I rinsed my mouth and washed my face, scrubbing myself back to what I really was, a mother—right?—a mother getting ready to greet her child, go downstairs, pour granola, slice bananas with a practiced hand. The mirror was foggy from someone else's shower. I started to wipe it off but suddenly felt too tired, and I leaned my head against the wall and shut my eyes. Hard tile wall, hard shell of skull. The contact, cold and impersonal, soothed me. I must have stood there longer than I meant to, for when I went to find Max, he'd already gone downstairs.

We ate, now, at a smaller table in the living room, often in informal shifts. With so many people gone, the lodge felt even more massive, the hallways longer, the echoes louder. Still, the place was full of reminders of the previous weeks. The bulletin board near the phone was covered with photographs. On the living room wall hung a row of papier-mâché masks I'd made with the kids, and their drawings decorated all three refrigerators. Outside, we left the backdrop for the play slung between two pine trees, a long white swath. In the evening, the phone rang frequently. Sara had forgotten her sneakers; had anybody seen them? Étienne was at the airport about to board a plane to Paris and wanted to say good-bye one more time.

Mostly we answered the phone, but sometimes, if no one was near it, we let the machine pick up. We did our own dishes in the sink. We ate sandwiches for dinner and kept forgetting to harvest the tomatoes in the garden, though the branches dragged with fruit. On Tuesday, after the sun went down, I went with Max and Alida to the garden, and we bit into warm, overripe tomatoes, one after another, the seeds running down our chins. There would be a nearly full moon that night—already you could see by its watery light—but the tomatoes tasted entirely of sun.

"You're a mess, Anna!" Alida said, aiming her flashlight at me. I shielded my eyes and laughed.

Max fished in his pocket and held out a wadded tissue. "Here, Mom."

"What? For my face? Thanks." I wiped my chin and started to return the tissue to him, but he brushed my hand away.

"What about you?" I pointed to his chin.

He sniffed. "Kids are supposed to be a mess."

"But not grown-ups?"

"No."

"Why not?"

"It's *gross.*"

He grabbed the tissue from me and flung it, and it landed by my foot, an exotic bloom, a piece of trash. His disgust was palpable, and underneath it I could feel the simmerings of what I only half understood, then, to be rage. Alida looked back and forth between us. I bent for the tissue.

"We don't litter here," I said, sounding like a humorless version of Hal. "Talk about gross."

"*We* litter," said Max. "*I* litter."

"I litter!" Alida flung down her flashlight. "Ha! See?"

Suddenly Max was upon her. For a moment I thought he might be trying to hurt her, but then I saw he was tickling her—on her neck, under her arms, on her belly, which showed pale and chubby with leftover baby fat when she raised her arms. Alida squealed and writhed, nearly choking with laughter. "Stop!" she gasped, but when he did, she lifted her arms for more. I stood and watched, the Kleenex in my fist, the odd man out. A taste of your own medicine, I told myself, but of course they were only children, playing children's games. And so beautiful. I tried to hold them in my mind so I could draw them later—the blur of legs, her bent back, the intersecting tension of their mirth. "Children Playing," I'd call it, though I didn't usually title my drawings. I'd give it to Hal—here, your girl, my boy. But of course it might have been anyone; that was the pleasure, the danger of a drawing. Two bodies yielding and resisting. How much it looked like sex. *Stop*, I told myself, or them. I clapped my hands together, and they looked over, startled, and stepped apart.

"Enough romping, puppies," I said. "We need to go back to the lodge."

"Why?" asked Max.

"Because," I said stupidly, "we have a lot to do."

He squinted. "Like what?"

"Like . . . braid my hair," said Alida.

"Yes," I said.

"Oh." Max nodded. "That's very important. That's, like, earth-shattering."

"It is." Alida took my hand. "It is, Anna, right?"

"Definitely. Come on, possum." I reached for Max, and surprisingly, he let me hold his hand. The three of us walked this way for a few steps before Alida remembered that she'd left her flashlight on the ground, and then, like the flimsiest of paper chains, we broke apart.

Often, now, it felt like we were only four: Max, Alida, Hal and me. Just like at home, except it was a different four. Of course there were other people around, too. Marnie and Tommy stayed on, as did Helen and her parents, and Anil. Jess and Amy still came to help out, but most of the volunteers had left to go back to college or work, their daylight lives. The two women Hal had hired as cooks were gone. Fewer paths were hung with lanterns. No clowns or fencers showed up, no drumming teachers or doctors. I stopped ordering art supplies. Hal stopped organizing events. Marnie stopped going running—too hot, she said—and it was, the last week of August, the weather so muggy that even the lake turned lukewarm except for the odd current threading—cold, surprising—around your legs.

Each night around seven, Max and I called home. How was the drive back? How was soccer practice? Was everything fine with the house? With Arno? What else was going on? During these conversations, Adam and Ian were brief with me, perfunctory, and I dreaded the calls in a way that left me feeling guilty and burdened at the same time. *Talk* to me, I wanted to shout—so curt they were, so stiff—and yet I knew I could demand nothing from them. We're having fun, I'd announce brightly, blandly to Ian in the absence of his questions. I'm doing a fair amount of painting. Max and Tommy are still having a blast, practically living in the water. Are you sure everything there is okay? Sometimes I'd suppress a rising desire to confess to him, ask for his forgiveness. Other times, I'd find myself wanting to talk to him in the way of an old friend, for he, of all people, had known me the longest, in the steadiest way, and I couldn't help thinking that as my friend, my longtime companion, he might be able to bring some helpful perspective and locate my actions inside a stream of time, of life.

Of course, I said nothing. He was my husband, my lover. If I was, in some fashion, hurting him by keeping things from him, I would hurt him more if I confessed. Or so I told myself as, meanwhile, my silence allowed me to return to Hal's arms. After I'd finished talking, I'd step outside the wood-paneled cubby, and Max would slide in and get on the phone. "Hey, Dad," I'd hear him say and, on the second night, "Hi, Daddy, I miss you"—though he rarely called Ian *Daddy* anymore. He doesn't know and so he won't tell, I reassured myself that night. Or did he know? Or didn't he? As Max talked to his father, I took a daisy from a vase in the living room and plucked its petals off, reciting the possibilities to myself—he knows, he doesn't—again and again, until I was left with a powdery yellow nub and a bare-plucked, last-ditch answer: *He doesn't know*.

It seemed like the truth, but I couldn't be sure, for Max wasn't spending a lot of time with me and there was something opaque about him when we were together. Hal and I were careful around the children, never touching, almost avoiding each other, but still, Max had a radar for my moods, my ways. As I gathered the petals from the floor and went to throw them away, a memory came to me: my brother Matthew and two of his friends plucking the legs off a daddy longlegs by the municipal pool, then leaving the brown rabbit turd of a body to roll, limbless, on the hot cement. I had hated to watch and been compelled to, wanted to intervene and been afraid to. I must have been eight or nine and was used to thinking of myself as a girl incapable of cruelty. I rescued worms from puddles, after all, and defended the retarded girl at school. But a week or so later, alone behind our garage, I came across a spider and did the same thing, plucking off the filament legs, one by one. Then I smashed what was left beneath the heel of my sandal, kicked dirt over it and ran into the house.

At the time, I had no idea why I'd killed the spider; looking back, I'm still not sure. Maybe I was just copying my brother. Maybe I did it because there was something fascinating, stripped-down, at once awful and awesome about how, with a few quick plucks, a spider could become a ball. Or was it more my own transformation that interested me? Cruel girl. Secret girl. I never told anyone what I'd done. I didn't stop rescuing worms. But I knew myself, at least for that instant, as somebody completely different from the person I presented to the world.

A girl incapable of cruelty. A good mother, partner, wife.

Straightforward, mostly. I disliked pretense. I believed—I thought I believed—not so much in the sanctity of marriage as in the value of the love and friendship that could come with it, the worth of a life built carefully together, piece by piece, over many years. That was something hard-earned and precious, I knew, not to be taken lightly. Ian was something precious. No wife-beater, he. No philanderer, drunk or distant father. Years before, just after we'd moved out of our first rented apartment—a shabby walk-up with a dark shotgun layout—he'd made me a diorama model of it in a wooden wine crate: here our old bedroom, here our living room, the galley kitchen, the celery-green bathroom with its window overlooking an airshaft. Here, our futon bed, but made of Popsicle sticks. Cotton balls for pillows and a paper-towel quilt. My porch garden jutted off the end, a cigar box with amber pill-bottle chairs and plastic flowers stuck in real soil.

It was all so carefully wrought and, at the same time, so flimsy. It came with no card, no words or explanation. We were unmarried, still. We had sex the way we had dinner, almost every night. I remember leaning over the diorama to kiss him and feeling a tenderness for him that I'd never felt before for anyone. *Treasure* was the word that came to mind. Treasure as both noun and verb. I was so lucky to have found him, and I knew my luck to be extraordinary, unearned. When did you make this, I asked. At night while you slept, Ian said, and I realized he'd been living a sort of secret life, yet one which (what could be better?) had everything to do with me.

Now Hal and Alida, Max and me. If there was cruelty in this new formation, it was complicated by the fact that there was also love and many kindnesses. It was hard to feel unloving, betraying, when my hands were so open and my heart—or wherever love takes up residence in the body—so full. This was not a new family we'd made, surely not that, nothing so fast or easy, but for a short while, when I focused hard enough, I could almost imagine it, and then the other people at the camp grew faint, ghost bodies on the edges of my vision. Ian, even Adam, grew faint. Our house at home. My recent past. Another life, it began to feel like, when I plunged far enough. When had I lived there? Why? It almost seemed like someone else's story—a woman I'd read about, or one whose life I had encountered in a dream. A cramped but serviceable house in Massachusetts. A bathtub she retreats to when she needs to be alone. Somewhere in the attic, a model of an old apartment. Paintings, too, rolled and stacked. Don't undo me, don't unroll me. And on the door to the older boy's room, a Magic Markered sign. It was years old, but it might have spoken, now, for every member of this little family: PRIVATE PRIVATE, KEEP OUT.

THIRTEEN

Max made a beautiful girl. His brown curls and thick fringe of lashes, the pixie shape of his nose and chin. As I walked in and saw him sitting among a thicket of lights and wires, it took me a moment to absorb the fact that the child in front of me was, in fact, my own, holding court before a crowd. He was wearing his own blue shirt, but he had on a short flowered skirt and barrettes in his hair, and his cheeks were the fevered high pink of rouge. A microphone attached to a long pole hovered above his head. "It's kind of hard," he was saying. "Sometimes I want to go outside during the day, but I know I'd just die"—the *just die* a little breathy, a little Marilyn Monroe: *I'd just die for a slice of cherry pie*. "The other girls get to lie in the sun," he added. "And play on soccer teams and stuff." Beside him on the couch, Alida nodded. "Except here," she said, "we have lots of games, like badminton with glow-in-the-dark birdies." The interviewer leaned forward. "Oh, lovely! And what else do you do?"

I'd come up from the crafts room, leaving Hal there, his cigarette a red tip in the dark. We'd gone there—truly we had—to clean up the place for winter. No touching while the kids were awake; it was our rule. We'd worked quickly, silently, storing pom-poms, felt and pipe cleaners in plastic bins. Then, just as quickly and quietly, we'd made love. I'd been planning to take a shower before I went to find Max. Maybe, I'd thought, we could go canoeing or walk along the lake, if I could coax him away from his friends. Ian had been gone for four nights by then, and we'd found an informal rhythm, dispersing and meeting up without any particular plan. I was enjoying myself; I had to admit it. More than enjoying myself—I was happy, sated, though part of me also knew I was living in a dream.

Now this: the lodge taken over by strangers and equipment, lights trained on the kids. Of course, the BBC film crew—they had shown up. Without phone call or warning, they had arrived, installed themselves in the living room and started interviewing my son. Who was dressed up like a girl. Okay. Was it a joke? I wanted to step forward: Excuse me, I'm his mother, I'd like an explanation. But the camera might turn, the microphone dangle expectantly over my head: *We'd* like an explanation, Mother. Speak. I'd come in from the night. My feet were bare, my skin warm. Beneath my shorts, my pubic hair was slick with sex.

I stood off to one side and watched. There was equipment everywhere—light stands, thick black cases, leggy tripods that looked as if they'd topple in a breeze. On the floor, orange extension cords crisscrossed like cartoon snakes. One man carried an enormous camera on his shoulder; another, wearing headphones, held the microphone boom. A young woman squatted behind him with a clipboard, her ponytail high on her head, a spray of blond. I was quite sure Max hadn't seen me yet, for the lights were bright and he was focused on the interviewer, a tall, elegant woman in a crisp safari outfit—khaki vest and pants, a white shirt, a red bandanna tied jauntily around her neck.

"You've both," she said in her British accent, "been living with XP for your whole lives. And for most of that time, until very recently, you didn't know any other children with the illness. What was that *like*?"

"Lonely," said Alida cheerfully, as the microphone turned her way.

"Oh, I'm sure," said the woman. "And for you, Maddie?"

"Um . . ."

Max—Maddie—paused to think, and I leaned forward to listen. Would I hear it now—a summary, a backed-up, bare-bones appraisal of his life? The costume seemed suddenly insignificant. *Actually it's been all right*, I wanted quite desperately to hear him say. *I have my family and they love me so it's been all right*. Max fiddled with his barrette, crossed and recrossed his legs, glanced up at the mike. The light on the side of the camera shone red and steady, a bloodshot eye, a tiny sun. It was then that I spotted Marnie sitting on the floor in a corner of the living room, convulsed with silent laughter.

"It's hard," Max said finally.

The reporter nodded. "How is it hard?"

"Well, like, you want to say someday I'll grow up and be . . . whatever, an astronaut or doctor or something, but you might not grow up at all, and if you do, you've got to stay inside. So you've got to say *maybe* I'll grow up and be—" He shrugged. When he spoke again, his voice was flat. "Just me."

The reporter bobbed her head, the motion almost spastic. For god's sake, was she about to cry? I felt a rush of hatred for her, with her glossy black hair, chiseled jawline and BBC-Goes-

Camping outfit. How thrilling for her to be getting this footage, so real, so *moving*, docudrama at its very best. And something else: Max talking this way to a pretty, nodding stranger, speaking his mind, his soul. Except of course it wasn't Max at all, but "just me," just Maddie, a sick little girl in purple barrettes and a too-short flowered skirt. *But you might not grow up at all.* If the messenger was an impostor, the message was too true. I'd never heard him speak it out this way, so stark, so plain.

"How has camp changed things for you?" the woman asked.

Max considered. "Well, my friends here are my real friends—or my family, even." He leaned forward. He had uncrossed his legs, and you could see an edge of his white jockey briefs, which for some reason made me want to weep. "My parents, um, they got divorced this year, but Alida's like my sister and Marnie over there"—he pointed—"is like my mom."

No, I thought. No no. Just that, a nothing of a word. I looked at Marnie, and when she met my eyes, I saw she knew everything. Please, I thought. Turn the world back. Girl back to boy. Max back to me. Me back to . . . what? A time and place before, clean and windswept, free of complications. A baby just born and yet to feel the sun. A handshake in a classroom: I'm Ian. A face in a car window: I'm Hal. A boy who could say—and mean it, and hold it as his gift, his saving grace—I have my family and they love me so it's been all right. Had that child ever existed, or was I making him up, prone as I was to revision, invention? It is *not* okay to lie, I wanted to tell Max. You are not a girl. Your parents are not divorced. It is not okay to lie.

Except.

Turn the world back—to the shiver before the action, the thought before the deed. For years they had kept me happy enough, my shivers and my thoughts; they could have been feeding me still. There was judgment in Marnie's eyes, if I looked carefully. Kindness and understanding, yes, but also judgment. You've made your bed. You've cooked your goose. Things are bound to catch up with you. Or was this my own self speaking, wagging a finger at me from across the room?

"Children of the night. . . . An enormous burden. . . . A daily, or should I say a nightly, challenge."

The reporter had repositioned herself and was talking straight to the camera now. Nearby, two people scurried about, adjusting lights. I moved forward, stepping over wires and past the cameraman, bumping his arm with my own. When I got close to the couch, I positioned myself to block Max and Alida from the camera's eye. Then I spoke.

"I'm his mother. How could you—" I froze. "Please. Could you turn that thing off?"

With a whirring sound, the camera stopped. The man set it down on a tripod, and suddenly my load, too, felt lighter, and I could breathe again. "I don't understand how you could come here and just start filming," I said. "These lights are hot—they could damage their skin. And don't you need some kind of parental release form? There are privacy issues here. And he's not—"

I turned toward Max. I might have been Ian; I sounded just like him. Max's face was stony, his eyes, when they locked with mine, unblinking. If he'd begun this as a game, he was far from that by now.

"He's not a girl," I went on. "Maybe you were playing a joke, sweetie, but these people have come all the way from England to film us and teach people about XP—"

Max stood and brushed past me. "I *know*."

"Then why did you pretend—"

He turned to face me. "I know they came from England, Mom. I'm not an idiot."

"Max, I didn't—"

All eyes were on us. The reporter stood, too.

"Well." She laughed nervously. "We don't mind, do we? We love a good joke, it keeps us on our toes. How about we take a break? I want to talk to the parents anyway—off-camera." She smiled at Max. "You're a terrific actor. You had me quite tricked."

Max blushed and ducked his head, and I saw that he was smitten. From the far side of the room, I heard another laugh, familiar, deep.

"From gatekeeper to girl, Max," Hal said as he stepped forward. "You keep us guessing."

His shirt was untucked, his hair mussed by my hands. He was lovely; I would always think so. He looked right past me at the reporter. He wants to sleep with her, I thought. It couldn't have, somehow, been more clear. He was arrogant, self-absorbed, profligate, fickle. He was an asshole, loser, creep. Oh, the words I could summon. How easily they came to me—and with them, in equal measure, sorrow and relief.

"Welcome, BBC," he said. "I'm Hal. You must be tired. I'll make some tea."

And so the scene broke into movement again. Marnie stood. Alida ran to Hal. Tommy appeared and joined Max. The BBC people shook hands with the camp people: Hello, I'm Imogen. I'm Jack. Oh, Hal, it's great to meet you, we tried to call ahead but couldn't get through.

I stood. In the middle of it all, I stood, stunned and speechless. I knew I needed to talk to Max, but I had no idea what to say. *Not divorced? I'm sorry?* Might that be enough for now?

After a few minutes, Marnie came over. "Are you all right?"

I turned away from the camera crew. "How can they just barge in? It's unbelievable."

"Actually they didn't, exactly," she said. "I was here. I checked out the lights. They're fine. Then I went to round up some kids." She smiled, but wanly now. "Max was all dressed up."

"So they just started filming?"

She looked at me oddly. "We did sign releases."

"What? I didn't."

"Ian signed. I figured he'd told you."

"He *signed*? Where was I?"

She looked down. "You weren't around."

Does everyone know, I might have asked. Was it that obvious? Did all the parents know, all the children? For how long? "Max is furious at me," I said instead. "And he has a right to be."

Marnie touched my arm. "It won't last. You'll make things better."

"How?"

"Go talk to him."

"What do I say?" I swiped at the tears that were starting down my face. "What a mess I've made. I'm so sorry."

"No," she said. "Don't apologize, not to me."

I saw myself through her eyes, as passive and muddled and without a compass of my own. And crying now, as if I were the one who deserved pity.

"Look," she said. "He's watching us. Go on."

I went. Past the strangers, over to Max, who was sitting beside Tommy on the couch. "Hi," I said.

He waited, watching.

"Can I talk to you for a minute?" I asked, though what I really wanted was to hold him, my chin resting on his head. Years before, when he was an infant, there was one night when I was lying in bed with him racked with worry, and I realized that he—the smell of his skin, the heat he gave off—was the only thing that could soothe me, even as he was the precise object of my fears. I had known there was something wrong, or at least unwise, about this, but I couldn't help it. As for Max, he had trusted me completely back then, because he'd come from my body and lived at my side, because he had no choice.

"Come upstairs for a minute?" I said now, as gently as I could.

He shook his head.

"Please?"

"I'm busy."

"But this is important." My voice came out imploring. "Really, Max. I need you to come with me."

"No thanks," he said lightly.

For a second, I saw him as a grown man—how charming he would be, slippery and charismatic, stubborn and difficult to catch, and, underneath it all, as deep-feeling as they come. He had taken the barrettes out of his hair. He was still wearing the skirt but sat like a boy now, his legs spread wide. Out of long habit and because I couldn't help it, I bent to touch his arm.

"*No,*" he said.

I sprang back. "Come with me," I told him sternly. "I'm not asking. I'm *telling* you to come."

"Well"—his voice was singsong, mocking—"I'm *telling* you I'm going outside with Tommy."

I looked at Tommy. Tommy looked at Max. I was no longer a

mother talking to her son or even an adult talking to two children. I had forfeited all that, and I didn't care. Divorced? Fine. So what if we were? Along with half the rest of the Western world. Ian could take the kids; he'd do a better job. Go, I thought to Max. Outside with Tommy. As far as you like. Leaving me with . . . what? Not Hal, who was prostrating himself before the BBC, serving tea with milk and making labored, cheery jokes. Not Ian or Adam, who couldn't manage a decent conversation on the phone. Alone. Perhaps it was what I'd wanted all along, had wanted, in a way, for years—the floaty feeling of a wanderer, a nomad, tent on my back, water in my gourd. My body contained inside itself, healthy and durable, all mine.

"Fine. Go outside," I said, and as soon as I spoke, I wished my words back, for the pain on Max's face was pure and raw and I knew then that we'd never quite return from this moment, no matter how hard I tried (as was my job, my choice, my lot and, yes, my love) to patch and mend.

"Wait—" I said.

But I was talking to the air.

FOURTEEN

I went to meet him to tell him I could not. It was morning, finally, after what had felt like an endless night. I had followed Max onto the lawn; he'd run from me; I'd let him go for a while and then found him again outside the hangar with Tommy and Alida, throwing pebbles against the metal walls with a gaiety that let me think, for a moment, that everything was all right, and a violence that told me it was not. Bedtime, I said in my Mother Voice. Dawn coming, getting light. I herded the children back to the lodge, and like docile cows they tromped along, all of them suddenly quiet, Max dressed like a boy again—my boy and yet so clearly not.

When we reached their room, he and Tommy got into bed, and I kissed their brows and left, just as Marnie appeared to say good night. I went downstairs. I sat. In the kitchen, with a full glass of water in my hand. In the living room, among the cameras and black boxes of the BBC. Everyone else was sleeping, and I could hear what Hal must have said: Plenty of extra bedrooms, you've come so far, you're exhausted. Stay. I poked my head inside the phone cubby, went upstairs to check on Max, then came back down again, unable to stay still. As I wandered, I remembered a stray tomcat I'd brought home once as a child, how he'd run about in a nervous frenzy, peeing in the fireplace and potted plants, on the kitchen floor, on rugs, his urine a fecund, spreading pool. He's marking his turf, my mother had said, surprising me with her understanding. To me, though, the cat had looked not dominant, but frantic and unhappy, literally leaking sadness. When my mother threw him out, I cried so hard my throat was sore for days.

Even then, I knew how hard it was to find a home. Now I had one, and I'd scrambled it; or I didn't have one, not really, just a series of habits, of well-worn treads; or I had several homes, *we* had several, this place more Max's than mine, and yet I'd stolen it from him, from my own child, while my other boy was far away, all of us forever leaving except I was the mother, the grown-up, supposed to be the still point, fixed.

I went into the piano room, the screened porch. I was barefoot, still in just shorts and a T-shirt. Even on the porch, the air was humid, close. I walked into the dining room and pressed my fingers to the copper windowsill, leaving silvery-blue smudges. Built on blood, Hal had once said of the lodge. At the time it had sounded hyperbolic, but now I could see it: the miners' dusty feet, their scraped hands and bowed bones, and how easy it must have been, as you sat in this handsome room, in this green wilderness, to keep your thoughts here, on the taste of the wine, the face of the man across from you, the smell of pine and pitch. I rubbed at the copper with the hem of my shirt, then, and dabbed at it with my spit. Still, my fingerprints showed through, evidence of—what? My presence, maybe. My absence. The quiet, unconsidered violence of my acts.

Finally, when even the lodge felt too small to house my thoughts, I went out to the dock and sat with my legs hanging over the water. It was late dawn, the air still and heavy, its sounds muffled as if passing through a scrim of gauze. Then day broke—first slowly, and then with a confidence I had nearly forgotten—the bright, bold sun, the dazzling light. The water was glinting, gorgeous, but in daylight my arms and legs were pasty, and my face, reflected back at me, was pocked with sparkling holes. A motorboat passed by; without thinking, I lifted my arm to wave. Somewhere down the lake, I knew, a teenage girl was getting ready to bare her belly and offer her body to the day. The sun was hot but it could not warm me. For a long time I sat, my mind and body shivering, and then, when finally it was time, I went inside.

No. No longer, I planned to say to him. Too many things gone wrong, too much at stake, how could I not have seen it until now? *Time to go time to go*, I practiced as I walked down the hall, Hal already in my line of vision, waiting for me by the maid's room door. It was eleven o'clock, the hour when, each day now, we'd been meeting. Hal opened the door, and we stepped through. Lock through bolt, then through the second door, and hook through eye.

"I'm not staying," I blurted when we were inside. I meant not staying here, right now, in this room with you, but it sounded larger than that, and I felt a wave of shame. *Not staying*, as if this had been anything other than a tryst for him, and as soon as I left, he'd be on to someone else.

Hal stood by one eave, his back slightly bent under the garret wall. "I figured you'd say that," he said calmly. "You seemed pretty out of sorts."

Suddenly my anger was with us in the room—another figure, a lunging shape.

"*Out of sorts?*" I said. "That's what you have to say?"

"Okay, Anna." He stepped forward as if to touch me, but I moved aside. "Let me rephrase that," he told me. "Upset. Unhappy. Am I wrong?"

"No," I said. "No, you're not wrong. I come in from . . . from being with you, and there's Max telling strangers his parents are divorced. On film, he's saying it. And then you step forward like—like Mr. Hospitality and offer them tea, and I'm thinking, where *am* I? Who is this man, this . . . *cheerleader*? I mean, are you that desperate for publicity? We'd just been together, Max knew we had, he knew something, and you're joking and smiling like you're on top of the world."

"I was," he said softly. "I had been."

"Don't. That's not what I mean. It was a disaster, can't you see that?"

"Was it?" He seemed genuinely confused, and suddenly I was too. "Maybe it was," he said. "I saw—I don't know, I saw a playful, funny kid. I love Max, I just—" He shrugged. "I love him. Yes, he said that thing about divorce, but he was playing. He had them eating out of his hand, he and Lida. I can't help it, Anna, I thought it was funny—the skirt and barrettes and oh-we-have-such-a-hard-life, we-poor-sick-little-urchins, very tragic, very dreadful." He started to move toward me but stopped partway, snorting with laughter. "You have to admit they were *good*, putting on that show."

"It wasn't funny," I said, but soon I was laughing despite

myself. And then we were pressed together, holding each other in the center of the room where the ceiling was at its highest, our legs jammed up against the bed. I leaned against him, laughing so hard that my eyes ran tears—the kind of runaway, gut-twisting mirth that can flip, in an instant, into grief.

"I'm not staying," I repeated when finally our breath had evened out and nothing seemed funny anymore. My hands felt like someone else's, plucking at his shirt, tenting the fabric—so jangled, as if electrical impulses were misfiring in my brain. And then his cheek was on my cheek, his hands on my back, ironing me out until it all seemed smaller, the night I'd come from, the child I'd hurt, the lives I'd disregarded and undone. Maybe I *had* lost my sense of humor, my perspective. A little thing I had one summer. A joke my kid made, one night when he was dressed up as a girl. How I longed, then, to be able to back up and see a map of our lives—a bird's-eye view, the shapes like pastel continents; a time-line view that followed our human tribe, our little clump of people, through days and months and years. The figures on the time line would be rendered with a botanist's detail, in India ink, and when you looked at the whole picture, you'd be able to trace patterns—this gone wrong, this set right—all of it as clear as (dare I say it?) night and day.

"He knows," I said, and then I was crying again, moving away from Hal, sitting on the edge of the bed where we had fucked and fucked, two animals giving in to impulse, pretending knowledge of each other, pretending love.

"I've spent his whole life trying to protect him," I said, "and this was supposed to be his place, not mine, where he could be, you know, safe and happy, and I've taken that from him, so *carelessly*, for my own stupid pleasure, because I was"—I shrugged—"bored and confused."

As soon as I said it, I heard how cruel it was and how, in many ways, untrue. Hal was turned away from me, facing the tinted window.

I stood. "I didn't mean that."

He turned. "Oh no?" he said. "Mr. Hospitality. Glad to have been of service to you in your time of boredom." He made a flicking motion toward the door. "Just go now. Stop discussing it and go."

"No," I said. "Please."

"Then what? What do you want from me? *Good-bye, farewell, auf Wiedersehen, good night?*" He took a bow and let out a choked noise.

"Oh, Hal." I went to him. "I'm sorry, I am. I'm saying things I don't mean. I'm upset—that's no excuse, I know, but I'm so worried about Max, and . . . us, what I should do now, how to go back. I think I need to, but the thought of leaving is—"

"So?" He put his hands on my shoulders. "Come to California. We're all set up for you. You'd like it there. So would Max."

"Are you serious? What about Adam? And . . . and Ian. I mean, it could never—"

"We have hot springs," he interrupted, "and trails and beaches, right outside the city. I'm building a cabin in the mountains—I already have the land. We can eat pomegranates and mangoes. Alida really likes you, you know, more than anyone since Robin."

I tried to find the solid ground beneath his words. To California. A place I'd only visited a few times—first in college and again a few years ago, when my mother had hip surgery and I flew out for a weekend by myself. Before Ian left, Hal had asked me to stay at camp for a few extra weeks, but not once, in all my talks with him, had we broached the possibility of a life beyond camp.

"You don't mean it," I told him. "You love to fantasize, but our lives aren't filled with . . . you know, milk and honey and exotic fruit. They're just our lives."

"I eat pomegranates almost every day," he said. "Fifty cents each, sometimes less. Come with me to the land of cheap exotic fruit."

But then he sighed. Already I could see his enthusiasm waning. I was too difficult, too focused on practicalities. I would be, we would be, a lot of work. Then again, he was hardly offering to yank up his life by the roots and come to me.

"I can't," I said. "Can I? Of course I can't."

In another life, I might have said yes, even with two children, even with a husband. At least for a visit, a trial separation. People reshaped their lives, married and remarried, coupled and uncoupled, all the time. It sounded so easy, in a way. We would wait a little while (all right, four years, it wasn't so long) until Adam was in college. Perhaps he'd go to California. I could picture where we'd live, a gingerbread house built on a steep hill and painted bold colors. A girl and a boy, our children. We'd take them up the coast; they would be strong and barefoot. We'd have plenty of money and spend it freely. I'd start painting again for real, and Hal would like my paintings—for their strangeness, for how far I went with them. I might visit my parents and brother now and then, repair things a little. And eat pomegranates with my new family until our fingertips ran red.

Except for an X, a P. Except for a man, the father of my children. Not until we were apart from Ian had I quite understood how vital he was to Max, or how far he and I had drifted from each other. I *could* leave him. The thought surprised me in its concreteness, though I'd been living it for weeks. I *could* live without him, feeling him grow dimmer, vaguer, wishing him, always, the best, for I would never not love him in some way or find it in myself to think poorly of him. We had been through so much together, Ian and I. We had not been graceful, much of the time—and I less so than he. We had not shouldered each other's burdens enough, or let down our guards, or found, in the rare moments when we focused on each other, the generosity and patience that we hoarded like rare jewels for our boys. Not often, not enough, especially lately.

Still: days, months, years. A handshake in a classroom, a body whose scars and slopes it seemed I'd always known. A voice, its particular timbre, the way he spoke so steadily, rarely faltering, his sentences, when we first met, like stepping-stones to me, and my own a headlong brook. Milkweed and camping and the sense (how innocent it seemed from here, a blind dumb faith) that our life together would unwind easily, an infinite, light-soaked chain.

None of it was his fault. I knew that. But I could leave him.

Hal sat down heavily on the bed. "Once," he said, "my father woke me up in the middle of the night and asked if I wanted to go on a boat. I thought he was drunk—sometimes he drank too much—and I was furious. I mean, we never went on boats, it was a city kid's dream, but for some reason I thought he was taunting me with some warped adult joke I didn't get."

"Was he?"

He shook his head. "I said no, I didn't want to go, and he said, What're you, crazy, I'm offering you this fun thing, you're such a *weird kid*, he got really pissed at me. Years later, after he died, I found a brochure in his desk about some sunrise boat trip, a Statue of Liberty thing. It was probably what he meant, or maybe he was drunk or having a vision—he was verging on insane for a few years." He paused. "If I woke Alida up for an adventure, she'd know I wasn't kidding."

I nodded.

"But not you." His voice was bitter. "You think I'm all talk."

"She's your daughter. I'm—" I shook my head.

"Weird kid, weird kid."

Hal spat the words. I turned away. The expression on his face was too much for me, too private, too frightening. I didn't, when it came right down to it, want to see. I looked at my watch. "We need to go."

"Has the world turned you this tough?" he asked. "Or were you always this way?"

"They'll be waking up."

I stared at the wall across from me, the trophy list of animals tacked up by their hunter, who was probably dead by now himself. *15 deer, 9 pheasants, 23 ducks.* I sat back down.

"I wasn't always this tough," I said under my breath.

"I know," he said.

We made love. For the last time, I kept telling myself, mostly believing it was true. We didn't speak or even take off all our clothes. We didn't use a condom or look at our watches or ask each other how it felt. We pressed into each other—our hands, his penis, my pelvic bone, our teeth, which felt suddenly like the bones they really were, elemental, lasting past the rest of us, and clicking, now, against each other as we kissed.

And then I got up, got dressed and left, my legs shaky, his sperm still inside me and damp on the inside of my thigh. To check on my boy, a mother's ritual. One time, two times, sometimes three or four. Is he breathing, is he covered, is he waking, is he there? Which he always was, always had been, until now. No joke, this. No children's costume drama. I was right. Outside, the sun was bright, the kind of weather the forecasters call a beach day. High August, high noon. Inside, Tommy slept with his head buried in his pillow, but Max's bed was empty, he was gone.

FIFTEEN

High and low, I looked: *Max* in the bathroom, *Max Max* in the kitchen, piano room, front hall. At first I tried to tell myself that my worry was for nothing; he must have gotten up early, headed down for breakfast, gone somewhere with Alida. Max? I called, my voice a question mark, my footsteps steady, but he wasn't there and he wasn't there, and as I kept not finding him, the house started to seem bigger, flimsier than before, a Jell-O sculpture wobbling in the heat. If it weren't for my fear, like paste on my tongue, it might have been a game we were playing, Hide and Seek, or Capture the Flag, or Sardines. Under the bed, in the closet, on the attic stairs, until finally, got you, found you, olly olly in-come-free, you're It!

Around the next corner. No. And the next. Not in the living room. Not in the kitchen. Not in the laundry room, where the washing machine shuddered, unbalanced, and started to bang. I did not stop to fix it. I turned away. Was he there, by the window? Or there, behind the dryer—imp, you ran away from me, where have you been, *come here*, for suddenly my need was enormous, impossible, and all for my boy. Not in the doorway. Not behind the dryer. I steadied myself on a chair. You lost him, I told myself. Can't find him. Because you stayed too long.

The longer I looked, the less I felt able to negotiate the furniture, the maze of house, the people I kept passing, everyone starting to get up now, holding towels, contact lens solution, a bristled brush. Have you seen—? No. Selfish. Careless. Bad. We haven't seen. And suddenly I could see it, the bird's-eye view, the time-line view. One little mother, one little boy, if only I could know for sure that I would die before him, after he was full-grown, one small light extinguished, no big deal, the natural order of things. If only I could know. *Ma-a-a-x*, I was calling in the basement with its chalky pillars and cement floor, Max by the stern gray fuse box, Max under the stairs, crouched like a wild child, his eyes full of injury and heat. I'm sorry, love. I scared you, wronged you, lost you.

Not there. Not anywhere. Which left outside.

I went up to the dining room. By then Marnie was there, eating eggs. And Tommy, Anil, Alida, Hal, nearly everyone but Max. Plus strangers. The ABC, the BBC. I stopped on the threshold. "Have you—has anyone seen Max?"

No, no, they shook their heads.

"I can't find him. He must have gone outside. I need to—"

I watched as Hal took a sip of juice.

"He wouldn't go outside," Marnie said. "He knows better."

"He's not here. I've looked, I've been everywhere, and he's not—"

"Anna," Marnie said. "Don't panic. He's a smart kid. He's never gone outside like that before, right? You must have missed him."

"Did you see him leave your room?" I asked Tommy. "Did he tell you where he was going?"

No, no.

"Has anybody seen him?" I turned to the strangers again.

Nobody has the answer. Nobody can figure it out except you. Up to you, up to you, but I was paralyzed, incapable (I am four years old, I am seven, the choices at once insignificant and huge: this girl or that to my birthday party, these shoes or those; or I'd have lost something—my favorite feather, my piggy bank—and beg my mother to find it, convinced she had the power to lift up the rug or reach into a vase, restoring order to my world).

Marnie stood. "I'll go look upstairs."

"Thank you," I said. "I'll—I'll try outside."

I started to walk away, and as I did, my mind returned to me in its entirety, stocked with all its hard, cold facts. Everything felt clear now, clearer than usual. Even the shapes in the room had a cartoonlike quality, as if they were not so much themselves as what they stood for. Table. Wall. Reporter. Mother. That was me. At times I had tried to convince myself that it was a costume I could take on and off at will, but I saw now that it had entered me, become me, at some point when I was only half paying attention. I turned back.

"I need your help," I said to Hal.

He looked at the others, his gaze making a swift circuit. I may as well have announced our morning coupling; my words came out that close, that slick with need. Marnie looked down. Anil looked down. The BBC reporter studied her nails.

"I—" Hal shrugged helplessly. "I'm sure he's fine, Anna. He's not a baby."

"He's *missing*."

"Just because you haven't seen him doesn't mean—"

"I searched all over the house."

As the words left my mouth, I understood: He wanted to be there for the BBC. He wanted to make it onto the show (brave man, widower, he lost his wife, he founded a camp for sick children). He was wearing a white button-down shirt with the sleeves rolled up, and khaki shorts, and buttery leather sandals I'd never seen before. He had showered and shaved since I'd last seen him. He was fine-featured, articulate. He loved an audience and would do well on film. I had a flash of Ian, how he would already be outside, opening doors, combing the grounds. Calling. As I turned again to go, I felt a hand on my back.

"I'll meet you outside," Hal said, and as he spoke, everything realigned again, and I let myself lean toward him.

"Thank you," I said.

"I'll get Lida her pills," Hal added, "and then I'll come."

A child gets lost. It isn't a girl and it isn't a boy, just a child, a baby, before gender even was, way back in the womb, that small, that absolutely significant. A child gets lost and so do you. Mother. The second skin. It floats away and what's left? Webwork, only. Frail, branching filaments of vein.

Like that, I went outside and felt the sun as if for the first time—not on my skin but inside me, the heat entering the dark dots of my cells, the eye of the nucleus, and it burned. This is what Max feels, I thought as I parted bushes and peered under the porch and felt a spider mincing over the stone of my elbow with its skinny, jointed limbs.

Hal joined me, our voices traveling out into the heat, but he was not fully beside me, even though he was. I saw how he looked in a desultory way, his eyes flickering toward the lodge where the cameras waited, along with his own flesh and blood. I missed Ian then with a stab. I thought of calling him—"It's me. Max is missing"—and the pause on the other end of the line, a pause brief but dense in which small things swam packed together: bitch, you are not, I am not, I am, mother, help me, no.

We went down to the lake. I had brought an oversized towel to shield Max, and Hal took it from me and draped it around his neck. The sun was high in the sky, the strip of beach a brilliant white. Far out, a sail like a child's triangle walked on the water. Closer to shore, there was not a ripple, the liquid glassy and still, more like wax than water, and when I touched it with my finger, I was surprised to find how thick and warm it was, how *wrong*.

And that was when I saw it, a bubble, a little ring of bubbles rising up a few feet from us, but far enough, in the deep part, over his head, you're in over your head.

"Hal," I said. I whispered it. I poked his arm. We were standing close together, too close, if anyone was watching. "What's that?"

He looked. "Nothing. You're panicking, because"—he sighed—"for various reasons. You feel guilty about where you were."

I hit him, then, on the chest, not hard but suddenly, a flailing out. I didn't mean to, my hand just swung out—a thump, an empty sound—and with it, days, months, years of anger, only a fraction of it actually aimed at him. It was the first time in my memory that I'd hit someone, and as I made contact, I felt so exhilarated, so *distracted* by my own action, that I thought I just might do it again.

Hal caught my hand in his fist and gave it back to me. "For Christ's sake, Anna. What did I do to deserve that?"

I couldn't answer. My hand, as I lowered it, was a knuckled ball of shame. I pointed toward the water. It wasn't Max, of course not, but then why were the bubbles still rising, why had he never learned to swim, not well, no more than a sloppy dog paddle and thrashing crawl, arms churning, chin held high?

I started into the water, my sneakers still on, but before I could get there Hal had kicked off his sandals, taken off his shirt, and plowed into the lake, leaving the towel on the shore. He bent over, scanning with his hands. Then he swam deeper, went under, and came up, finally, holding a hunk of snarled grass like something scalped and fresh. He dropped the weeds into the water and waded back out, and for an instant, as I stood ankle deep in the lake, I wanted to stop everything and just touch him, for his chest was bare, his eyes hurt, and wary now, as if he no longer knew who I was.

I went toward him, my sneakers sopping, and wrapped the towel around his shoulders. "You think I'm crazy, don't you?"

He shook his head, water spraying. "I think he fell asleep inside someplace. But no, I get it. If it were Alida—"

He hesitated, and I saw that he was worried now, too, and my own fear rose.

"We'll find him." He reached for his shirt, turned away from the lake. "We'll just keep looking until we do."

He cupped his hands to his mouth, as he had on the night we

first met. "*Ma-a-a-x?*" he called now, we called together, walking the shoreline to where the woods met the water, parting branches—*Max, Max*—the name a plea aimed east and west, north and south, but no.

"Maybe we should split up," Hal said when we came to a clump of cat briar too thorny to pass through. "It'd be more efficient."

"I can't."

I knew it was the wrong answer, for Max, for everyone, but I felt too slim, too slivered, to make my way alone. Tell me he's fine again, I wanted to say. Tell me I'm crazy, guilt-ridden, whatever, I don't care. Say he's inside, sleeping like a baby. Hal squeezed my hand. Like a friend, he squeezed it, or a husband, and his hand was damp and firm and kind.

"We'll stick together, then," he said.

I hit Hal and he didn't deserve it. He stayed with me, looking in the brittle August grass and along the flagstone path and behind the crafts shed where the earth was cool. After a while, he went inside to call Jess and Amy and ask if they could come watch the kids, and when they arrived, Marnie joined us, and then the reporters, and finally, after I called 911, two policemen from the station twenty minutes from us, more boys than men, really, their faces young and scrubbed, though they both wore wedding bands.

A sick child. Missing. Maybe upset. Yes, there'd been an argument. Sort of. Not exactly. Hard to explain and we don't have time. I stumbled as they asked me. They stood by the couch in the lodge's living room and wrote things down, and I pictured gates clanging shut, a gavel smacking wood. They had arrived with a search dog, who sniffed at Max's sweatshirt and flip-flops while I instructed myself to breathe. Then they divided us up, spread us out over the property, Max's name everywhere now, buzzing, crossing as the dog ran nose to ground. No one was behaving, anymore, as if my child were in the house. No one was telling me to calm down. At one point, as I walked across the lawn, I ran into the BBC cameraman with his camera on his shoulder. "Put that away," I told him, my voice surprising me with its authority. He looked down at me, a tall man with broad shoulders and a ruddy oblong of a face. *All's fair in love and war*, his expression seemed to say. I looked back, unwavering, until he lowered the camera and turned it off, and then I continued on.

By the hangar, by the garden, along the road. Back in the house again, in the shed next to the stone cottage, in the cottage itself. As the hours went by and still we didn't find him, a strange thing happened to me. I could feel time slipping away. I mean that literally. I never knew what that phrase described, but now I do. Time is a lot of beads on an oiled string, and each bead just slips and falls, rolling across the floor; you can hear it—there goes a moment, there goes another moment. You can hear it and see it and there's nothing you can do. The necklace is endless until it ends, and then a life is gone.

I saw all that. I saw my life, exactly what it had been and what it would be. The cliché of it, and then the tragedy rushing to crescendo. I was watching the lurid drama and critically appraising it, both—a movie review, the BBC, let's get it on camera, let's add it to our film. I saw that I was a bored, unfulfilled housewife who'd fucked a quirky ex-hippie and, as punishment—how symmetrical, how tacky—sacrificed her kid. And at the same time, a second story: a room within a room, two people touching. And a third story, even harder to translate, simply this: I missed my child. I missed his father, who was my child, half his DNA coiled in every one of Max's genes. I went back inside. In the sudden darkness, I could hardly see, but I knew the way to the phone by heart. At first I couldn't remember my own number, but then my fingers—my faithful, faithless body—found it, and I called.

Lost him. I have lost. Something like this, I said to Ian. Can't find him, looked and looked. He answered the phone on the fourth ring. It's me, I said, and when he didn't answer, It's Anna, and when he said, I know, I said I have to tell you something, I have to . . . Max is missing, I can't find him, we've looked everywhere, we've been looking all afternoon. . . .

He let me go on for some time. About the cops and search dog, the house, the grounds, the lake. He let me start crying, bent over the phone, holding the receiver as if it were—black plastic stump—the last thing left in the world. He let me go on and on. I have done things that Ian may never forgive me for; I will never forgive him for this. Finally, I stopped for breath.

"He's here," Ian said flatly into the silence.

"What?" I pressed the phone to my ear. "What did you just say?"

"He's here." Now he sounded casual, almost flippant, with just a trace of triumph in his voice.

"There, with you? That's impossible, how could he be—"

"He called and asked me to come get him, so I did. I've got to go; the kids are hungry."

For an instant, my relief. I sat down on the bench, my ankles buckling. "He's home? He's not outside? Oh my god. Is he okay?"

"No broken bones. I'm hanging up now. The grilled cheese is burning."

"Wait, Ian. I need—I'd like to talk to him."

A mistake, of course. I'd like to talk to you, I should have said. Or I'm sorry. Or I know we have a lot to discuss. Or even, why didn't you tell me right away? But I hadn't stopped looking yet, not fully. I would never stop looking again. I was still parting leaves, calling Max's name, thinking *around this corner, around this corner*, as the dog smelled dirt and grass and rock and piss and shit and even blood, but not the particular nameless, necessary scent that was my child.

"We're about to eat," said Ian, and then, in a lower voice, "He doesn't want to talk to you. I'm hanging up."

"Please," I said. "Don't—"

A silence followed by a dial tone, and then another silence and a ringing inside the phone; for a second, I thought somehow I'd called them back. Then I heard the crackle of static, followed by a woman's voice, nasal and familiar: *If you'd like to make a call, please hang up*. Those words had never made much sense to me, and they made even less sense now. Still I sat there, listening as the woman repeated herself, and the static scraped, and she repeated herself again, as if with enough repetition, she might eventually be understood. Finally, I hung up the phone and left the cubby. From upstairs, I could hear Jess reading a story to the kids. A clarion call, I would need to sound now. He's all right, he's home with his father, stop looking, he's okay! I tried out a smile. I'm going now, I would have to say. Of course I was. Home. If they would have me. Not a choice, exactly. An exigency. A shamed return, my tail between my legs.

As I walked by the dining room, I saw the megaphone that

Hal used to call the kids in from outside. I took it out to the front steps. It was late afternoon, the heat softer now, the light less shearing. I raised the megaphone to my mouth, and for a brief moment, it was joy I felt, my lips in the space that had held his lips, my voice the bearer of good news.

SIXTEEN

And so the woman packs her bags and slips away. The road is curved but her thoughts are straight—unwinding, lengthening, pulling her along as afternoon becomes evening and evening night, and still she drives, both hands on the wheel, the headlights peeling back the dark until finally she reaches her town where the turns are deeply familiar—left by the Mobil station, right on Sycamore, left on Acorn—and there it is, just as she left it, the place where she has made her life. If this were another house, she could look in a window and see them eating a late supper, their three heads, a hand lifting a fork, a nod. But this place is sealed—an unbroken egg, film inside a camera, spooled tight. She turns off the engine. Her own breath is loud. She will enter the privacy of it all; she will shut the door behind her. For a moment, as they look up and see her, things might go any way at all. Then, abruptly, she will find her place—the chair by the stove, the left side of the couch, the right side of the bed. She will find her bureau with its socks, shirts and underwear, her basket of earrings, row of shoes. She will find her boys and draw them to her. Find their father. Once upon a time, she married him. They will make room for her again, instinctively, and because they cannot imagine another way, and because amid the barbs and wires, sticks and stones, there is, between them all, a pulsing love. She will enter their privacy—the gift of it, the airlessness. Like a scar healing or water closing up around a skipping stone, the house will seal itself again.

Or the road takes her elsewhere, west or south or north. She travels mapless, alone, going nowhere in particular, just someplace new, and she might be twenty again, she might be twenty-two, sitting on a bar stool listening to the rise and fall of another language or riding a train to a place she's never heard of, her body young, the eggs that will make her babies still tucked inside her, and each night she cleans her paintbrushes as carefully as a mother cat cleans her kittens, until they are smooth and glossy, pale points. Or she is older now, traveling with another. Let me show you, this and this and this. He cares about the earth, its damages and beauties. The earth swings wide for him, an open door. They take food into their bodies, and wine, and each other, and always, as they leave one place and go to the next, they carry the shared knowledge that they are losing something; at every moment they are losing it, as skin sheds and cells sluice off and her eggs—what's left of them—drop down, drop out. They might whittle down to nothing, a feather, a tumbleweed, legs wrapped around hips, pure thrust. Except there, in the backseat, a child, and another, and a third. It's crowded, too many feet and elbows. The children are tired and hungry. The girl misses her mother, the boys their father. When will we be there? Soon. When? Try to sleep, it'll go faster. And their rage, a jab against the seat, a kick. They have not asked for this. Now are we almost there? I told you, soon.

That evening, after everyone came back inside and the police drove away with their dog, I went upstairs. Slowly, I packed, methodically, folding and stacking clean clothes, filling a garbage bag with dirty laundry. I snapped shut the box that held my drawing pencils, put my sketch pads in their carrying bag, tied twine around some canvases and stacked others in a corner to throw away. When I had piled everything in the hall, I stripped the bed, dusted the furniture with my dirty pillowcase and shut the closet door.

Then to Max's room. It was dark by then. Max's duffel bag was still in the closet; his dresser drawers—the top three—were full. One by one, I emptied them. I packed the sweatshirt we'd gotten him on our Maine vacation, his Camp Luna shirts, his jeans, passed down from Adam, the knees patched with red bandannas. I packed his windbreaker and shorts, his ski masks, gloves and wraparound sunglasses, his sneakers and flip-flops but not his sandals; he must have worn them home. He was home, he was all right. Not in the sun, his fingers splayed to shield his eyes, not in the woods, searching for shade. His possessions, like this information, soothed me. Don't forget Who, I reminded myself at one point, part of my every packing routine. I looked under the pillow, under the bed again, beneath the chair, in a pile of Tommy's dirty clothes. No owl. But of course—they'd taken him. Where had Ian met Max? How had no one seen them leave? They must, I told myself, have snuck out somehow, a clean escape. For a moment, I caved in at the thought of it all. Then I was back up again, stripping Max's bed, removing our traces like a good houseguest. When I knelt to check for things under the bed, I found a baseball cap, socks, a feather, two identical Pokémon cards and half a bagel. I left a Pokémon card under Tommy's pillow and threw out the bagel. The feather, cap, socks and other card, I took.

And went down, lugging one load, then a second and third, depositing it all in the front hall. The lodge was empty again, even the cameras and tripods gone from the living room, though their cases remained. When everything was downstairs, I went outside. I could go get the car and take my leave quietly—the most graceful and perhaps least painful way to go. Or I could find them, one more time. Say good-bye. Not just to Hal but to the rest of them.

Everyone was at the trampoline; I could see them from the bottom step. The BBC was there, setting up lights and cameras while Tommy jumped and Alida asked to join him from the ground. I started toward them. Hal was talking to Imogen, the reporter, his back to me. He will sleep with her, I thought again with chilly certainty as I approached, and just as I finished thinking it, he touched her arm to emphasize a point. "Whatever," she said, laughing, in her British accent. "You know them better than we do," she said. She was young and beautiful and had long ringless fingers, and Hal—Hal was what? Beautiful too, in his way. A man who loved women, who drew people toward him like moths toward a length of lit cloth. They would drink wine and stay up talking about XP and then start touching, because he was missing me, but also because she moved like a dancer and loved children and had come from far away to tell the world about our disease. And he was free, betraying nobody, not with me going back home the way I was. Still, for a moment I felt a jealousy so fierce it was almost cleansing.

I went to Marnie first. "I'm going," I whispered. "I wanted to say good-bye."

She turned, her face stark in the sharp lights, and drew me into a hug. "Call soon," she said. "Okay?"

I nodded and handed her a rolled-up drawing of Tommy and Max playing chess on the porch.

"What's this?" she asked.

"For you to open later."

I said good-bye to the others quickly, promised I'd write and call. Alida wrapped her arms around my waist when I bent to hug her.

"Why are you going?" she asked. "Where's Max?"

I brushed her hair off her face. "At home."

"But he never said 'bye to me."

"Because"—I spoke for Max though I had no right to, and my words were lies—"he knows he'll see you soon."

I turned, then, away from the trampoline, away from Hal. There was a period in my childhood when I didn't like to say good-bye on the phone, found it too wrenching, the end of the call, the silence after it. My best friend at the time and I had a system—ask what the other one would wear the next day to school and when the answer came, state your own outfit and hang up. Blue-jean skirt and fisherman's sweater. Leotard with cords. Nothing, I'll wear nothing, dressed only in your body, the way we hid together, lay together, and now I could not turn or look or say good-bye. I went up the hill, past the lodge, down the road that led to the field where the van was parked. Enough. I would drive back to the lodge, load our stuff and go.

It was only when I was halfway to the field that I realized that Ian must have taken the van, for his own car did not have tinted windows and couldn't carry Max. For a moment, I felt relieved:

I was stuck, I couldn't leave. Still, I walked on, and when I got to the field, I saw his rusty Subaru, its metallic blue visible in the moonlight. I opened the door. The car smelled like Ian and like Adam, soccer balls, cleats and uniforms covering the backseat, and I reached for one of Adam's jerseys and pressed it to my nose—my older boy's sour sweetness, his grassy, fervent sweat. The keys were not in the ignition, or on the dashboard, or on the floor by the pedals. I went around to the other side and opened the glove compartment. There were maps in there, and sunglasses, and a half-eaten Slim Jim. There was a red flashlight I'd given Ian for Hanukkah the year before. I turned it on. It worked. Awkwardly, folding myself small, I shone it under the front and back seats on the passenger side, then got out to search the other side.

Which is how Hal found me, doubled over, looking. He touched my back and I got out, and then he knelt with me and helped me search. It was he who finally found the keys, in the grass a few feet from the car. Ian must have dropped them or tossed them, lost them or intentionally made them difficult, but not impossible, to find. I set the key ring on the seat.

"Can I write you?" Hal asked. We were standing a few feet apart, our hands dangling at our sides.

"No," I said. "I don't know—I have to see where things are. It might be too hard. For you too, don't you think?"

He shook his head. "I only want the best for you, for all of us, but I'd like to be somewhere in your life."

"What does that mean?"

"Not much, maybe. But a little something. Somewhere."

"I'm not so good at a little something with you." I reached across to touch his cheek, his lips.

"Anna." He returned my hand to me.

I nodded, though I was stung.

"You know you're always welcome here," said Hal. "And so is Max, with or without his parents. This"—he waved at it all—"was supposed to be for him, and now I've gone and wrecked it."

"You didn't wreck it. I did. I'm his mother." The words sounded oddly reassuring to me, so set, so sure.

"In another world," Hal said, "we might have grown old together."

"You don't mean that," I said.

"I do and I don't."

"Precisely," I said sharply, and in my mind, a wrecking ball—the smooth, clean arc of it, the smash. Get over it. Let him, make him, let him go. My words came fast, then. "Who else will be there, in this other world? Imogen? I saw how you were touching her—it's hardly subtle. You might at least have waited until I was gone."

"What? What are you talking about?"

"Don't tell me you're not attracted to her. Anyway, I'm not the first person you've had a thing with here, that's pretty clear."

He stepped away, his face blurry now in the dark. "Oh?" he said. "Oh, really? You mean you've figured out that I'm not a virgin, that I've had other lovers—besides Robin, I mean—and right here at the *lodge*? My god, I should have told you! How unfair of me. I take it you disapprove?"

I knew I wasn't being logical, but I couldn't stop. "It just makes me question your intentions," I said, "and your . . . your grand proclamations. You talk so easily, you have so many plans, and when I leave you'll just pick up right where you left off, cast your eye around—"

He laughed. "And if I do? Good for me, good for fucking me. In case you didn't notice, I'm a single man, a *widower*, as my great-aunt Lily likes to say. Look in the mirror, Anna, if you want to question somebody's intentions." He stepped closer, and for a second I thought he might be about to hit me. Then he shook his head, and I felt the wash of his disappointment. "Clearly," he said, "you care a lot about my happiness."

"I do care. That's not what I meant."

"So what did you mean? That your little fantasy of me is broken? You want me to sit around, before I even knew you, and pine for you, poor Anna with her two great kids and nice husband, I think I'll just save myself for her, maybe she'll give me an hour or two because she's *bored and confused*, how generous of her, I'll just wait, it'll be worth it."

I shook my head. "You're twisting things."

"I'm quoting you."

"I know I've said some stupid things. I—" I searched for words. "This . . . it was about you, for me. Specifically. It's never happened with anyone else."

"Oh, and you could have been anybody."

"That's not what I'm saying."

"You're saying nothing," he said. "You're saying bullshit. You're the one with a screwed-up marriage who was acting out god-knows-what with me. Now I know what Ian has to deal with."

We had entered a thicket, though we stood there in the open field. It was an intimate place, and terribly lonely. I had been there before with Ian and found my worst self, his worst self. I would go there again, I realized, with any lover; give me enough time and I'd go. Now that he was no longer speaking, Hal looked not so much angry as defeated, caved in. I touched his arm. He let me. For a long moment we stood like that, my hand unmoving on his arm.

"This isn't how I want to leave," I said finally.

He shook his head.

"Can we erase this conversation?" I asked.

He shrugged but placed his free hand over mine. "We can try."

"Will you be all right?"

He nodded.

"Can I—" I stepped forward, and he pulled me toward him, and we held each other, swaying. This, the smell of him, this, the taste. I pressed my mouth to his neck. How many cells would rub off there, between the two of us? Would it be weeks or days, hours or mere minutes before we shed all traces of each other? I would be smaller, then, invisibly reduced.

"I still have to pick up my things at the lodge," I said when finally we broke apart.

"I'll help you."

"No, no. Stay here while I go. Just"—I looked at him—"like this."

And so he stood as I got in the car and drove away.

Our street, when I got home, was dark. Our house was dark, like all the others. The porch steps seemed tiny, shrunken. I unlocked the little red door with Ian's key. Inside, I went upstairs, stood by Max's bed and watched him, stood by Adam's bed and watched him, willing myself not to touch them, for if they woke, we'd have to talk. Max was buried underneath his covers. Adam looked even taller than before, his hair shaggy, books and magazines piled at the foot of his bed. I cleared a space and sat down. He was breathing steadily, peacefully, his mouth slightly open, and for a while I just sat there near him.

Then to the room that Ian and I had shared for thirteen

years. Ian, too, was asleep. How well their bodies guarded them, giving them respite, the sleep of the innocent, *Sleep, my love, and peace attend thee, all through the night.* I had sung it to my boys, just as my father, in a rich singing voice he rarely used except when he thought he was alone, had sung it once or twice to me, so that when I came across the song again as an adult, I thought, learn it, keep it, and I did. Ian was facing the wall, one arm crooked over his cheek. I sat on the bed and then slowly, carefully, lay down on top of the quilt, keeping my limbs to myself.

In the morning, when the boys were still sleeping and the sky was getting light, Ian and I would have to wake, to talk. I want you to leave, he'd say after he turned and saw me, and I'd say no. Leave, he'd say again, louder this time, his knuckles knobs, his face so familiar yet deeply unknown to me, a plate broken and mended, the lines askew where the pattern was supposed to meet. Fine, he'd say, stay then, I don't care what you do, just leave me alone, don't talk to me. And I'd say no, I'm leaving and taking the kids, you let me think he was missing, he might have been dead. You can't, I can, you can't. Listen, I need to explain, Hal, don't tell, not enough, too late, sorry, stop saying that, I am, am not, nothing to say, never listen, never have, selfish, sorry, oh you really *sound* sorry, you didn't tell me, *I* didn't tell *you*, lied, never would have thought, talk quietly, they'll hear, just stop, no you no you no you. And again: Leave, Anna, I mean it, I can't be with you right now. Meaning what? Meaning—are you deaf, woman? are you crazy? get out of here. Go. Leave.

All of this would happen. All of it did. But for a moment, lying there, I could pretend it was just an ordinary night, we were just an ordinary couple sleeping in our bed while our children slept down the hall and our gerbil—the only truly nocturnal one among us—ran his wheel. The sleep of the innocent. It was not mine to have, but still it found me. I slept for hours next to Ian before he realized I was there. He did not wake; I do not think he did. He was used to me, after all—my smells, my breath, the space I occupied in bed. We were used to each other. There were few gifts during this time. Max not being lost was one of them, this brief, shared sleep another. A lull, a lullaby. Then daybreak with its shattering light.

SEVENTEEN

To wake alone is the strangest thing, even stranger than waking to sunlight and shadows on the wall. It has been almost three weeks now that I've slept here, and still, before I even open my eyes, my mind starts reaching down the hall, and then, when it finds nobody, moving down one street after another, navigating the distance—eight blocks in all—between Carly's apartment and my house. I get up early if I sleep at all and wash myself in Carly's shower while she showers at her lover's, an older man she met when he took her painting class; he has a farmhouse, three grown children, three young dogs. I won't go so far, she said to me the other day, trying not to smile, as if to say I'm in love.

I make tea in her teapot, sit at her table. Sip. Then I walk—out into the morning, past children waiting for the bus and parents dressed for work, past the post office and dry cleaner, around the corner to the bakery café. Four of those, please.

Croissants the first day, sticky buns the next. I do not hesitate. I choose. Inside the bakery, the people drinking coffee and reading the paper look terribly composed, all of a piece, as if they know exactly who they are. Outside, the leaves are starting to turn, falling waxy and yellow at my feet.

I arrive at the house at seven forty-five, to have fifteen minutes with Adam before he goes to school. I ring the warning bell, let myself in, shut the front door, open the door to the kitchen. "Hi," I say cheerfully—each day the word shreds the air—and the boys mumble something, and Ian nods vaguely in my direction. I pull a chair out next to Adam. Do you have your biology test today, I ask. Are you ready? I take four lemon scones, still warm, from a paper bag. We need a plate for them, but opening a cupboard in front of Ian feels daunting, so I flatten the bag and place the scones on top. Adam reaches for one. Max reaches. I take the third. Time to go, says Ian, though it is not.

After they leave, Max and I share Ian's scone, dry crumble mixing, in my mouth, with gulped-back tears. Let's go read, I say to him—all we can manage for school right now. We go upstairs. Max reads out loud to me from *Stuart Little*, his head bent over the book, his voice my steady pleasure.

"'So Stuart and Margalo told all about the ocean, and the gray waves curling with white crests, and the gulls in the sky, and the channel buoys and the ships and the tugs and the wind making a sound in your ears. Mr. Little sighed and said some day he hoped to get away from business long enough to see all those fine things.'"

At her new lover's house, Carly is getting into her car to drive to the apartment I've just left, uncover her palette and begin her morning's work. In San Francisco, Hal and Alida are sleeping, or listening to music, or . . . what? I know so little. They are home now, and while I could picture them at the lodge—he's waking, she's eating, he's trying to braid her hair—I cannot picture them in California, and this bores a hole in my thoughts, a cavity scraped out but not yet filled.

And Ian. And Adam. They are also far from me, though only blocks away. Some nights, now, when Ian is home with Max, I take Adam out to dinner or to a movie, or once, to Carly's apartment, where he stood for a long time before her canvases—a brick wall half in shadow, a series of nude self-portraits, her breasts long, her belly flat. He says little on our outings, and I talk too much about nothing, but twice he has stood near me in a way that's let me know I'm allowed to touch him.

Days are mine with Max, at home, like before, except our cycle is reversed now; we've joined the rest of the world. It's temporary. I tell myself that every day. A temporary reversal, a temporary stay in Carly's apartment, a few weeks for Ian and me to find our balance, if we can. Then Carly will tire of lending me her place; I'll come home, though I can't picture much beyond this—how the past will fit inside the present, how we'll live. Still, sometimes, when I'm with Max, the sun blocked out, our hours long and full of stories, food, more stories, I can almost forget where we've been and what I've done. I'm a mother here, his mother. I know how to feed him. I am patient with explaining. I laugh at his jokes, which I find truly funny. I never get over his body—how strong it is and yet how fragile, how it issued from my own. And he is Max, still, though more aloof. He is Max reading aloud in a clear, high voice, squirming away from me as I check his skin, resting a hand absently on my elbow as I sit beside him on the couch. That he could be so forgiving, so elastic, both moves and reproaches me. Yet he also fled from me that day at camp, and it will be a long time, if ever, until I know what he is really thinking.

Sometimes, small hard clues. He doesn't talk about camp, hardly at all, and then only of his friends there, never of Hal. One day he handed me a sealed envelope and asked me to send it to Tommy. Another day he asked for Alida's e-mail address. Last year, his windowsills were lined with bits and pieces of camp—acorns, pennants, photographs. This year, nothing. I've stolen it all from him, though his souvenirs sit in a box inside his closet. I've stolen it, but he has to forgive me because I'm his mother, and he's sick, and he needs me too much to risk crushing me with his anger—this perhaps the saddest thing of all.

It's only for a little while, I tell him and Adam each night when I go to Carly's. Every time I leave, I want to invite them to come along; we could get Max home in the early morning, before sunrise, when it's still safe. We could sleep, all three of us, in Carly's king-sized bed, and play with her potter's wheel, and watch TV. But I do not, cannot. I'm on probation. Why are you leaving, Max asked, just once, as I was going out the door. Daddy and I need to work a few things out, I told him. Like get divorced, he said. No, sweetie, no. Ian was standing there too. I looked over at him. *Ask me to stay*, I thought, but he would not.

And then alone at night at Carly's place. I enjoy it there. Should this trouble me? I long for where I'm not—at home with my family, or with Hal, but still, I like it there. I do. I enjoy how one room is a bedroom, the other a studio with a trim galley kitchen; how there are just enough plates, cups and spoons for yourself and a friend, but the bed is big enough to swim in and the TV has a wide screen and a cable box on top. Each night I check to see what Carly has done that day on her painting, and though sometimes her progress is invisible, I have a funny feeling of accomplishment, even of pride, as slowly the colors deepen, the picture grows more complex. I enjoy the smell of paints, the orchids, ivies and ferns, and how, when, unable to resist, you slide open the night-table drawer, you find a nail clipper, a small white vibrator, a black-and-white photo of a lanky girl who must be Carly, sitting with a large cat on a step.

I had been at Carly's for three nights before I logged on to her computer and found Hal. Just to see how you are, I wrote in the first e-mail, knowing it was a mistake. His response came an hour later; he was still at camp, then. Missing you, worrying, missing you. We went back and forth five times that night. Need to stop, need to stop. Now he is in California, and we're down to one exchange a night, sometimes e-mails and twice, when he set them up, live chats, the messages bodiless but full of our bodies, the smell, the taste of you. Could I have this, I wonder. Might I not keep just this, a handful of words on a screen? Over, I write. Over, it must be. I know, he writes. But friends? I think I still love him, I write, meaning Ian, though I might just as well mean Hal. I still care about his happiness and want to find him again in some way, if that's possible. Do you think it is, he asks. Maybe. I don't know. He's furious, and so shut inside himself, which was always part of the problem. Are you talking? Trying, but talking to you is much easier. But you haven't lived with me; we have no history; believe me, I'm no picnic. To me you're a picnic, exactly that, with pomegranates and Jerusalem artichokes. No, Anna, really, I'm not. Me either. But who is, he writes, in the end? I want to be home again, with my kids, I write. I feel like someone else here, and it's not a bad someone, it's a person I might have been, but my life went another way and I need to be back there now, don't I, do I, do you think I do? And then his blessing, at once generous and rejecting: Go, Anna—it's what you want. If he'll have me. He'll have you. And we'll need to stop this, even these messages. Silence on his end, then, until I write again. Are you there, Hal? Yes, he writes. Just that.

Several times, now, Ian and I have gone on walks in the late afternoon. We leave Max—how extraordinary—with Adam. We go around the reservoir or walk the trails in the woods behind the library. These meetings feel oddly like blind dates; I'm nervous before them, nervous during them. He asks me questions. I try to answer. He tells me things I don't want to know—how four years ago, he fooled around with his friend Iris, just once, when they were at a conference. It might have gone further, there's always been a strong attraction, but he wouldn't (better person, pious person) do that to me or to the kids. He told me yesterday that I wasn't the only one to have given things up, to feel hemmed in, compromised. We were standing in the woods at the intersection of two trails. On one tree, a smudged red spot. On another, a blue.

"I know that," I said.

"Well, you don't act like it."

"I do know. You gave up getting a PhD and . . . camping and traveling—"

He stiffened. "I knew you'd say something like that. That's not the main thing."

"All right, then, help me." My irritation crept into my voice. "What have you given up?"

When he answered, I could hardly hear him. "Not being scared all the time."

"Scared that . . ." I echoed, out of some long-standing habit of speech, though I knew precisely what he meant.

"That he'll die." His face twisted. "You want to me say it,

don't you? You have some sick need to make me say it. That Max will be dead. That he'll kick the bucket. Throw in the towel. Die. Are you happy now?"

Happy, no, not that, not exactly, but in my rib cage, an opening out, a spaciousness, despite (or was it because of?) the ugliness of the words he chose.

"He'll die," he said again. "And then you'll die, and I will—our spirits anyway, how could they not? And Adam"—he shrugged—"will be alone."

For a moment, I could hardly breathe. I wanted to touch his arm, his face, something, but as I tried, he raised his hand to stop me. It was a light-soaked September afternoon. A woman and her dog ran by us on the trail, then a teenager with a Walkman, singing along to a song only he could hear. We left the woods and went back to the car. When we got there, I turned to him. "If I—if I wanted to move back in soon, maybe for a trial run," I said, "what would you think?"

His mouth twitched. "I'd be nervous."

"But not opposed?"

"I'd want to know why."

"To, you know, be with you all," I said. "To have our life."

"Lives."

"Yes, but also the one we have together."

"Had."

"Okay." I felt my fists curl and shut my eyes. Still, I could feel him watching me—suspicious, vigilant. "I want," I said, opening my eyes, "to be together."

"You want to be with the kids? Or with me for the kids? Or with me?"

All of the above. Some of the above. Suddenly I felt faced with a logic question I couldn't entangle: If the bucket is half full and you put two apples in it, if the sun shines ten hours a day for half the year. With you, I knew I was supposed to say. With you, the kids aside, because I love you, because you're the person I want to spend my life with, Hal just an error in judgment, a spasm without meaning, a fluke. I opened my mouth but the words refused to come. "I can't divide it up like that," I said. "I can't think of you without thinking of them, and of you as their father. It's like"—I started walking again, around the parking lot, and he hesitated, then followed me—"if a genie came to me and said would you prefer to have a healthy child, to have Max, even, but without XP."

"You'd say yes," said Ian. "If it was Max but healthy. How could you not?"

"I don't know. He wouldn't be Max."

"He's not his illness."

"It won't go away," I said. "We can send him to school and get him space suits and . . . and all the friends in the world, but it's who he is, for as long as he lives, and it's brought us—"

Gifts, I was tempted to say, but wouldn't that mean the camp, the lake, Hal? Wouldn't it mean, too, my nights alone with Max—like lovers, almost, we'd been for a time, that insular, that insistently focused on each other?

"It's brought us to where we are," I said. "It's made us give things up, but it's also brought us things we never could have imagined." I could feel how I was pushing him, perhaps unfairly, could feel how our days, forever, if we lived them out together, would contain many moments like these—two wills, intransigent, resistant. Two circling, stumbling selves.

"What's your point?" asked Ian.

"We—" I shrugged. We were back at the car now. I didn't

know how to explain it, even to myself. "We made our kids together. And our lives, with their good parts and their flaws. We're right"—I looked around the parking lot, at the minivans and bicycles and a mother helping her child into a car—"in the middle of it all. And they need us to be together."

"They'd survive," he said, surprising me, and then, more quietly, "I did."

He turned to me. His eyes were bright, and when he spoke, it was in a fast, loud voice I didn't recognize. "Say they were gone," he said. "Moved out, grown up, or even say one of them had died, not necessarily Max, and it was just"—he dropped his hands—"us. Alone in the house. What would we do?"

For a moment I couldn't answer, too shocked at the thought of it, and at his voice bringing me there. But then, as I stood, I started to picture it, and in my vision we were old, our bones and hair thinning. We had our projects—he his history books and dioramas, I my painting and my garden. We had some clear windows and others that were tinted; a bed we shared, held each other in, and other beds in the boys' rooms for when someone was visiting or we wanted or needed to sleep alone. We had our children, alive or not, near us or not, and they filled the rooms with their voices, with their lean, lithe bodies.

"We'd live together," I said. "And be kind to each other."

"Would you be kind to me?" he asked, and I knew he was exacting a promise from me, a sort of vow.

I took his hand. It was the first time we had touched since I'd been back. "Yes," I said.

"No matter what happened?"

"I'd try my best."

"I might need more than that."

"I'd try more than my best," I said, hoping I meant it.

"I might," he said, and then he let out a bursting laugh that reminded me more of Adam and Max than of the man I'd come to know, or unknow, these past years, "need more than that."

Carly's brother will be arriving from Japan in a few days to spend a week with her here. She has said I can stay until he comes and return after he's gone, but tonight I wipe her table clean and sweep her floor for the last time. I go to the Laundromat and wash her sheets, stop by a store in town to buy a wooden bowl for her, and new candles to replace the ones I've burned down. Back in her apartment, I give each of her plants a good soak, spray the leaves and turn the pots. I make the bed, scrub the sinks and toilet and empty the trash outside, where the night is cool and vast. When I'm ready—as ready as I'll ever be—I go back inside, log on to the computer and tell him I'm going home. Can't write, not anymore, I type. Not for a long time anyway, until it feels less necessary. I wish him and Alida all happiness, all love. Then I sit by the screen for an hour, maybe two, waiting for a message, but nothing comes.

They are sleeping when I get there. I tiptoe. I make some tea. It's a mug I don't recognize, blue with a rough, raised pattern, and heavier than you might expect. As my fingers trace the bottom, they find Adam's name, scratched into the clay when it was wet. I go outside and sit on a lawn chair on the back porch. The chair is damp. The sky is charcoal, then indigo, then smeared with white, then bluish gray. The house is breathing; even from here I can feel it, so full it is, so stuffed with daily life. Is this my return, sneaky, sidelong, in the dwindling dark? My limbs feel stiff, my mind unsure. My suitcase waits, still, in the car. Perhaps I will look back one day and see that no matter what I wanted, it couldn't have gone otherwise, no room for splitting off or changing course. Or perhaps I will look back and call this a choice, clear-eyed and lucky—if they will have me, if he will. Once upon a time, we made these boys. Once upon a time, we filled this house. Now, though I have been here many times, I cannot with any certainty say where I am. A long road leads to it. There is no sign. I go inside and wait for them to wake.

ACKNOWLEDGMENTS

The characters and camp in *Awake* are products of my imagination. Xeroderma pigmentosum, however, is an all too real disease. A visit to Camp Sundown, a summer camp for children with light-sensitivity disorders, contributed to my understanding of life with XP. I am very grateful to the camp's co-founders, Caren and Dan Mahar, for allowing me to spend a night there. I also learned a great deal by reading the XP Society Listserv, whose members gave me generous access to their discussions. Camp Luna, my fictional camp, owes some of its physical contours to the Blue Mountain Center, where I had an artist's residency some years ago.

The strong faith and sharp analysis of my reader friends were vital companions to me during the writing of this book. Everywhere in these pages are Lauren Slater, Bridgette Sheridan, A. Manette Ansay, Kathy Waugh, Suzanne Matson and Alexandra Chasin. Richard Parks is, as always, both a wonderful agent and a dear friend. My editor, Jennifer Barth, has brought extraordinary perceptiveness, patience and care to this novel, as she did to my previous two books. I am grateful, as well, to her assistant, Ruth Kaplan, and to Rachel Kadish, Francis

Bégué and Eric Grunebaum, all of whom helped me with technical details. Thanks, also, to Boston College, for granting me a faculty fellowship and sabbatical, which gave me the time to write *Awake*.

I began this project just before I got pregnant with my first child and finished it eight months after the birth of my second. My daughters, Chloe and Sylvie, have brought me daily joy and taught me, already, many things. Jimmy Pingeon, my husband, has been my gentle, daily supporter and valued final reader, with his awareness of both darkness and light. While I was writing, Joanna Howe cared for our children with great intelligence and love. Lawrence, Suzanne and Ruth Graver have all helped this novel grow at every stage and are, as always, a sustaining presence in my life.

ABOUT THE AUTHOR

Elizabeth Graver is the author of two previous novels, *The Honey Thief* and *Unravelling*—both *New York Times* Notable Books. Her short-story collection, *Have You Seen Me?*, was awarded the 1991 Drue Heinz Literature Prize. Her stories and essays have been anthologized in *Best American Short Stories; Prize Stories: The O. Henry Awards; Best American Essays* and *Pushcart Prize: Best of the Small Presses.* She teaches at Boston College and lives near Boston with her family.